DARK PRINCESS

ASCENDING

THE CHILDREN OF THE GODS
BOOK NINETY-ONE

I. T. LUCAS

Dark Princess Ascending is a work of fiction! Names, characters, places, and incidents are products of the author's imagination or are used fictitiously and are not to be construed as real. Any similarity to actual persons, organizations, and/or events is purely coincidental.

Copyright © 2025 by I. T. Lucas

All rights reserved.

No part of this book may be reproduced in any form or by any electronic or mechanical means, including information storage and retrieval systems, without written permission from the author, except for the use of brief quotations in a book review.

Published by Evening Star Press, LLC.

EveningStarPress.com

ISBN: 978-1-962067-64-5

1

KIAN

After Brandon had whisked the panicked and shaken Morelle away, an uneasy silence fell over the living room, with everyone who had witnessed the brush with disaster processing it in their own way.

Kian's gaze drifted to the heavy stone fragment lying on the floor and then to the fine web of cracks spreading across the remaining mantel. The physical evidence of what had transpired made him seethe with rage at the negligence of the stone supplier, the contractor who'd installed it, and himself for not noticing anything was wrong.

If not for Morelle's extraordinary display of power, the child would have died, a blow so devastating that none of them would have ever recovered from it, especially Darius's parents.

In fact, he was surprised at how calm Amanda was in the aftermath.

She'd lost her little boy a long time ago, and it had not only destroyed her but had affected the rest of the family as well. His little nephew's death was a big part of why Kian had been so disillusioned and almost nihilistic until Syssi entered his life and brought the sunshine back with her.

Perhaps Amanda hadn't internalized what had happened yet, the scientist in her dedicating the full bandwidth of her mind to dissecting and deciphering Morelle's incredible ability.

"I want all the mantels removed as soon as possible," Syssi said, bouncing Allegra on her knee the way she used to do when their daughter was younger. "Including the one in our bedroom. I don't want this stone anywhere in the house."

Kian nodded. "I'll have the community service crew start on it first thing tomorrow morning. For now, let's just keep the children away from all fireplaces." He pulled out his phone to send a global message to the community about the potential hazard.

When he was done, he glanced at Jacki to check on how she was holding up. Her tears had dried, but she still looked shell-shocked as she clutched Darius to her chest. The boy, however, seemed unaware of his close call, with his smart, dark eyes fixed on the stone fragment with curiosity rather than fear.

"We should take Darius home," Kalugal said

softly to his mate. "After all this excitement, a warm bath and a bedtime story will do him good."

The one who needed to get home and take a warm bath was Jacki, but Kalugal was the quintessential diplomat, and he knew how to frame his suggestion to avoid implying that she was not handling their son's brush with death as well as he was.

"Yeah." She nodded. "We should go."

"Thank you for dinner." Kalugal wrapped an arm around Jacki's shoulders. "We'll talk more about this tomorrow."

As they headed for the door, Darius lifted his head from his mother's shoulder and waved. "Bye-bye."

The sweet gesture hit Kian hard, and he had to fight the urge to snatch Allegra from Syssi's arms and encircle her in the protection of his embrace.

Instead, he tightened his hold on his wife's waist.

Once the door closed behind them, Amanda let out a long breath. "That was the most incredible display of paranormal power I have ever witnessed. Not to mention the level of control Morelle demonstrated. It's hard to believe that it was her first time."

"She acted on instinct," Annani said. "And what is even more incredible is that she displayed several talents at once. None of us noticed anything was amiss with the stone, and we are all paranormally talented individuals, at least to some extent."

"Not me," Alena said. "My only talent is producing babies."

Orion leaned over and kissed her cheek. "That's the most important talent of them all."

Their little boy had slept in his stroller throughout all the commotion, and although Alena looked a little paler than usual, she seemed to have recovered from the shock.

"You are right." Amanda tapped a long-nailed finger on her lower lip. "I mean about the multiple talents. To sense that the stone was about to get loose, Morelle has to have at least some precognition ability, but all the tests I did on her revealed the absolute lack of it." She turned to Syssi. "Do you think she was faking it in the lab?"

Syssi shook her head. "She seemed frustrated when she didn't do well on any of the precognition tests. Perhaps it has something to do with her telekinetic ability. Maybe she can sense faults in materials because she can manipulate them with her mind."

Throughout the exchange, Kian observed Ellrom from the corner of his eye to see if he knew or suspected something about his sister that he was not sharing, but he seemed just as stunned as the rest of them.

Amanda considered Syssi's suggestion but shook her head. "The way she redirected that stone reminded me of Ell-rom's ability, though obviously with a different application. Both seem to involve manipulation of physical matter through sheer force of will."

Ell-rom frowned. "I don't think my ability manipulates matter. I think it manipulates energy flow."

Amanda waved a dismissive hand. "It's all the same. Matter, energy, it's all interconnected, and I think that the same principles are involved."

"Ell-rom's power is purely destructive," Annani said. "What Morelle did was protective—saving a life rather than taking one." She paused. "Not that Ell-rom's ability couldn't be used to protect, but its primary function appears to be offensive."

Syssi set Allegra down on the couch and handed her the phone to play with, which she rarely did, no doubt because she didn't want their daughter to get anywhere near the fireplace.

Perhaps after their guests left, he should push the couch against the fireplace so they wouldn't have to restrict Allegra's mobility until the mantel got pulled down. Their daughter wouldn't like having to stay away from her favorite room in the house.

"Their abilities could be connected somehow," Syssi said. "They're twins, after all."

"It's possible," Amanda said, reaching into her purse and pulling out her tablet. "Right now, I'm still struggling with understanding how Morelle's nullifying ability relates to the telekinetic force, but I cannot think of what the two could have in common. On the face of things, they seem to be opposites."

Evie had fallen asleep in her father's arms, and Amanda went to take her, but Dalhu shook his head. "It's okay. I've got her."

Amanda smiled fondly at her mate. "It's also okay for you to admit that you just want to hold her because you got scared."

"I'm not denying it." Dalhu turned to Annani. "If it's okay with you, Clan Mother, I would like to start bringing Evie over to you much more often. I want her to transition as soon as possible."

A pang of guilt shot through Kian. Dalhu, along with every other clan member except for Kian and Alena, still believed that the little girl Dormants transitioned just from being around Annani. Kian carried the burden of keeping the real method a secret, but since his mother's safety was at stake, he preferred to feel guilty rather than expose his mother to peril.

Her blood's ability to induce the transition of young female Dormants would have to remain a secret.

With five gods in their community, the secret was a little less daunting now that Annani was no longer the only source of the miraculous healing godly blood, but Kian still wasn't going to reveal it even to his two other sisters. It was up to his mother.

Amanda detached the stylus and started jotting notes on her tablet. "I'm already brainstorming ideas, so I'll have something by Monday to start testing." She lifted her head and smiled. "But it's going to be a busy weekend, so I don't know how much I will manage to do."

"Oh, right. Tomorrow is Rob's induction ceremony." Syssi turned to Kian. "Do you have anything special planned?"

He frowned. "Should I? I always say more or less the same thing." He looked at Amanda. "Are you in charge of organizing that event as well?"

She was arranging a wedding party for Marina and Peter nearly singlehandedly, so he doubted she would have the time or energy to organize a party for Rob as well.

"Not this time." Amanda put the tablet on the coffee table. "Since Arwel is Rob's inducer, Jin took it upon herself, and Margo and Frankie are helping."

"I should offer to help as well," Jasmine said. "After all, I feel responsible for getting Rob here. I pressured Margo to confront him with what she knew about Lynda to save him from a disastrous marriage."

"That's right." Amanda cast her a smile. "Rob owes you a big thank you. The dude is so happy now with Gertrude."

"He moved on fast," Syssi murmured. "I would have expected him to mourn his doomed relationship a bit longer."

"He dodged a bullet," Amanda said. "Speaking of which, I wonder if Morelle can deflect bullets." She picked up the tablet and started writing again. "I have a feeling that she can only summon her telekinetic energy in an emergency, so I might have to trick her into thinking that someone is about to get shot and see what she does."

"Is that wise?" Syssi asked. "What if she decides to snap the neck of the shooter instead of intercepting the bullet?"

"Good point." Amanda waved with her stylus. "I'll need to come up with a nonlethal experiment. Maybe throwing a ball at someone's head or something like that."

As a soft groan escaped Ell-rom's throat, Kian chuckled. "Don't get carried away, Amanda. Start slow and increase the stakes gradually. We don't know the extent of Morelle's powers yet, and we don't want any fatal accidents."

Amanda winced. "Yeah, you are probably right. I wonder if Ell-rom and Morelle's abilities are complementary." She turned to Ell-rom. "Your power destroys, while Morelle's seems capable of averting destruction. It's almost like they're two sides of the same coin. We should explore whether there are other paired aspects to your abilities. The nullifying power doesn't seem to fit the pattern, though."

"Unless it does," Annani said thoughtfully. "If Ell-rom's power is purely offensive, perhaps Morelle's nullifying ability is its defensive counterpart. She stops others from using their powers while he..." She trailed off, glancing at Allegra, who was still within earshot. "Sometimes others need to be stopped." When Ell-rom winced, she continued. "With great power comes great responsibility, and I am glad that both you and your sister are conscientious, good people. You make our family stronger."

2

MORELLE

As Brandon carried Morelle into his home, their home now, she rested her head on his chest, and when he headed straight for the master bedroom, she expected him to put her down on the bed. Instead, he settled onto the couch in the seating area, keeping her cradled in his lap.

"How are you feeling?" he asked.

Morelle lifted her head and smiled apologetically. "This wasn't the way I wanted to spend our first night together in our home." Losing the fight against the waves of exhaustion that threatened to pull her under, she put her head down again. "I'm completely drained. I don't even have the energy to take a shower, let alone do anything else."

She'd wanted tonight to be special and had planned to seduce Brandon properly to celebrate this important step in their relationship. Instead, she felt like her limbs were as limp as noodles and her eyelids as heavy as the curtains in the Mother's temple.

To perform such a powerful feat of telekinesis she'd pulled energy from everyone present, probably mostly from Annani, but a significant portion had come from her, and what was left was barely enough to keep her alive.

Or at least it felt like that.

Could expending too much energy kill her?

Drain her of her life force?

Or did she have a safety mechanism that stopped the process when it reached a critical level?

It was also possible that she didn't have enough power of her own to affect physical objects. Perhaps she could only do it by stealing power from others.

But wait. Physical objects were not the only things she could affect. Her so-called nullifying gift wasn't really the ability to block others' paranormal talents. She simply drained them of their ability, rendering them temporarily inert.

She didn't know that for sure, but it made sense to her that the two abilities were actually one. Still, without further testing it was all speculation at this point.

Had Annani noticed the drain on her power?

The thought made Morelle's stomach clench. Thank the Mother that her sister had been there.

The combined energy from the other immortals might not have been enough on its own to move that heavy piece of stone.

"I will gladly help you in the shower, but if you don't even have the energy for that, I will just undress you and tuck you under the covers." Brandon pressed a kiss to the top of her head. "As I've said many times before, I will be overjoyed to just have the privilege of having you in my bed and holding you in my arms."

Guilt crashed through Morelle at his words. He was so loving and devoted, and yet she couldn't bring herself to trust him completely.

They had something special going on, but Brandon had known her for mere days, while he'd been part of the clan for centuries, and he was a councilman. Of course, he would side with the clan and not with her.

He wouldn't keep her ability secret if he thought that it could potentially endanger Annani.

Morelle comforted herself with the thought that the energy drain hadn't seemed to harm her sister, but what if it had diminished her abilities somehow?

Then again, when she had *blocked* Jin earlier, the female's tethering ability returned as soon as she left the room, which indicated that the effects were temporary. The same had also been true of the others she had tested her power on.

"I know that you haven't fallen asleep." Brandon

rubbed soothing circles on her back. "Are you so quiet because you are still bothered by your foiled plans for tonight?"

Morelle chuckled without opening her eyes. "I'm upset by that, but it's not why I'm quiet. I'm trying to process everything that occurred. I'm still shaken by what might have happened if that power hadn't manifested out of nowhere."

His arms tightened around her. "You saved Darius's life, and no one will ever forget that, especially his parents, but you are exhausted and should go to sleep. We can brainstorm what happened tomorrow over a cup of coffee."

He was so good to her. Too good. Too trusting.

Didn't he realize what she'd done?

"I moved without thinking," she murmured. "Pure instinct. I sensed the flaw in the stone, and it was like I knew that something was going to happen. I braced for action, and when the stone started falling, I reacted as if I'd done something like that many times before, but I haven't. I didn't know I could do it."

Brandon's chest rose and fell with a deep breath. "Do you believe in reincarnation?"

Morelle opened her eyes. "I used to be a skeptic who believed the universe was pure chaos and that there was no divine intervention in anything, but then my mother appeared in my dream and told me so many things I couldn't have known. She was proof that the afterlife exists."

Her mother had also told her about her father, about the head priestess being her sister, and that the head priestess had been reborn almost immediately after dying. Curiously, her mother hadn't mentioned Ahn reincarnating, and she hadn't said anything about him being with her in the Fields of the Brave either. But she had said that even though they hadn't been fated for each other, as Ahn had believed, they were bound together in life and death by the two wonderful children they had produced.

"Bonds of love never die," her mother had said, perhaps to encourage her to wake up and find love.

Morelle lifted her hand and cupped Brandon's cheek. "My mother told me that life was worth living. She told me to listen, and I did. That was when I heard you talking to me."

He dipped his head and kissed her forehead. "I should thank your mother. Is there a ritual in your religion for thanking ancestors for their guidance?"

"Not that I know of. I wasn't a very good acolyte. But I guess you can offer a prayer to the Mother of All Life and ask her to convey a message to my mother." Morelle regretted her suggestion as soon as she voiced it. "On second thought, maybe that's not such a great idea. The Mother might not appreciate being asked for favors."

"Good point. From what I've heard about the

Kra-ell deity, she's not the kind and forgiving type."

Morelle nodded. "She's both kind and harsh, but she's not forgiving, that's for sure. The Mother of All Life doesn't offer second chances, and the only redemption she accepts is through the ultimate sacrifice of one's life. Still, she gave me the ability to save Darius, and I'm grateful to her for that."

"Maybe the gift was always there," Brandon said. "The reason I asked whether you believed in reincarnation was that you might have possessed the ability in a previous life, and perhaps it has lain dormant until a life-or-death emergency forced it to the surface."

His words resonated with her.

"I've always felt there was something more inside me, waiting to emerge," Morelle admitted. "It felt like something big, but I dismissed it as wishful thinking."

Brandon nodded. "I suspect we've only scratched the surface of what you're capable of."

If he only knew. Morelle suppressed a shiver.

"Are you cold?" He shifted as if prepared to stand. "I'll get you a blanket."

The only warmth she wanted was that emitted by his body. "Just hold me. Please."

His expression softened. "Always."

They sat in silence for a while, Brandon's steady breathing and warm embrace almost lulling

Morelle to sleep, but the questions that kept circling in her mind prevented her from truly relaxing.

"Brandon?" she murmured.

"Hmm?"

"Do you ever keep secrets from the clan?"

His hand stilled on her back. "What do you mean?"

If she didn't want him to guess her motive for the question, she had to be careful with how she worded it.

"Let's say you knew that a good friend of yours thralled someone they were not supposed to, but it was for a good cause and not for their own benefit. Would you report the transgression?"

He was quiet for a long moment, and Morelle held her breath, waiting for his answer.

"That's a complex question," he said finally. "It would depend on the situation and the potential consequences." He shifted slightly to look down at her. "Why are you asking?"

It seemed to her like he was evading a straight answer, which led her to believe that he had transgressed before and hadn't told anyone about it.

"So basically, what you are telling me is that if the unauthorized thralling results in a positive outcome, you approve of bending the rules?"

He chuckled. "You are a smart lady, Princess Morelle, and if you can detect my deflection even while half asleep with exhaustion, I need to be very careful about what I say around you."

Morelle took that as an answer to her question that didn't necessitate his admission of guilt. She also took it as proof that he trusted her but not enough to give her a straightforward answer that could implicate him.

"You are a smart male, Councilman Brandon," she mimicked his response. "And I too should remember to be careful about what I say around you." She shifted in his arms so that her head was higher, and their eyes were level.

His lips lifted in a half smile. "We make a great pair. So, why the sudden concern with my ethics? Are you afraid that you have moved in with a scoundrel?"

"I'm still learning about clan dynamics." She rested her head on his chest again. "As a new member, I should be aware of the rules, which ones are set in stone and which are bendable. I also need to know what the rules are between mates. If I know of your minor transgressions, am I obligated to report them? Or are mates excused from such obligation?"

He regarded her for a long moment, his eyes calculating. "Everyone knows that mates do not keep secrets from one another unless the secret can endanger someone's life. My first loyalty is to you, Morelle, and unless your transgression might cause someone's death, your secret is safe with me."

3

BRANDON

Brandon found Morelle's questions about clan loyalty, minor rule-bending, and keeping secrets suspicious. They could have been just part of casual conversation, if they hadn't followed right after tonight's events when she was so exhausted that she'd barely kept her eyes open and was now dozing off against his chest.

He'd never actually explained the code of conduct to her, so this was an odd time for her to ask about it. She'd picked up bits and pieces from overheard conversations, like the prohibition against unsanctioned thralling, and perhaps he should have been more thorough in explaining clan policies, but tonight wasn't the time for a lesson in clan bylaws.

Morelle had been testing the waters, trying to gauge how he might react to whatever she was hiding, and he suspected that it had to do with what she had done earlier. Something other than telekinesis had been at play, and it had scared her.

After that incredible display of power, Brandon had seen the panic in her eyes, and at first he'd attributed it to the shock of what had almost happened. Everyone's hearts had been racing, and even now, he still felt the lingering lethargy that followed the adrenaline spike.

Given Morelle's obvious soft spot for children, her strong reaction seemed natural and warranted, but her subsequent questions suggested there was more to it. Something about that display of power had frightened her deeply, and not just because of the near tragedy she had prevented.

As Morelle stirred in his arms, he kissed her temple.

Whatever was troubling her, tonight wasn't the time to press her for answers. She needed rest and time to process everything that had happened so she could address it with a clear mind tomorrow.

Still, even in her exhausted state she remained incredibly sharp, and he couldn't help but admire her for it. She'd caught the evasiveness in his answers, proving her mind was still razor sharp despite her fatigue.

His tactical mind wanted to let this play out, to give her enough rope to—no, that was wrong. That was how he'd think about an adversary, not the woman he loved. With Morelle, it wasn't about manipulation or strategy. It was about giving her space to realize that she could trust him completely.

When she stirred again and sighed, he leaned and kissed the top of her head. "How about a bath?" he suggested. "It will help you relax and fall asleep."

Morelle's eyes fluttered open, and a weak laugh escaped her. "That might lead to things I have no energy for."

"Just a bath," he promised. "I want to pamper you. No ulterior motives."

She narrowed her eyes at him, but it wasn't in anger. "On one condition."

"Name it."

"I get to return the favor when I'm feeling stronger."

Heat coursed through him at the thought, but he kept his voice steady. "I eagerly accept."

She was really big on fairness and reciprocation, and he admired her for that as well.

"Then we have a deal." She lifted her head just enough to kiss his jaw. "Thank you."

"Don't thank me yet." Moving carefully, he stood with her still in his arms. "Thank me after the bath if you are still awake."

She wound her arm around his neck. "That's not what I'm thanking you for. I'm thanking you for being so patient with me. I don't know if I would have done the same for you."

"I'm sure you would." He carried her to the bathroom. "Perhaps I need to stage a scenario when I need you to take care of me."

She frowned at him. "Are you so infallible that you never need help and have to fake it?"

He paused. "I've never needed it before, but it's nice to know that now I have someone who has my back." He kissed her forehead before setting her down on the counter.

She leaned back, her legs dangling over the edge. "Doesn't the clan have your back?"

"It does." He started the water in the large freestanding soaking tub that could easily fit two people. He'd never used it before, always preferring quick showers, but tonight, it would serve its purpose perfectly. "But it's not the same as having someone at home who I can talk to, who listens to all my crazy ideas and gives me immediate feedback without caring whether she offends my feelings or not."

She chuckled. "Is that what you think of me?"

"Am I wrong?" He checked the water temperature and turned to look at her. "Would you give me platitudes instead of the naked, harsh truth?"

She pursed her lips. "You'll get no platitudes from me, but if I didn't like your ideas, I would try to soften the punch."

"That's exactly what I need, and it's such a good feeling that I have someone I can rely on who wants only what's best for me."

Morelle lifted a hand and put it over her chest. "I vow that's what you will always get from me. I will always tell you the truth, and I will do my best to provide constructive criticism."

"I appreciate that." He chuckled. "My mother's motto is that if you don't have anything nice to say, say nothing at all, but that's not constructive when I need feedback."

Morelle paled. "Your mother? Is she here in the village?"

He stood up, moved over to her, and when she made room for him by spreading her legs, he walked between them and wrapped his arms around her. "My mother does not live in the village. She lives in Annani's sanctuary in the north, and we are not close. She has her life, and I have mine. That being said, she has no doubt heard about you and me being together and is biding her time, waiting for me to call her and tell her the good news."

She arched a brow. "Are you sure she will think I'm good news?"

"Of course. You are a princess and a half-goddess. What mother wouldn't want that for her son?"

"I'm also half Kra-ell and know next to nothing about Earth and its customs. She will think that I'm an ignorant savage."

"I promise you that she will not." Brandon glanced at the rapidly filling tub and the steam rising from the surface. "Do you want me to add bath oils?"

"Yes, please."

He kissed the tip of her nose before leaving the enticing comfort of her thighs and walking over to the tub.

As he added the foaming bath oils, the air filled with a subtle floral scent. He looked at Morelle, expecting her to smile as she inhaled the soothing smell, but instead, she was slumped against the mirror with her eyes closed.

Brandon turned off the water, walked over to her, and began unbuttoning her blouse.

"I thought you said no ulterior motives," she murmured, though there was a smile in her voice.

"Just practicality," he assured her. "I don't think you have the energy to undress yourself."

"True," she admitted.

He helped her out of her clothes with as much clinical detachment as he could manage, then supported her as she stepped into the tub.

A soft sigh escaped her as she sank into the warm water. "This feels amazing," she said, her eyes drifting closed.

Thankfully, the soapsuds covered her nudity, or he would have needed to take a cold shower to keep all the blood from leaving his brain and pooling in his groin.

"Do you want me to shampoo your hair?"

He hoped she would say yes because he had

never done that for a woman before, but Morelle was sensitive about the appearance of the new hair growth, so she might not want him to touch it.

"Yes, please." She smiled. "The advantage of having such short hair is that I don't mind washing it every night. In the temple, it was a complicated process to untangle my long strands, so I didn't wash it as often. Having to do it with cold water was another deterrent."

Brandon paused with the shampoo in his hand.

"Why cold water? Was it only you that had to go without, or was everyone in the temple required to bathe in cold water?"

She opened her incredible blue eyes. "The inhabitable area of Anumati is hot and humid, so the water was never freezing, but since it came from an underground reservoir, it wasn't warm either. Still, no one ever thought about heating up water for bathing, and since the Kra-ell didn't need hot water for cooking either, it just wasn't done."

He shook his head. "I have to admit that the Kra-ell physiology lends itself to an uncomplicated life." He began working the soap through Morelle's short hair.

Actually, it was growing out nicely, already thick enough to run his fingers through.

"I love the way your hands feel on my scalp," Morelle murmured.

Brandon smiled, massaging it gently. "I love

taking care of you." He reached for the handheld to rinse her hair. "Close your eyes."

She did as he asked.

When he was done with her hair, he reached for a washcloth. "Lean back," he instructed.

As he began rubbing her shoulders, he said, "You know what I think?"

"What?" she asked sleepily.

"I think that you are incredible." He ran the washcloth down her arm. "I've watched you adapt to this new world with grace and courage. I've seen your fierce protective instincts, your deep capacity for love. My mother will fall in love with you at first sight."

Just like he had, but he was too much of a coward to admit it yet.

She caught his hand and pressed a kiss to the back of it. "Thank you. It means so much to me that you think that."

"I know." He leaned over and kissed her forehead. "You are the most amazing person I've ever met. I feel blessed and incredibly lucky that, for some reason, you want to be with me."

A smile tugged at her lips. "The reason is that you are a great storyteller."

She was teasing, he knew that, but he also wanted to give her many more reasons for wanting to be with him.

When Morelle's breathing became deeper,

Brandon patted her shoulder. "Let's get you dried off and in bed."

She didn't protest as he helped her out of the tub and wrapped her in a thick towel. He dried her carefully, trying to stay indifferent to her nudity, and then slipped one of his t-shirts over her head.

By the time he carried her to bed, she was barely conscious. He tucked her in, then quickly changed into sleep pants before sliding in beside her.

She curled into him, fitting against his side as if she'd been designed for that space. "Thank you," she mumbled.

"For what?"

"For not pushing. For being patient with me. And for all the lovely compliments. I might get used to that."

"Please do." Brandon gathered her closer, pressing a kiss to the top of her head.

4

MARINA

Marina attacked the bathroom tiles with a vengeance, scrubbing at nonexistent spots as if they had personally offended her. The sharp scent of cleaning products made her eyes water, but she couldn't stop. Peter's mother would be here in less than three hours, and that wasn't enough time to make everything perfect.

If there was even a speck of dust anywhere in the house, Marina was sure that Peter's mother would spot it with her immortal vision and use it to put her down.

"You missed a spot," she muttered to herself, spraying more cleaning fluid on the already gleaming surface.

Did immortals even care about things like that?

The Kra-ell had, and Marina had gotten scolded more than once when her cleaning hadn't been up to their standards. Naturally, it had also resulted in a loss of privileges and a cut in her allowance.

In her experience, the immortals were not as cruel, and Wonder had forgiven her many mishaps, but then she wasn't about to marry Wonder's son. Peter's mother considered her an inadequate bride, and she wasn't wrong.

From the bedroom, she could hear Alfie packing up his things, humming some upbeat tune that only heightened her anxiety. At least he had somewhere to escape to. He'd be staying with two other Guardians while Peter's mother occupied his room for an entire week after the wedding.

A whole damn week.

Marina's hand stilled on the tiles as the reality of that sank in again. She'd given up having a honeymoon to accommodate Peter's new position as head of the Avengers, and now, instead of enjoying private newlyweds' time with her husband, she'd be stuck playing hostess to her mother-in-law.

Why had Peter agreed to host his mother in their house?

Not that his mother had given him a choice. When he'd called to invite her to the wedding, she'd said she would come for the weekend and stay with a good friend, but after booking her flight, she'd called to inform him that she would be staying until next Sunday and that she wanted to stay with him and his bride so she could get to know Marina better.

What could Peter have done? Said no?

Well, yeah. If her mother had made such an unreasonable demand, Marina definitely would have told her that it wouldn't work and that she should find another solution. In fact, her parents and Larissa were arriving in the afternoon, and they were staying at a house that Ingrid had prepared for them.

The sound of a drawer closing in the bedroom jolted Marina out of her thoughts, and she returned to the task, rinsing the tiles one more time.

Alfie poked his head into the bathroom. "Did I really leave it that dirty? You've been in there for over an hour."

"Not at all." Well, it had been only surface clean, and barely that either, but she wasn't going to say that. Marina straightened and stretched her aching back. "I just want everything to be spotless for Catrina."

"Oh, I see." He ran his fingers through his hair. "She's not as bad as you think."

That didn't sound encouraging at all. He hadn't said she was nice or that she shouldn't worry about her, just that the female wasn't that bad.

"I know." Marina forced a smile. "I'm just nervous."

"Understandable." Alfie slung the strap of his

duffle bag over his shoulder. "I'm off. I guess I'll see you at the wedding." He walked over and gave her a quick, one-armed hug. "Try to relax, okay?"

She forced another smile. "I will try."

Right.

As soon as Alfie was gone, she rushed to the linen closet and pulled out a change of bedding. He'd offered to do that, but she preferred to do it herself to make sure everything was perfect.

The entire house had to be scrubbed from top to bottom, every surface polished, every corner dusted, every pillow fluffed to maximum fluffiness. Yet she knew it wouldn't be enough.

The real problem wasn't how clean the house was or how tasty the roast Marina had made for the occasion would be. Meeting her mother-in-law along with her very human, elderly parents was a testament to Marina's mortality, and that was something she couldn't erase.

She straightened up, catching sight of herself in the spotless mirror. Her face was flushed from exertion, her hair escaping its messy ponytail, and her old t-shirt was spotted with cleaning solution.

"You can't clean away the fact that you're human," she told her reflection.

No amount of scrubbing would change the fact that she wasn't immortal and wouldn't be transitioning. Peter's mother would never accept a human wife for her son, no matter what Marina did to impress her.

"Hey, cleaning lady!" Lusha's voice rang out from the hallway. "Where are you hiding?"

"In here," Marina called back.

Lusha appeared in the doorway and let out a low whistle. "I think I can see my reflection in those tiles."

"How did you know that I was cleaning? Did you see Alfie leaving?"

Lusha chuckled. "I could smell the Pine-Sol from the walkway. You know that stuff gives immortals headaches, right?"

Marina's eyes widened in horror. "Oh, dear Mother of All Life, I didn't think—I need to air out the house—"

"Relax." Lusha grabbed her arm before she could rush past. "I'm kidding about the Pine-Sol. But, immortals don't like strong smells of any kind, so go easy on the perfume as well."

Marina shook her head. "I'm not in the mood for jokes. I'm going out of my mind with stress."

Lusha's smile slid off her face, and she looked Marina up and down critically. "What you really need to worry about is yourself. You look like you're auditioning for a cleaning service commercial."

"I just want everything to be perfect."

"If you want to impress Peter's mother, you need to stop acting like the maid and start acting like the lady of the house." Lusha steered her toward the door. "Go take a shower—in one of your other pristine bathrooms—and put on something nice. I'll finish changing the bedding."

"But—"

"No buts. You can inspect my work later if you don't trust me to make a neat bed. Right now, you need to apply all that nervous energy to making yourself look good. You need to project confidence and poise, not desperation."

Marina hesitated. "My parents and Larissa are arriving later this afternoon."

"All the more reason to get yourself together." Lusha started pushing her toward the master bedroom. "Where are they staying?"

"Ingrid prepared a house for them."

"That's great. Give me the address so I can stop by and say hello."

A thought struck Marina, making her stop short. "Maybe I could visit them and stay away from this house as long as Peter is not here. I don't want to be stuck with his mother without him running interference for me."

"You can escape for a little bit when you feel like you can't take it anymore, but don't overdo it." Lusha's tone was serious. "You can't show fear by running away from your own house. Immortals are predators, and when they sniff fear, they pounce."

Marina frowned. "Really? Because that wasn't my impression. Everyone I meet is nice to me. But then I'm not marrying their son, so they don't have skin in the game."

Lusha laughed. "That's because you are not afraid of them. You are the mate of a well-liked Guardian who has just been promoted to head a new division. No one would dare to mess with you."

"Well, that's not true. The Kra-ell—"

"Marina." Lusha gripped her shoulders, meeting her eyes. "I know you're nervous, but you need to snap out of it. You didn't kidnap Peter or put a gun to his head, forcing him to marry you. He chose you, and his mother needs to respect his choice. If she has any brains in her head, she will realize that you are the one who holds real power here, and that antagonizing you might cost her the relationship she has with her son."

"I would never—"

"I know that." Lusha's eyes softened. "You are a sweetheart. But Peter's mother doesn't know, and as long as you project confidence, she will be afraid to try anything and will be on her best behavior."

What Lusha was saying actually made a lot of sense. Bullies went after those they deemed weak.

Marina took a shaky breath. "When did you get so smart?"

"I've always been wise. You've just been too busy cleaning to notice." Lusha winked. "Now go get ready. And wear that blue dress—the one that makes you look like you could command armies."

"I don't have an army-commanding dress."

"Trust me, you do. Blue dress, subtle makeup, and those pearl earrings Peter gave you. Once I've done your hair, you will look like a boss lady."

Marina snorted. "A blue-haired boss?"

"Why not?"

Why not, indeed?

5

MORELLE

The aroma of coffee and something sweet and buttery greeted Morelle and Brandon as they emerged from their bedroom in the morning. Following the enticing scents, they found Jasmine in the kitchen, wearing an apron and sliding brown circular things onto plates.

"Good morning!" Jasmine beamed at them. "Come and enjoy a breakfast worthy of kings, or as it may be, a prince, a princess, and an honorable councilman."

"Good morning. Those smell delicious," Morelle said. "What are they called?"

"Pancakes," Jasmine said.

"That makes sense. Cakes that are made in a pan." Morelle took a seat at the table. "Pan cakes."

"Try to say that as one word. I wonder if the translation earpieces will pick up on that."

"Pancakes."

Jasmine grinned. "Perfect. It's amazing how smart these things are, given the tiny chip that powers them."

"Would you like some coffee?" Ell-rom asked.

"Yes, please."

He poured her a cup from the carafe and another one for Brandon. "I feel bad about Jasmine doing all the cooking. I told her that I want to learn to cook so we can take turns."

"We should all learn," Brandon said. "I know how to make coffee and order takeout, but since I've moved into the village, takeout is not an option."

"What's takeout?" Morelle asked.

"It's food prepared by professionals and either delivered to your residence or picked up by you. It's called takeout because instead of eating it in the restaurant, you eat it at home."

"That sounds convenient." Morelle cast a sidelong glance at Ell-rom.

In the temple, they had been lucky to eat raw fruits and vegetables. Cooked food had not been an option. She was still getting used to the variety and abundance of dishes in the village, and now Brandon was saying that there was much more out there for them to sample.

"We should all go to a restaurant in the city." Jasmine looked at Brandon. "What say you, Councilman? Can you take us out of here to the city?"

Brandon let out a breath. "I will need to clear it with Kian. He will probably insist on a Guardian escort."

"Why?" Ell-rom put his cup down. "Outside of this village, no one knows who we are. Why should we need an escort?"

Brandon took a sip from his coffee, probably to give himself a moment to think. "Frankly, I don't know. I guess he's a little jumpy after what happened to you in the alley."

Ell-rom flinched. "I've learned my lesson. I'm never going to take shortcuts through back alleys again."

Brandon cut a piece of his pancake and dipped it in some kind of gooey sauce that he'd poured from a glass container. "Perhaps if I tell Kian that I'll drive us straight to the restaurant and back without stopping anywhere on the way, he will be okay with us going without an escort." He turned to Morelle. "One of the clan members owns an exclusive restaurant. Dinner there is an experience that is hard to describe. Gerard is an incredible chef."

"I would like that." Morelle lifted the glass container with the gooey amber liquid and poured some in the corner of her plate as Brandon had done.

She cut a small piece of the cake, dipped it in the sauce, and put it in her mouth. It was much too sweet, but she chewed and swallowed it, nonetheless. She wasn't going to offend Jasmine by spitting it out or making a face. She was just going to avoid the sweet sauce and eat the cake dry.

When, for the next few minutes, no one said anything, Morelle wondered if that was because they were busy eating or because they were thinking of a way to bring up what had happened last evening.

She hadn't talked with Brandon about it this morning yet, and she knew that he had more questions, and Jasmine and Ell-rom would probably want to talk about it, too.

As if reading her thoughts, Ell-rom said, "Amanda and the others talked quite a bit about your talent after you left last night."

Morelle's fingers tightened around her fork. "What did they say?"

"Amanda's already preparing a whole new battery of tests for Monday."

"Great," Morelle muttered, then forced a smile when Brandon squeezed her shoulder.

"Amanda thinks that you have multiple talents," Jasmine said. "You sensed that the stone was about to get loose, which means that you have at least some precognition ability."

"I don't." Morelle lifted her coffee cup. "I failed miserably at all the precognition tests. In fact, I performed worse than what's expected from talentless humans."

"Ouch." Jasmine scrunched her nose, which

made her face look funny. "That sucks. Anyway, Syssi suggested that perhaps it has something to do with your telekinetic ability and that you can sense faults in materials because you can manipulate them. Then Amanda said that your ability and Ell-rom's are similar because you both manipulate physical matter."

Ell-rom cleared his throat. "My ability is still hypothetical." He cast Brandon an apologetic look. "Kian insists on keeping it a secret until it is proven."

"That's okay." Brandon waved a dismissive hand. "I know you have some secret talent, and I'm dying to know what it is, especially since Kian is being so secretive about it, but I know him well enough not to push. If he decided to wait to inform the council, then he has a good reason for it."

Ell-rom dipped his head in appreciation. "Thank you for being so understanding."

Realizing her mistake, Jasmine didn't continue recounting what everyone had said. Instead, she loaded her plate with two more pancakes, poured a generous amount of the gooey sauce on them, and got busy eating.

"Syssi thinks our abilities are connected somehow," Ell-rom said. "Because we are twins. Then Amanda suggested something crazy to test your telekinetic talent."

Morelle tensed. "What does she have in mind?"

Ell-rom chuckled. "Don't worry. Syssi managed to convince her that she shouldn't do it."

"But what was it?" Brandon asked.

Ell-rom took a sip of his coffee before replying. "Amanda thinks that your telekinesis is triggered only in an emergency because it only manifested when a life was in danger. She wanted to simulate another emergency by staging someone with a weapon shooting at another person to see if you could stop the bullet."

Brandon shook his head. "That's truly insane. What if Morelle can't stop the bullet? What if someone gets shot?"

"That's one of the reasons why the idea was scrapped," Ell-rom said. "The other was that Morelle might choose to attack the shooter instead of trying to stop the bullet."

Nodding, Morelle took a bite of pancake, trying to think of a way to get Ell-rom alone so she could tell him the truth about her ability. With Brandon and Jasmine hovering nearby, she couldn't risk it.

"I have a meeting with my teenage consultants about InstaTock this morning." Brandon looked at his watch as he finished his coffee. "Want to come along? They're lovely kids, and you'd enjoy meeting them."

Morelle seized the opportunity. "Actually, I should start learning English on my new laptop." She turned to her brother. "Ell-rom, could you help me? By now, you probably know everything there is to know about the program."

"Of course." He smiled knowingly.

Brandon seemed disappointed. "Are you sure? I'm meeting them in the café, and it's such a lovely day outside. You will enjoy the walk."

Normally, she would, but she really needed to talk to her brother.

"Some other time," she said. "I'm still tired from yesterday, and I'd prefer to stay home and take it easy, as you like to say."

He studied her face for a moment before nodding. "Alright." Leaning down, he pressed a kiss to her lips. "I won't be long."

"Don't rush," she said. "Take all the time you need. I'll keep myself occupied with learning your language."

After Brandon left, Jasmine began clearing the dishes. "I promised to help Margo with the decorations for Rob's induction ceremony," she announced. "So, I should head over there and see if we can get an early start." She turned to Ell-rom. "You don't mind, right? You'll be busy teaching Morelle about the program."

"Not at all." He rose to his feet and wrapped an arm around her middle. "But I will miss you."

Morelle wasn't sure if Jasmine had sensed her need for privacy with her brother or if she truly needed to help Margo, but either way, she was grateful.

Once Jasmine left, Morelle stood and leaned over to whisper in Ell-rom's ear, "Is it safe to talk here? Do you know if there are listening devices in this house?"

"It's doubtful that a councilman's home would be bugged," he said in a whisper. "But just to be safe, we could study outside in the backyard. As Brandon said, it's a nice day."

"Great idea." Morelle pushed to her feet. "Let me get my laptop."

A few minutes later they were settled at the outdoor table, laptops open but powered off.

Morelle leaned close to her brother, lowering her voice despite the privacy of the yard. "I need to tell you something about what happened last night." She swallowed hard. "The power I used wasn't mine."

Ell-rom tilted his head. "What do you mean?"

"I didn't just move that stone." She glanced around nervously before continuing. "I pulled energy from everyone present. Mostly from Annani, but also from everyone else. That's how I was able to do it."

Her brother's eyes widened, but he didn't immediately reject the idea. "That...actually makes sense."

"Did you feel it? I mean, the drain?"

"I felt something," he admitted. "But I thought it was just the shock of what almost happened to Darius. Whatever it was, it passed quickly, though."

Morelle let out a long breath. "I didn't tell Brandon. I'm scared."

"Why?"

"Isn't that obvious? I'm a parasite, a vampire. I feed off other people's energy."

To her surprise, he laughed. "A vampire? Where did that idea come from?"

This was no laughing matter. "What else would you call it? I drained energy from people to power my ability."

"That doesn't make you a vampire." He frowned. "How do I even know what a vampire is?"

She'd forgotten that Ell-rom remembered next to nothing from their childhood, and it seemed that those memories were forever lost. She really needed to spend more time with him and tell him about his past.

"When we were kids, we read legends about soul-sucking vampires." She shuddered at the memory. "You were terrified of going to sleep for weeks afterward."

A thoughtful expression crossed his face. "I wonder if those legends were based on people with abilities like yours."

"That doesn't make me feel better." She slumped in her chair. "What if I take too much and kill someone? I call it energy; the ancients might have called it a soul, but the mechanism of stealing it is the same."

Ell-rom regarded her with a serious expression

on his face. "You have to tell Amanda so she can help you figure it out. Your ability is not any worse than mine, and they accepted me despite it. They will accept you, too."

Morelle considered this. It was true—the clan hadn't rejected Ell-rom despite the devastating potential of his power. Instead, they were working to help him understand and control it.

"But your ability is straightforward," she argued. "You don't need to drain anyone to power it. Mine is strange and parasitic."

"Our abilities are complementary. Mine destroys, while yours averts destruction. I'd say that yours is the positive side while mine is the negative."

She shook her head. "There is more. My so-called nullifying power is not based on me blocking someone's paranormal ability. I nullify it by sucking the paranormal energy out of the person, thereby temporarily making them incapable of using their talent."

Ell-rom leaned forward. "So what? You didn't harm anyone. The energy drain was temporary, and yesterday, you used it to save a life. That's not parasitic—that's symbiotic."

She blinked at him. "That actually makes sense, and I definitely prefer to think of it as symbiotic rather than parasitic."

"You are welcome."

This was why she needed to talk to her brother.

He could always help her see things from a different perspective.

"What do I do now?" she asked.

"First, you need to tell Brandon. He loves you, and he will be hurt if you tell Amanda before you tell him."

She leaned back. "If I tell anyone, he will be the first to know. But I'm still not sure that I should. What if he starts to fear me?"

Ell-rom shook his head. "Does Brandon even have a special ability?"

A smile tugged on her lips. "Many, but not of the paranormal kind. He can thrall and shroud, like other immortals, but nothing more than that."

"Then he has nothing to fear from you, right?"

She shook her head. "I don't know about that. His shrouding and thralling might be enough, and I might also draw on just any life energy in my vicinity. Even that of humans." Morelle snorted. "For all I know, I could suck the life energy from a field of flowers and see them wilting in front of my eyes. Wouldn't that be something?"

"It would." Ell-rom shuddered. "You really need to test all of that."

6

PETER

Peter leaned against the wall of the international arrivals area, sipping a large iced caffè mocha through a straw, and mentally rehearsing all the things he wanted to tell his mother about Marina. He needed his mother to understand why he was so completely, irrevocably in love with her, but how could he explain that she was his soul mate?

His mother wouldn't accept that explanation. To her, the very idea that a human with no godly heritage could be his destined mate was laughable.

He could tell her about Kaia's research into the secret of immortality and tell her that there was a chance she would find a way to turn Marina immortal while she was still young enough to undergo the transition, but that wouldn't change his mother's attitude either.

She'd already made up her mind that Marina was an opportunist who had ensnared him with great sex.

Well, there was some truth to that. The sex was incredible, but that was just one small part of why he loved Marina. How could he make his mother understand that Marina made him happy? That coming home to her was the highlight of his day and that his heart felt lighter the moment he pulled her into his arms?

Marina wasn't an opportunist who wanted him just because he was an immortal Guardian with a large bank account and a hefty investment portfolio. She just wanted him, Peter, and she proved it each time he walked through the door with an expression that was pure joy.

He'd never made anyone as happy as he made Marina.

The arrivals board showed his mother's flight had landed twenty minutes ago, but she still needed to go through immigration and then collect her suitcases. He'd wanted to get her an American passport so she could skip the line, but she'd refused, saying that it wasn't worth the trouble.

Almost an hour later, she finally appeared, pushing a cart loaded with two massive suitcases, a carry-on, and a duffle bag.

Peter tossed his empty cup into the trash bin

and rushed to embrace her, wrapping her in a bear hug that had her laughing.

"So, you missed me after all." She pushed out of his arms.

"Of course. We didn't get to spend a lot of time together on the cruise." He kept the accusation out of his voice as he took control of the cart and started pushing it toward the exit.

She'd been busy hanging out with all her American cousins, but if he said that, she would accuse him of spending all his time with Marina.

Peter really didn't want to play the blame game with his mother.

He also needed to remember not to address her as Mother in public because she looked younger than him.

His mother threaded her arm through his. "We are going to spend as much time together as you can spare. Congratulations again on the promotion."

"Thank you." He looked at the mountain of luggage piled on the cart. "That's a lot of stuff for one week."

"Actually, darling, I've decided to stay a little longer, or much longer, depending on how I like it in the village."

Peter nearly lost his grip on the cart. "What?"

"Well, with your new position as head of the Avengers division and everything else going on..."

she patted his arm, "I think you need my support. What kind of a mother would I be if I didn't rise to the occasion, right?"

He was speechless.

Marina was going to flip. She was nervous enough about having his mother stay with them for a week. Now, she'd never have a moment's peace, especially if his mother expected to stay in their house.

He loved his mother, but he could only tolerate being with her in small doses. He had been very glad to have an ocean separating them.

"You've said time and again that you have no intention of leaving Scotland and even refused to get an American passport. What's made you change your mind?"

His mother turned to him, reaching up to cup his cheek in a gesture that had comforted him countless times in his youth, but he was a man now, and it felt condescending rather than loving.

"You will need me once this blows up in your face. I'm here for you."

Her words felt like a slap.

Rage surged through Peter so quickly that his vision blurred red, and his hands tightened on the cart handle until the metal groaned in protest. He forced himself to remain silent, though, waiting for the anger to subside before he said something he couldn't take back.

The walk to his car passed in tense silence. He opened the passenger door for her, then loaded her luggage into the trunk, and by the time he settled into the driver's seat, the rage had receded just enough for him to be able to speak calmly.

"Explain to me why you think this is going to 'blow up in my face.'"

His mother sighed as if he were being deliberately obtuse. "You know I only want what's best for you. But Marina is human. Her lifespan is a blink of an eye to us." She reached for his hand, but he pulled away. "And if you have children, they'll be born human too. Can you imagine how devastating it will be to watch them grow old and die?"

"There are solutions—"

"Theoretical solutions," she cut in. "Possibilities and maybes. But the reality is that you're setting yourself up for heartbreak. That's why I decided to move here and strengthen our relationship. When the time comes, you'll need someone to lean on. I don't want you to have to deal with the pain alone."

Peter's hands clenched on the steering wheel. She wasn't wrong, and he could understand where she was coming from, but she shouldn't have dumped all that on his head the day before his wedding.

Then again, his mother had never been good at thinking things through and realizing the impact of her words.

"You could have waited a few days before dumping ice on my head."

She shrugged. "Hiding from reality is not going to do you any favors, and wishing for miracles will just bring you disappointment. You must have angered the Fates for them to saddle you with a human." She said 'human' like it was a slur. "You're blinded by love right now, but—"

"Stop." Peter's voice cracked like a whip. "Just...stop."

"Peter—"

"No." He turned to face her fully. "You don't get to belittle my feelings, and you don't get to reduce my relationship with Marina to some temporary infatuation. And you absolutely don't get to plan for its eventual demise before we've even gotten married."

His mother's lips pressed into a thin line. "I'm your mother. It's my job to protect you from making mistakes that will cause you pain."

So that had been her plan. It was a last-ditch attempt to make him reconsider the marriage.

"Marina is not a mistake." The words came out as almost a growl. "She's the best thing that's ever happened to me. She makes me happy, and she makes me better and stronger. Do you think it's a coincidence that I got such an incredible promotion just as I was about to marry her? That's her influence on me. Her support makes me a better man."

"It's a mother's worst nightmare," his mother said quietly. "Watching her child walk willingly into heartbreak."

"No." Peter shook his head. "You see what you want to see. You see a human girl who isn't good enough for your immortal son. You see an ending before we've even had our beginning."

"That's not fair."

"Isn't it?" He started the car, needing something to do with his hands. "Tell me honestly—if Marina were immortal, would you have welcomed her with open arms? Or would you still have reservations about her?"

His mother's silence was answer enough.

"That's what I thought." He pulled out of the parking space with more force than necessary. "Well, I have news for you, Mom. Marina is who she is, and I love her exactly as she is. If you can't accept that, at least try to be happy for us..."

"Then what?" she challenged.

Peter took a deep breath. "Then maybe moving to the village isn't the best idea. In Scotland, you won't have to suffer seeing us together, being happy and all that."

His mother was stubborn—it was where he had gotten it from—and once she got an idea in her head she rarely let it go, but he couldn't let her intimidate Marina, which she obviously planned to do. He wouldn't let her poison their relationship.

How the hell was he going to break the news to

Marina that his mother was moving in and had no intentions of leaving?

He couldn't allow it to happen. If his mother wanted to live in the village, she would have to do that in a house of her own, and he would make sure that it was far away from theirs.

7

KIAN

Kian rarely took meetings on weekends, but when Eleanor requested to see him while she was in the village for Peter's wedding, he couldn't refuse. She and Emmett had made the trip from Safe Haven, where they jointly managed both the spiritual retreat program and the government's paranormal research facility, and this wasn't a social call.

The café was relatively quiet for a late Saturday morning, and as Kian approached the table where Eleanor and Emmett were already seated, sipping on coffees from the vending machine, he was glad to see that a third cup was waiting for him.

"Hello." He settled into the chair across from them. "It's good to see you."

"It's good to be here." Emmett extended his hand. "How are things in the village?"

Kian smiled as he shook the Kra-ell hybrid's hand. "Never a boring moment."

"So I've heard," Emmett said. "Is there a chance I can meet the famous royal twins?"

Kian leaned back in his chair. "They will attend the wedding tomorrow, and I'll gladly introduce you."

Emmett grinned. "Looking forward to it."

Eleanor rapped her fingers on the table, looking impatient. She was not the type to indulge in small talk or tolerate it for long. It was one of the things he liked about her, and probably why he was in the minority of those who did.

"So, what's happening at Safe Haven?" Kian asked.

"The government has decided to terminate the paranormal program," Eleanor said. "They're offering severance packages to all participants and sending them home."

"When was that decided?"

"I got the call Friday."

"Did they say why?"

"Budget cuts." She winced. "My contract is terminated as well."

Emmett put a hand on her shoulder. "Don't worry about that, love. You have enough work helping me manage the resort. I promise that you won't be bored."

"Yeah, but it's a shame. I liked my fake title."

Kian chuckled. "The clan arranged for a fake

doctorate for you so you would meet the government's requirements and could apply for the job of heading their paranormal program, and no one is going to take it away from you. As far as the world is concerned, you've earned the title."

"I know, but I liked being in charge of the program. Is there a chance the clan can take over? I want to keep my team."

The program's participants were all genuine talents, though most of their abilities were relatively weak. More importantly, though, they were all potential Dormants who had never been tested.

"What do you suggest we do with them?" he asked, though he already had a good idea of what Eleanor would propose.

"I think it's time we get everyone tested. Most of them are in committed relationships with each other, which is partly why I never pushed for Dormant testing before. But now it's decision time."

"The Guardians could handle the inductions," Emmett said. "They can induce the males, and those who get activated can induce their mates in turn."

Eleanor nodded. "There are two complications. Andy, who's only fifteen, and James, who might be too old at fifty-six. He's a weak telepath, and his partner, Mollie, has post-cognition abilities. She's forty-seven, which is borderline for transitioning, but neither she nor James are in as good health as

Ronja, who, as far as I remember, transitioned at fifty-seven."

"You remember correctly," Kian said. "Ronja was in great shape even before Merlin put her on a health regimen in preparation for her induction, but she was in an even better condition by the time he was done with her. You can do the same for Mollie and James."

"There's one more issue." Eleanor removed the lid from her cup and took a sip. "If they start transitioning, they'll need proper medical care. We have a clinic at Safe Haven, but no one that's qualified to handle transitions. Unless you want to send one of the doctors and a nurse there, it might be better if I bring my paranormals to the village."

Kian was not at all enthusiastic about that. "Remind me who we're talking about." He reached for his coffee. "Besides James, Mollie, and Andy."

"Jeremy is my top suspect for dormancy. He's twenty-six, and he is a remote future viewer." Eleanor pulled out the phone, scrolled for a moment, and showed Kian the guy's picture. "Unlike James, who can view the present, Jeremy sees possible futures. His ability would be more useful if the futures he saw were definite, but there are always multiple possibilities."

"Good-looking guy," Kian said. "Who's his partner?"

"He's with Naomi, twenty-two, whose ability is psychometry—she can get information from objects." Eleanor scrolled through her photos again and lifted her phone to show Kian.

It was a good tactic for her to attach a visual to the story.

"This is Abigail." She showed him another picture. "She is thirty-three, and she's an energy healer who's particularly good at diagnosis. Her partner is Dylan, thirty-one. His talent is claircognizance."

"The ability to acquire psychic knowledge without knowing how or why it was acquired." Kian impressed himself by remembering what the term stood for.

"Exactly." She chuckled. "Although that's the least exact of the talents. And finally, we have Spencer, who is nineteen and can read auras. His girlfriend is Sofia, twenty, and she has a weak telekinetic ability—mostly just affecting the trajectory of small objects like dice or coins when they are already in motion."

Kian's interest sharpened at the mention of the young woman's talent. With Morelle's recent display of powerful telekinesis, having another telekinetic talent to study, even a weak one, could provide valuable insights.

"I'm sure Amanda will be thrilled to have more test subjects." Kian took a sip from his coffee. "You can fly them to a local airport, and Okidu will pick them up with the bus."

"Hold on." She lifted a hand. "What do I tell

them, and what can we offer them? They are all out of a job as of Monday."

Kian snorted. "Isn't immortality enticing enough? I don't have anything to offer them other than that. If they turn immortal, they will stay in the village rent-free, and I can give them a small living allowance, but they will have to figure out what to do with the rest of their long lives on their own. Those who do not turn immortal will be thralled to forget their visit and sent home."

Eleanor leaned back and crossed her arms over her chest. "There is a big problem with that plan. The females need to wait for the males to transition first and for their fangs and venom glands to become functional, which takes six months at the minimum. If the females fail to transition after waiting so long for their partners to be able to induce them, they will have too many memories of the village to thrall away. We can compel them to keep the village a secret, but that will require periodic reinforcements, and that complicates things."

"So, what do you suggest?" Kian asked.

"I'm not suggesting anything. I'm brainstorming with you. Maybe we can put them up in the clan's hotel. If they start transitioning, they will be close enough to bring to the clinic in the keep, and we can get one of the clan doctors to take care of them."

"What about you?" Kian asked. "You are their leader, and I'm sure that you don't want to leave

Emmett in Safe Haven and come live in the keep or the clan hotel with your paranormals."

She winced. "I don't. That's why I'm so conflicted. Perhaps the best thing would be to send one of the doctors to Safe Haven. Do you think Julian would mind?"

"He would, but I can ask him. The other option is to get someone else to manage them." Kian raked his fingers through his hair. "That's a lot of effort for people who are not likely to benefit our community. They are already in relationships, so they are going to become someone's truelove mate, and their talents are negligible. I wish there was a simpler solution."

"Perhaps there is," Emmett said. "If you gift us a helicopter, we could just airlift the transitioning Dormant when the time comes. That way, we don't need to move them anywhere, and you don't need to send us one of your doctors."

"It's too far away for a helicopter," Kian said. "You would need a small jet, and I'm not too keen on lending you one of ours, but it's an option. I need to sleep on it."

Eleanor let out a breath. "We don't have a lot of time."

"What about Andy?" Emmett asked. "He's so young..."

"Thanks for reminding me. We need to send him home," Kian said. "We'll wait until he's of age and then make him an offer."

8

MARINA

Marina tried to keep her expression amiable as she pushed open Alfie's former bedroom door. "I hope you'll be comfortable here," she said, stepping aside to let Catrina enter.

The tension radiating from Peter behind them was palpable. Something had happened during their drive from the airport—something that had put that tight, controlled expression on his handsome face.

What had his mother said about her?

"It's nice," Catrina said, scrunching her nose as if she smelled something foul.

Marina tried to ignore that.

After Lusha's comment about harsh cleaning product smells, she'd opened the window and aired the room. If Catrina still had a problem with that, well, too bad.

"The bathroom is through here," Marina said, proud that her voice was remaining steady. "Fresh towels are in the tall cabinet next to the vanity."

Catrina nodded, then turned to her son. "Can you bring my luggage in?"

As Peter moved to comply, his mother's attention shifted back to Marina. "I think I'll unpack and shower. Will you need help setting up for dinner?"

The offer caught Marina completely off guard. "I...thank you, but I have everything under control."

"Are you sure? It's no trouble."

Was this some kind of test? And if it was, what was the required answer?

"I'm sure," she said. "Please, make yourself comfortable. You must be tired after such a long flight."

Catrina smiled indulgently. "I flew first class and had a lie-flat seat. I slept my standard four hours, and I'm good to go. I'll just shower and put on a fresh outfit for dinner. After all, I'm about to meet my in-laws. I want to look presentable." She gave Marina a subtle once-over, her gaze stopping for a moment on the piercing in her left brow.

The female was a master at acting polite and friendly while delivering dozens of subtle but perfectly aimed paper cuts.

"Very well." Marina forced a smile. "I'll leave you to it. I need to run to meet my parents and my best friend at the parking garage."

"How exciting," Catrina drawled. "I can't wait to meet them."

The moment Marina closed the bedroom door behind her, she shook her head and let out a breath. "I'm going to meet my family," she told Peter. "They should be arriving any minute now."

His expression was apologetic as he touched her cheek. "I'm sorry about—"

"We'll talk about it later," she cut him off. "I really need to run. Do you want to come with me?"

"I wish I could, but I need to stay in case my mother needs anything. I can't just leave her alone. Not yet."

"Of course." She cast him a weak smile and practically fled the house, grateful for the excuse to escape.

The afternoon sun was warm on her face as she hurried toward the glass pavilion, and being out of the house was a relief.

Her heart lifted at the thought of seeing her parents, but mostly Larissa. Her best friend would know how to handle a situation like this. Larissa had life smarts that many didn't, and she saw through the façades and walls that people put up.

When Marina reached the garage level, they weren't there yet, so she waited a few minutes for the car to arrive.

As soon as the Guardian driving the vehicle parked it, Marina rushed forward to greet them. Her mother emerged first, and Marina threw herself into her arms with more enthusiasm than she'd shown since she was a child.

"Sweetheart!" Her mother hugged her tight. "What's wrong?"

"Nothing," Marina said quickly—too quickly.

Her father was next, wrapping them both in a bear hug. "There's my girl!"

Larissa emerged last, raising an eyebrow at Marina's unusual display of affection. "Okay, spill it. You've never been this happy to see any of us before. What's going on?"

Marina pulled back from her parents, trying to smile. "Can't I just be excited to see my family?"

"Please." Larissa crossed her arms. "I know that look. Something's up."

Marina glanced around, but other than the Guardian, who was busy with their luggage, they were alone in the parking area. "Peter's mother is here."

"Ah." Her mother's expression turned knowing. "And she's making things difficult?"

"Well, not really. She just arrived, and she hasn't said anything offensive, but she's giving off those subtle hints that are all aimed to show how unworthy I am of her son." Marina wrapped her arms around herself. "I hate how tense it is with her in the house."

"What's her problem?" her father asked.

Marina let out a bitter laugh. "What isn't her

problem? I'm not immortal. I didn't go to college. And I'm not royalty. Take your pick."

"Hey." Larissa threaded her arm through hers. "You're amazing, and Peter knows it. Who cares what his mother thinks?"

"Peter cares," Marina said. "And I care that he cares. He looked so upset when they arrived—I don't even want to know what she said to him on the drive here."

Her mother's face hardened. "She has no right to make you feel less than worthy in your own home."

"I wish that was true." Marina blinked back tears. "I'm going to age and die while Peter stays young forever. Any children we have will be human. She's just saying what everyone else is thinking."

"Stop it." Larissa tugged on her arm. "Peter chose you. The clan accepted you. And your aging has slowed down." She tilted her head to look up at Marina. "I need to find me an immortal boyfriend. Any candidates that you can think of?"

Marina laughed. "You know the selection. You saw them on the cruise."

"It's all a blur now. I had my heart set on you know who, and I didn't pay attention to the others."

"What about all the Guardians who served in Safe Haven?" Marina asked.

Larissa shrugged. "They were all good-looking, but none stood out."

"Well, you can browse during the wedding," Marina said.

"Classic possessive mother syndrome," her father murmured under his breath. "She's worried about you taking her place as the most important woman in her son's life. Some women are like that."

"Dad..." Marina hadn't expected such insight from her father.

"He's right," her mother said. "And the immortal thing is just an excuse. If you were immortal, she'd find something else to object to."

"That's..." Marina considered this, "actually very possible."

Larissa nudged her. "Stop doubting yourself. You're about to marry the man you love, who happens to be smart and hot and totally devoted to you. Focus on that."

"And remember," her father added, "you have us in your corner. Always, no matter what."

As Marina led them toward the guest house, she felt some of her anxiety ease. Her father's insight about Catrina's true motivations had helped put things in perspective. And Larissa was right—she needed to focus on her relationship with Peter, not his mother's approval or disapproval of her.

9

SYSSI

The late morning sun warmed Syssi's back as she watched Allegra wet the sand with water from her bottle, carefully shaping it into what was meant to be a castle. Beside her, Evie seemed content to simply dig with her little shovel, occasionally showing her findings to Allegra with excited babbles.

During the weekends, the playground was Syssi's favorite spot for Allegra to play with her cousins and for her to catch up with Andrew and Nathalie, Eva and Bhathian, and have a chat with some of the Kra-ell, who brought their kids to the playground as well. Today, though, Darius's absence was a reminder of what had almost happened last evening, and it made her feel anxious all over again.

Amanda, on the other hand, seemed unaffected, her attention drifting from time to time to the village green, where Guardians were arranging tables and chairs for tomorrow's wedding according to the diagram she'd given them.

"I love this," Amanda said, her eyes sparkling as she watched the preparations. "The excitement in the air before an event. And this weekend, we get two. I just hope it doesn't rain tomorrow because I didn't order a tent." She smiled at Syssi. "I'm crossing my fingers that we won't have to dance in the rain."

Perhaps that was why Amanda didn't seem to be dwelling on the barely averted tragedy. She was focusing on reasons to celebrate instead.

Rob's induction ceremony was happening tonight at the gym, and Peter and Marina were getting married tomorrow on the village green.

"Speaking of celebrations," Syssi said. "Kian barely agreed to have a family get-together for his birthday, and I didn't argue with him since no one celebrates their birthdays in the village. But he is all in for a big party for Allegra because her first birthday is a milestone."

Amanda's face lit up. "I've been thinking about that. It needs to be a grand celebration. We should even invite Sari and David and anyone else from Scotland who wants to attend. And since it's going to be such a big event, you should probably start preparing Allegra for all the attention."

Syssi shifted on the bench. "I'm not sure about making it so elaborate. If we throw a big party for

Allegra, it sets a precedent. Other parents might feel pressured to do the same for their children."

"Exactly!" Amanda's grin was triumphant. "That's precisely the point. First birthdays should be grand celebrations. After that, they can be more modest affairs. With how few children we are having, each one is a miracle and should be regarded as such."

"Mama!" Allegra patted the top of her sandcastle. "Look!"

"That's amazing, sweetheart," Syssi called back, then lowered her voice. "Andrew and Nathalie didn't have a big party for Phoenix. It was just the close family, very intimate. If we do something elaborate for Allegra, my brother might feel guilty for not throwing a great party for his daughter."

Amanda rolled her eyes. "One has nothing to do with the other. But if you're worried, talk to Andrew. Check with him to see if it would bother him."

"He'd never admit it if it did."

"Then if he says go ahead, you have your permission." Amanda shrugged, then reached out to steady Evie, who had tried to stand in the sandbox. "Careful, baby."

Syssi watched her daughter pat more wet sand onto her castle. Allegra was so focused and determined to succeed, her little face scrunched in concentration, reminding Syssi of Kian when he was working.

"Besides," Amanda continued, her expression growing more serious, "as Kian likes to say, we should embrace every opportunity for celebration, and the bigger the better—meaning including the most people."

"He does say that a lot," Syssi admitted.

"And he's right." Amanda pulled out a tissue to wipe sand from Evie's face. "The world is full of sorrows, but we need to stay positive and celebrate our triumphs, big and small. To us, every child is a victory. You know that."

Syssi considered this as she watched the girls play. Allegra had abandoned her castle-building efforts and was now showing Evie how to make handprints in the wet sand.

"You're thinking too hard," Amanda said softly. "You always do that, trying to consider every possible ramification of every decision. Sometimes a party is just a party, Syssi."

She laughed. "Not in this village. In our community, everything sets precedents and becomes tradition."

"And that's beautiful." Amanda spread her arms. "Immortals live so long that we've stopped celebrating birthdays. I need to concentrate to remember my own. I don't think it's a good thing. It belittles the incredible gift of immortality." She leaned closer to Syssi. "We should know better than to take for granted what the Fates give us. They want to be appreciated."

"I agree." Syssi wrapped her arm around her sister-in-law's middle. "Big party it is."

A squeal of laughter drew their attention back to the sandbox. Evie had put her sand-covered hands on her head, and Allegra was trying to help clean her cousin off, but she was mostly just spreading the mess around.

"Oh dear," Syssi said, reaching for the baby wipes in her bag. "I think someone needs a bath."

"Two someones," Amanda agreed, watching as Allegra also became covered in sand through her helpful efforts. "But look how happy they are."

Syssi had to smile at the pure joy on the girls' faces. "I love seeing them together." She glanced in the direction of the café. "Kian is supposed to come over here when he finishes his meeting with Eleanor and Emmett. I want him to see the girls like this."

Amanda tilted her head. "Do you know what the meeting is about?"

Syssi shrugged. "They are here for the weekend to attend Peter's wedding, so I assume they thought it was a good opportunity for a face-to-face meeting with Kian. Probably something to do with the management of Safe Haven."

10

KIAN

As Kian walked over to the playground, the sound of children's laughter made him smile.

Was there a better sound?

But then he saw Allegra and Evie covered in sand and laughed. "What happened? Did they decide to swim in the sand?"

"Something like that." Syssi patted the spot next to her on the bench. "Allegra was building castles, and Evie was watching, but then she decided to put her hands on her head."

"They're going to need hosing down before you even get them into the bathtub." He settled beside Syssi.

"Noted," she said, leaning into him. "Maybe that's why Evie did that. She loves taking baths with Allegra."

"They are so cute together." Amanda looked at

the girls with a smile tugging on her lips. "I'm thankful to the Fates for granting us such an incredible boon as daughters who are close in age and will get to grow up together." She chuckled. "I can just imagine all the mischief they will get themselves into, with Allegra being the ringleader, of course. Evie is too sweet for her own good."

Kian couldn't argue with that. He loved Allegra's spunk and her strong personality, but he didn't look forward to her turning into a rebellious teenager who'd taken a page from her grandmother's book.

He wouldn't be able to sleep at all.

"What did Eleanor and Emmett want?" Amanda asked. "I bet they didn't request a meeting just to chat."

"No, they didn't." He smiled at Allegra, who'd just noticed that he was there, and pointed at her castle.

"Daddy, look!"

"It's beautiful, sweetheart. Daddy is so proud of you."

She beamed happily and went back to work.

"The government is terminating the paranormal program at Safe Haven," he said.

Amanda's head snapped up. "Are they moving it somewhere else?"

"No, they are terminating it. They are paying the participants part of their contract as severance pay and sending them home."

"Did they specify a reason?" Syssi asked.

"Budget cuts."

To his surprise, Syssi relaxed against him. "That's actually good news."

"How do you figure?"

"The less interest the government has in paranormal abilities, the better," she said. "Besides, these people deserve more out of their lives than spending them in near isolation and participating in experiments."

There was truth to that. He didn't think about the paranormal program often, but when he did, he felt sorry for the small group of people who were living in limbo. "What do you think we should do with them?"

"It's quite simple. First, we need to test them for dormancy like we should have done a long time ago." She lifted her head to look at him. "Those who aren't Dormants should be released to live their lives as free citizens, and those who transition will be welcomed into our community."

"It's not as simple as you make it sound," he said. "They're all paired up into couples. We can't exactly suggest the women have sex with random immortals in hopes of inducing their transitions."

Amanda snorted. "Why not?"

"Amanda!" Syssi looked scandalized.

"What? Human couples aren't as exclusive as immortals. Some of them might be perfectly okay with it once we explain the situation."

Kian rubbed his temples. "We can start with the males, who are easier to induce, but when they start transitioning, we will need a way to get them to a clan doctor as quickly as possible. That means either bringing them here, taking them to the keep, or sending part of our medical staff to Safe Haven."

"It was always the plan to test people at Safe Haven eventually," Amanda pointed out. "Maybe Merlin and Ronja wouldn't mind relocating there for a few weeks."

"Or we could bring just the males to the keep for testing," Syssi suggested.

Amanda shook her head. "That's not fair to the women. They should at least have the option. Explain the situation to them and let them decide. Those who refuse to have sex with anyone other than their partner will have their memories thralled away, and those who agree will be compelled to keep quiet."

"That's actually not a bad plan." Kian pulled out his phone. "Although, I hate to put them in that position. Imagine if someone told you that you had to choose between being unfaithful to your husband and losing your chance at becoming immortal."

Amanda cast him a hard look. "I would be much angrier if that someone decided that he wasn't going to tell me in order to save me the heartache and deprive me of my chance. In fact, I would be so livid that I could resort to violence."

He shifted his gaze to Syssi, but to his surprise, she nodded. "Amanda is right."

"Well, if you both agree, who am I to argue." He typed a message to Eleanor, outlining the suggestion.

"Mama!" Allegra called. "Castle broke!"

"That's okay, sweetheart," Syssi called back. "You can build another one."

The response from Eleanor came back quickly: *Will discuss options with participants after government contracts are dissolved and proceed from there.*

"Eleanor is on board," Kian reported.

"Of course she is," Amanda said. "It's the most practical solution."

Kian watched as Allegra determinedly began piling up sand for a new castle, and Evie tried to help her by digging out sand and adding a few grains to the pile while losing most of it by just lifting her toy shovel.

"Some of them have interesting abilities," he said. "One of them had a weak telekinetic ability, so she could be useful for your research into Morelle's talent."

"Speaking of Morelle," Syssi said, "did you notice how exhausted she seemed?"

"It was an intense situation," Kian pointed out.

"It was more than that." Syssi pushed a strand of hair behind her ear. "The expenditure of energy cost her." She turned to Amanda. "When you test her, be careful. I have a feeling that she might burn herself out by trying too hard. Don't push her, and don't let her push herself."

"I'll be careful," Amanda promised. "Having another telekinetic to compare her to will be very useful. I can measure the energy expenditure on the other female."

Kian watched his daughter abandon her castle-building efforts to help Evie dig a hole. "Sofia's ability is much weaker than Morelle's, but studying it might still provide insights."

"If Sofia transitions successfully," Amanda pointed out, "her ability might get stronger." She grinned. "It will be fun to have two strong telekinetic talents work together. They could throw a ball to each other without using their hands."

Kian laughed. "Let's not get ahead of ourselves. Sofia might choose to stay faithful to her boyfriend. Besides, we need to focus on getting through this weekend's events first."

"Speaking of events," Amanda said with a sly glance at Syssi, "we were just discussing Allegra's upcoming birthday party."

Kian recognized the gleam in his sister's eyes. "What are you planning?"

"Nothing too extravagant," Amanda assured him. "Just...special."

"Special is good," he said, watching his daughter laugh as she played. "A special girl deserves a special party."

Syssi squeezed his hand. "Amanda thinks we

should throw a grand party and invite Sari and David and anyone else from Scotland and the Sanctuary who wants to share in the celebration."

"Of course we should," he agreed eagerly. "The more excuses I have for dragging our stubborn sister to come visit, the better."

"That's what I said!" Amanda looked triumphant.

Syssi rolled her eyes. "I knew you'd both gang up on me about this."

"Because we're right," Amanda said. "Right, Kian?"

"Always," he agreed solemnly, then laughed when Syssi elbowed him in the ribs.

Their laughter was interrupted by a squeal from the sandbox. Evie had managed to dump a handful of sand down her shirt, and this time, she wasn't as happy about it as when she'd dumped it on her head.

Her little face was twisted in a prelude to crying, and then the tears came.

"Bath time." Amanda gathered up her daughter and lifted her shirt to dust off some of the sand, which made Evie cry even louder.

"It irritates her skin," Syssi said. "The sand sticks to her sweat and brushing it off hurts her."

"Right." Amanda just whipped the shirt off, leaving Evie bare-chested, and then blew air on her chest and tummy. "Better?" she asked.

Evie nodded and arched her little belly for more air blowing.

"Adorable," Syssi cooed.

Kian scooped Allegra into his arms and kissed her cheeks as Syssi collected the sand toys and dumped them onto the bottom shelf of the stroller.

"Daddy." Allegra cupped his cheeks.

"Yes, sweetie?"

She just smiled and planted a slobbery kiss on his cheek.

11

PETER

Peter placed four pairs of the latest model of translating earpieces on the dining table. William's team had developed them for the Kra-ell, and they weren't as sophisticated as the one that blocked compulsion, but they did the job of translating even better.

"What are these?" his mother asked.

"Marina's parents don't speak English. They can speak Russian, Finnish, and Kra-ell." He added the last part so his mother wouldn't get all snooty about them being illiterate or something.

For humans, who didn't have the immortals' innate ability to absorb new languages like sponges, speaking all three fluently was an impressive achievement.

"I see." She picked up a box and opened it. "They don't look like the ones you have in your ears."

"Mine are also compulsion blocking. William's team created a new, simpler, and less costly version for the Kra-ell. They can be set up to translate from Kra-ell or Russian into English. Marina's parents will set them up to translate English to Russian or Kra-ell."

Pulling out the devices, she examined them for a moment before sticking them in her ears. "What do I do now?"

"Tap on one of them." He demonstrated. "It will give you the selection and instruct you on what to do next."

She frowned. "But what will happen when you and I speak English? Will it automatically translate to one of the other languages?"

He chuckled. "No. It's a smart device. It will not translate my English to Kra-ell when you have it set up the other way around."

"That makes sense." She smiled sheepishly. "All this new technology just goes over my head."

As the door opened and Marina walked in with her parents, Peter walked over to greet them.

"Lara, Daniil. It's so good to see you again." He leaned to kiss Lara's cheeks one at a time and then offered Daniil his hand.

"How do they like the village?" he asked Marina.

"They love it," Marina said. "Did you get them the earpieces?"

"Yes." He led them to the dining table and explained how to put them in.

When it was done, Peter turned to his mother. "This is my mother, Catrina. Mother, this is Lara, Marina's mother, and Daniil, her father."

"A pleasure to meet you both." His mother offered her hand to Lara and then to Daniil.

So far, so good. Everyone was being polite, and his mother was making an effort to be civil and to not look down her nose at Marina's parents.

"I see that you've met my Peter before," his mother said.

"Oh, yes." Lara smiled. "Peter and Marina stayed in Safe Haven before they moved to the village, so, of course, we were introduced. And you met our Marina on the cruise, correct?"

"Yes." His mother forced a smile. "She was part of the crew and hard to miss with her blue hair and piercings."

Lara grimaced. "I don't like either of those things. But what can I do? When they are all grown up, they don't listen to their parents."

His mother laughed, and for a change, it didn't sound forced. "Tell me about it. Peter stopped listening to me when he was a wee lad of sixteen."

Peter lifted a hand to stop his mother from launching into more details about his rebellious teens. "Please sit down. You can keep entertaining Lara and Daniil while I help Marina serve dinner."

The house's open layout meant that they had no privacy in the kitchen, so he couldn't pull Marina into his arms and kiss her until the tension left her shoulders. All he could do was convey his feelings with his expression when his back was turned to the dining room.

Once the food was served and they'd taken their seats around the table, everyone got busy loading their plates.

Lara broke the silence first to compliment her daughter on the roast, and his mother echoed the sentiment, whether she was enjoying the food or not.

"Wine, anyone?" Peter asked.

Daniil regarded the wine with one raised bushy brow. "Do you have anything stronger?"

"I sure do." Peter got up and brought over a bottle of vodka. "Better?"

Daniil's expression brightened. "Oh, yes. Now you are talking my language."

Peter opened the bottle and poured the vodka into Daniil's wine glass and was surprised when his mother lifted hers.

"I prefer something stronger as well. I'm not a big fan of wine."

"Well." Marina lifted her glass. "When in Rome and all that. I guess I'll be drinking vodka as well."

"Not for me." Lara shook her head. "I'll have the wine."

For the next ten minutes or so, they ate in silence.

Daniil was done with his meal first. He pushed the empty plate aside, poured himself more vodka, and leaned back in his chair. "This was an excellent meal, Marina. When did you learn to cook like that?"

"The better question is not when but where, and I learned from the best." She lifted her glass at her mother.

"Oh, Marina." Her mother waved a dismissive hand. "You flatter me. You didn't learn from me. I never cooked just for my family. I always cooked for many people, and I still do." She glanced at Catrina. "That is what I do at Safe Haven. I work in the staff kitchen."

"And I work in maintenance," Daniil said. "It's the same job I did at Igor's compound, but now I do it with joy."

Peter watched his mother's expression shift as Daniil described their struggles—the constant fear, the oppression, the ways they'd maintained their sense of community and tried to lead as normal lives as they could.

Thankfully, he hadn't mentioned what Marina had been forced to do with the Kra-ell. Not that it was a secret, but he didn't want his mother to make her feel uncomfortable about something she had very little control over, if any.

"What about school?" his mother asked. "Peter tells me that all of you speak three languages. Did you have official schooling, or did you just pick it up?"

"We had schooling," Marina said. "But it was just the basics. Most of what I've learned has been from reading books. At least the Kra-ell didn't restrict that. We were allowed to order books from a catalog, and we had a system of borrowing books from one another."

Peter saw something soften in his mother's face. "Is that how you learned English?"

Marina set down her fork. "I learned some English while still in the compound, mostly by watching movies and reading children's books. But I learned the most after arriving at Safe Haven. I studied every free moment I had. I wanted to integrate, to be part of this wonderful new country the clan brought us to."

"That's admirable," his mother said. "What kind of work did you do at Safe Haven?"

Peter tensed at the question, seeing Marina's discomfort. "I worked in housekeeping," she said quietly. "Safe Haven is a resort, and they need people to maintain the guest rooms."

To Peter's surprise, his mother nodded approvingly. "There's no shame in any kind of work as long as it is legal. I've done my share of odd jobs over the centuries."

Peter stared at her. "You have?"

"Of course." She took a sip of her drink. "In my youth, which was a very long time ago, the clan wasn't nearly as wealthy as it is now. Everyone had to contribute however they could. I've done everything from serving ale in taverns to raising chickens and selling eggs."

"I remember the chickens," Peter said. How had he forgotten that part of his childhood? "You used to send me each morning to collect the eggs."

"And you hated me for it," his mother laughed. "But you did it, and we made do. Every morning, rain or shine, summer or winter, I walked to the nearby village with my basket of eggs and sold them until there were none left."

The atmosphere around the table shifted perceptibly as the three parents found common ground in their experiences of hard work and survival, and Peter watched in amazement as his mother engaged enthusiastically in swapping stories about the old times with Marina's parents. The walls between them were crumbling as they found unexpected connections.

Marina caught his eye across the table, her expression a mix of relief and wonder. He reached for her hand under the table, squeezing gently.

"Tell us about the tavern," Peter said. "I've never heard that story before."

He was fascinated by this glimpse into her past.

"Oh, those were interesting times," she said. "I

learned a lot about human nature during that time."

"The stories you must have heard," Daniil said. "The drink loosens people's tongues."

"Oh, I did, and the fights I broke up!" His mother laughed. "My immortal strength came in handy. I developed a reputation as Iron-fist Catrina. Men wanted to arm-wrestle me, and the barman took wagers, and he gave me a cut of the winnings after everyone left. I made more from those than from what he paid me and the tips combined."

This was a whole new side of his mother that Peter had never been aware of.

He shook his head. "I can't believe you did all that and never told me."

His mother shrugged. "It was a long time before you were born. I saw no reason to encourage your adventurous streak by telling you stories from my own somewhat scandalous youth."

"We all do what we must to survive," Daniil said. "To make better lives for ourselves and for our children."

His mother nodded. "Yes, we do."

Peter felt something tight in his chest begin to loosen. They weren't fully there yet—his mother hadn't completely accepted Marina—but this was progress. Finding these common threads of experience, these shared understandings, was a start.

As the conversation continued, flowing more

naturally now, Peter felt hope growing. His mother was seeing Marina and her family as people—complex, resilient, worthy people—rather than just humans who weren't good enough.

It wasn't perfect, but it was a beginning.

12

ROB

"Wow." Rob took in the transformed gym. "Look at what they have done."

Gertrude threaded her arm through his. "It's something, isn't it?"

"Yeah. Something."

Jin, Mey, and Margo had converted the space into what looked suspiciously like a teenager's birthday party. Colorful balloons bobbed against the ceiling, paper chandeliers twirled in the air-conditioning breeze, and ribbons festooned every available surface, including all the exercise machines that had been pushed aside to clear a large space in the middle of the cavernous room.

"It's very festive," he said diplomatically. "But it seems more appropriate for someone much younger."

"Well," Gertrude said, "technically, boys usually have their induction ceremonies at thirteen, so I suppose the decorations are appropriate. I just have to wonder how Jin knew that. We haven't had any boys transition since Parker."

Jin, who was packing up leftover decorations, turned at Gertrude's words. "These are the stored decorations Amanda told me to use. The boxes contained balloons, ribbons, chandeliers, and banners, but we skipped the banners. Those were really inappropriate for an adult."

"I have to admit that it does look very festive," Rob said.

In truth, he didn't mind the decorations. They were far from the most anxiety-inducing aspect of the evening ahead.

His eyes drifted to the buffet table being set up along one wall, laden with snacks for the guests. Thankfully, there were no tables and chairs for sitting. His upcoming humiliation wouldn't be a prolonged affair.

People were already starting to arrive, filtering into the transformed space with excited chatter and expectant faces. Rob shifted uncomfortably, unsure what to do with himself until the actual ceremony began.

"Just smile and say 'thank you' when people wish you luck," Gertrude murmured, squeezing his arm.

"I can do that." He plastered a fake confident smile on his face and assumed a strong pose with his legs slightly spread, one arm around Gertrude's shoulders and the hand of the other in the pocket of his sweatpants.

Bridget had promised to attend in case he needed medical attention, which had given him a fright until she'd explained that she hadn't meant him getting beaten up by Arwel but his reaction to the venom. Not that it was much better, but at least it didn't involve pain, and he wasn't really worried about his body reacting badly to the venom.

His test results had been fantastic, and Bridget had been impressed that a dude who until recently had engaged in very little physical activity was in such good shape.

William arrived with Roni, Kaia, and another female who was probably Roni's mate Sylvia. Rob hadn't met her yet, but he'd heard rumors about her extraordinary talent for disabling electronics.

"Excited?" Roni asked after introducing his mate.

"More like terrified," Rob admitted quietly.

Roni chuckled. "Been in your shoes, so I know how it feels."

"Yeah, but you were a kid, right?"

"Yes, but not the way you think. I was eighteen, scrawny as hell, and I was recovering from pneumonia. It took three attempts before I finally transitioned."

Rob blinked. "Three?"

"Yeah. Not only that, I also had to resort to

reciting vile slam poetry to get Kian riled up enough to bite me." Roni's grin widened. "I was too scrawny and weak to actually challenge an immortal to a fight. I had to make him angry enough to attack me."

"Wait—Kian himself induced you?" Rob couldn't imagine the clan leader agreeing to do that.

He was the master of ceremonies, not the biter.

Gertrude nodded. "As a demigod, Kian's venom is more potent than that of most immortals. He was the last resort after Roni failed to transition the first two times."

"Isn't Toven's venom even stronger?" Rob asked. "Being a full god and all?"

"Of course," Gertrude said. "But Toven wasn't part of the clan back then. He's a relatively recent addition."

Mia had told Rob about how she and Toven had been matched through a Perfect Match adventure, leading to the clan discovering the god's existence. He just hadn't realized Roni's induction had predated that.

Gertrude leaned against his arm, her eyes twinkling. "So, do you know any vile slam poetry? Just in case?"

"I'm offended," Rob said, drawing himself up. "I can provoke Arwel's aggression through actual fighting. I'm not a scrawny kid," he said, quietly enough for Roni not to hear him all the way from the snack table.

"Of course not." She laughed, the sound warming him despite his nervousness. "Still, maybe prepare a few verses. You know, as backup."

Looking at her bright eyes and teasing smile, Rob had a feeling she was just trying to ease his tension. It was working, too. The knot in his stomach had loosened a little.

"You'd be surprised." He wrapped his arm around her waist. "I did some slam poetry during my college years. I could compose something about Arwel's fighting stance," Rob mused, playing along. "Or maybe critique his footwork in rhyming couplets."

"Now, that I'd pay to see." Gertrude's eyes danced. "Though maybe save the critique until after you've transitioned. When you're immortal, and he can't actually kill you."

Rob's amusement faded. "Arwel is too kind to kill someone in anger, and I respect him too much to insult him even as a joke."

She arched a brow. "Haven't you ever watched roasting? I've forgotten the name of that show, but people roast their best friends. I've even seen a former president taking insults like a champ."

"The name of the show is *Between Two Ferns*, and I could never watch it because it just makes me anxious. I don't like it when people are forced to take punches, whether real or verbal. I don't watch boxing or wrestling either."

That wasn't a very manly admission, and Rob would never have said that to Lynda for fear of ridicule, but Gertrude accepted him the way he was, and he didn't have to pretend to be anyone he wasn't.

"That's so sweet." She cupped his cheek and kissed him on the other side. 'You are a good man, Rob. A really good man."

"And you are an angel." He lifted her hand to his lips and kissed her fingers.

More guests were arriving now—Guardians he recognized from training sessions, clan members he'd met through his sister, faces both familiar and new. Each arrival brought a fresh wave of nervous energy.

"I didn't expect so many people to come," he whispered to Gertrude.

"The clan loves celebrating new additions. Every transition represents hope, continuity, and growth. Besides, everyone likes you."

He chuckled. "I haven't spoken more than a word to most of these people. I'm a computer nerd who was never popular."

She smiled at him. "In our community, nerds are cool."

13

MORELLE

"Does the induction ceremony always take place so late at night?" Morelle asked as she and Brandon walked with Jasmine and Ell-rom toward the glass pavilion, where Rob was about to wrestle Arwel and get bitten.

"That's the custom," Brandon said. "The idea is that the Dormant enters the ring before midnight and emerges on the other side on a new day, but the truth is that the transition itself doesn't happen right away. It usually starts a day or two later."

"For males," Jasmine said. "For females, it's less predictable than that."

Brandon had explained to her the differences between male and female Dormants and their transitions, and in Morelle's opinion, the females got the better deal because they got induced through pleasure, but if the results were less predictable, then maybe they didn't.

Morelle still hadn't experienced those kinds of pleasures, and she was impatient. She felt much better today, stronger, and she'd taken a nap in the afternoon deliberately so she wouldn't be too tired after the ceremony to follow up with her seduction plan.

"Look," Jasmine said. "Syssi and Kian are right in front of us. Let's catch up to them."

As their group hastened their steps, Amanda and Dalhu walked out of their home and joined them.

"Good evening," Amanda said. "We have quite a turnout for Rob's ceremony tonight."

As more people kept walking out of the homes they were passing by, Morelle had to agree with that assessment. It seemed like the entire clan was heading to the gym.

"We do," Jasmine said. "Margo will be thrilled, but I'm not sure about Rob."

"Is Rob really this popular?" Morelle asked Brandon. "He's only been in the village a short time."

"Usually, these ceremonies are more intimate," Syssi said. "Just close family and friends. I'm not sure why the turnout is so large tonight."

Jasmine brightened. "I'm glad Rob is getting such a big audience. Brandon, do you think I should sing something for him before the ceremony begins?"

Brandon's eyebrows rose. "That's never been done before, but it's not a bad idea. Do you know any songs about friendship? The ceremony does cement a lifelong bond between inducer and inductee, so that would be appropriate."

"How about 'Bridge over Troubled Water'?" Amanda suggested. "Or is that too dramatic?"

"'Lean on Me' might be more appropriate," Syssi offered.

Jasmine hummed a few bars of each, her voice clear and melodious in the evening air, and Morelle found herself enchanted by the talent of her brother's mate.

"You should definitely sing," she encouraged. "Your voice is beautiful."

They had to pause their discussion as they reached the glass pavilion, where a crowd had gathered waiting for the elevators.

Being surrounded by so many people, Morelle felt the energy thrumming through her. She wasn't actively drawing on it, but it was somehow seeping into her, and she wanted it to stop. Remembering how she'd pulled power from everyone in Syssi's living room, she forced herself to focus on Brandon's solid presence beside her to ground herself against the temptation to reach for that power and pull.

When they finally made it to the gym, Morelle's focus turned to the colorful decorations hanging everywhere. The gym had been transformed, and in the middle of it, Rob stood inside a roped-off area, looking like he might be sick.

Her heart went out to him. She wished she had some way to ease his fear, but that wasn't one of her abilities. Though...her eyes drifted to the decorations bobbing against the ceiling.

Could she pop a few of those inflated containers?

She hadn't tried to use her newly discovered power again, and she was curious to see if it would be available to her without pulling energy from people around her, using only what was inside of her.

Would it amuse Rob if she managed to pop those decorations? Or would it just scare him more?

"Don't even think about it," Brandon murmured in her ear.

She turned to him. "Think about what?"

"Whatever mischief you're plotting." His eyes crinkled with amusement. "I saw that look."

"I just thought that a little innocent distraction might help Rob relax, and I'd get to test my ability on something harmless." She pointed at the ceiling and made a popping sound with her mouth.

He chuckled. "Exploding decorations might

have the opposite effect on poor Rob. Jasmine singing him a song is a much better idea."

She couldn't argue with that. "Does every male Dormant look so scared before his induction?"

"Most do," Brandon said. "It's a big moment even without taking into account having to fight a much stronger opponent. It's a life-changing event."

Beside them, Jasmine was still quietly singing, her voice barely above a whisper as she tested different lyrics. The sound provided a pleasant counterpoint to the nervous energy filling the room.

"What happens if he doesn't transition?" Morelle asked.

"Then he tries again another time," Brandon explained. "Some need multiple attempts."

More people continued to file into the gym until Morelle felt almost claustrophobic with the press of bodies. She breathed in and out steadily, reminding herself that these people were her community, and she had nothing to fear from them.

"Are you okay?" Ell-rom asked from her other side.

She nodded. "Are you okay with so many people around?"

He shrugged. "Not really, but with you and Jasmine beside me, I feel safe."

"Oh, sweetheart." Jasmine leaned her head on his shoulder.

"We can move toward the back if you'd prefer," Brandon offered.

"No," Morelle said quickly. "I want to be close to the stage where this will play out."

This was her clan now, her community, and she wanted to learn their traditions and their ceremonies because they were hers now.

"I think I know what song would be perfect," Jasmine said. "'With a Little Help from my Friends.' It's about friendship and support, and it's also upbeat."

"That's perfect," Amanda agreed. "But we should check with Kian first. He's the master of ceremonies, and he might object to deviating from tradition."

"I'm all for it," Kian said. "I'll introduce you." He walked over to where Rob was standing and lifted his hand high in the air to get everyone's attention.

"Good evening, everyone, and thank you for coming to witness Rob's induction ceremony. I'm thrilled to introduce a new tradition to our ceremony tonight. Jasmine is going to sing a song about friendship, and everyone who knows the words to 'With a Little Help from my Friends' is welcome to sing along." He turned to Jasmine and waved her over. "Next time, we will have a stage ready for you, but tonight, the best I can offer you is a chair to stand on."

She laughed as she made her way over to him. "No need. Thanks to the significant height increase following my transition and a pair of high heels, I will be seen by most even without standing on a chair."

She ducked under the rope to where Rob was standing and put her hand on his shoulder. "You are also welcome to sing along, my friend."

14

ROB

As Rob joined Jasmine, singing loudly and slightly off-key, it felt cathartic. Nearly everyone in the gym was singing with him, and the energy infusion was incredible.

These people cared about him for some reason. They had his back.

When she was done, the room erupted in cheers and applause, and Jasmine took a bow before turning to him. "Good luck, Rob." She patted his arm before stepping out of the ring.

Kian raised his hand again to shush the crowd. "Who thinks that Jasmine's wonderful song is a great addition to our induction ceremonies?"

As another round of cheers and applause ensued, Kian clapped along, and his butler rushed in with a tray of tiny paper cups filled with wine, distributing it amongst the guests.

Had he brought enough?

Surely, no one had anticipated such a turnout, especially not Rob. Margo and Gertrude stood on the other side of the rope like two lionesses guarding their cub, and when the butler reached them, they each grabbed a cup, and Gertrude took one more for him.

When everyone was served, Kian raised his cup, and the gym fell silent.

"We are gathered here tonight," Kian's voice carried clearly through the space, "to present this man to his elders. Rob is ready to attempt his transition. Vouching for him are Toven, Mia, and many others. Who volunteers to take on the burden of initiating Rob into his immortality?"

Arwel stepped forward. "I do."

Rob's heart hammered against his ribs. Despite knowing this was coming, everything suddenly felt terrifyingly real.

"Rob," Kian continued, "do you accept Guardian Arwel as your initiator? As your mentor and protector, to honor him with your friendship, your respect, and your loyalty from now on?"

"I do," he said.

"Does anyone have any objections to Rob becoming Arwel's protégé?"

When no one came forward, Kian raised his wine glass. "As everyone here agrees that it's a good match, let's seal it with a toast. To Rob and Arwel."

The assembled crowd echoed the toast, and Rob took a sip of the sweet wine, grateful for something to do with his hands.

Arwel approached him with a warm smile. "Ready, brother?"

The term of endearment, though part of the ceremony, still touched something in Rob's chest. "As I'll ever be."

They embraced briefly—the traditional gesture symbolizing their new bond—before taking positions on the mat. Rob was acutely aware of the crowd surrounding them, but he forced himself to focus on Arwel.

"You're ready," Arwel said with a smile. "Show me what you've got."

Someone blew a whistle, and suddenly, they were moving. Rob blocked Arwel's first strike more by instinct than skill, falling into the patterns they'd practiced countless times. But this was different from training—there was real power behind Arwel's attacks now, but Rob still suspected that the Guardian was holding back just enough for him to last longer than two seconds.

Rob managed to dodge a kick, but Arwel's follow-up punch caught him in the ribs. He heard Gertrude gasp, but he couldn't spare the attention to look at her.

Using his slightly heavier build to his advantage, Rob attempted to grapple Arwel to the mat. For a moment, he thought he'd succeeded, but then the world spun, and he found himself face down, arm twisted behind his back.

"That was very good," Arwel said, his words sounding slurred, coming from between his elongated fangs, but Rob could still hear the amusement in his voice.

He wondered how Arwel could be amused while getting aggressive enough to produce venom. The fight had been a joke, but he'd managed to last longer than two seconds, and maybe that had been good enough.

Despite knowing it was futile, Rob struggled against Arwel's hold, his pride demanding he at least put in an effort. Then Arwel pressed his knee between Rob's shoulder blades, holding him firmly in place, and a moment later came the sharp pain of fangs piercing his neck.

The world exploded into sensation. Fire raced through his veins, but it wasn't painful—it was euphoric, transcendent. Colors seemed intensified, sounds sharpened, and everything had taken on a crystalline clarity.

Then darkness swept in, and Rob fell into it willingly.

He came to with his head pillowed in Gertrude's lap, her fingers gently stroking his hair. "Welcome back," she murmured.

Rob blinked, trying to orient himself. His body felt heavy but not unpleasantly so, and the residual effects of the venom left him feeling oddly peaceful and content.

"How long was I out?"

"Just a few minutes, thank the merciful Fates." She leaned over him and kissed his forehead. "I would have freaked out if it took longer." She helped him sit up. "How do you feel?"

"Like I got hit by an ice cream truck," he admitted, "flattened but happy and satisfied."

Arwel appeared beside them, offering him a hand up. "That's normal. Come on, brother. Let's get you cleaned up."

Rob accepted the help, swaying slightly as he got to his feet. The crowd had thinned somewhat, though many still lingered, offering congratulations and good wishes.

"You did well," Arwel said, clapping him on the shoulder. "Now we just wait to see if it takes."

"How will I know?"

"Oh, you'll know." Arwel grinned. "Trust me."

Margo waited for Arwel to let go before slipping under Rob's arm to support him. "You're an impressive fighter, Rob. I didn't expect you to last that long."

"And there was no slam poetry required." Gertrude slipped under Rob's other arm. "Let's get you home."

Rob laughed, then winced as his ribs protested. "Maybe I should save that for next time if this doesn't take."

"It'll take," she said with certainty. "I can feel it."

"Me too." Margo cast him a confident smile. "Tomorrow morning, you'll start transitioning, which will be a bummer because you will miss Marina and Peter's wedding."

He chuckled. "I can live with that."

15

MORELLE

Morelle stood in front of the mirror in the master bathroom and ran her fingers through her short hair, which had grown a lot over the past several days. She assumed that since her body no longer needed to work on rebuilding itself from the skeleton up, it could finally dedicate energy to re-growing her hair.

She no longer looked bald, and that was a big improvement. Perhaps when it got a little longer, she could style it like Amanda's.

Curiously, no one had commented about their resemblance. Was she the only one who had noticed? Amanda was a little taller, though not by much, and they had similarly shaped faces, eyes, and lips.

Their personalities were different, though, and maybe that influenced how people saw them.

Amanda exuded an extroverted confidence, while Morelle was much more reserved, not just because she was still learning and was unsure about how to act and what to say. After a lifetime of isolation, she didn't feel comfortable surrounded by people, and today was no different.

She could only hope to one day exude confidence like Amanda's.

Sexual confidence.

Amanda looked like a female who knew what she wanted and didn't shy away from anything, and after tonight, maybe Morelle would feel the same.

Not likely.

Even if she succeeded in seducing Brandon, it would take many more nights of passion before she felt like she knew what she was doing.

With a sigh, she slipped on one of the modest nightgowns that Brandon's shopper had gotten for her. It was silky and sleeveless, so it wasn't completely devoid of allure, but it was floor length, and according to her new friends, sexy meant short.

It didn't matter.

Her plan was to whip the garment over her head and present Brandon with her nude body. Hopefully, he would find the sight irresistible, and nature would take its course.

When she entered the darkened room, though,

she was surprised to see him standing by the window instead of waiting for her in bed.

He must have overridden the automatic shutters that every house in the village was equipped with. They closed each evening at dusk so no light would betray the hidden village location.

"What are you doing?" She walked up to him.

"Watching the moon." He wrapped his arm around her middle and drew her against his side. "It's full tonight."

Morelle followed his gaze to the large disk hanging heavy in the sky and casting a silvery glow over the village below. "Does the full moon hold any special meaning?"

"Not really." He smiled at her. "Well, some say it's a symbol of everything mysterious and beautiful and that it represents connection, clarity, and things coming full circle. Others say it represents the goddess, the feminine power."

"What do you believe?"

"I believe in the power of beauty to move and inspire us." His eyes met hers. "To remind us that some things are worth stopping to appreciate."

The moonlight silvered his features, making him look otherworldly and yet somehow more real than ever. Morelle reached up, tracing the line of his jaw with her fingers.

"Indeed, you look very handsome and alluring in the moonlight." She laid her hands on his chest and pressed a soft kiss to his lips.

With a sharp intake of breath, he took over, devouring her as if he was starved for her. His frenzied kiss betrayed the desperate need he'd been hiding behind a veneer of civility, and it set her on fire. Molten heat rushed through her, turning her body liquid, and her knees buckled. If not for his arm holding her up, she would have melted on the floor.

He eased up then, teasing her lips with a swipe of his tongue before thrusting it back into her mouth and stoking the inferno once more. It was all-consuming, and yet not enough. She needed to bare him, to touch his skin, and to lick him all over.

Reaching for the buttons of his sleep shirt, her normally agile fingers turned clumsy as she tried to release the first one, and she groaned. "I need to feel you."

Without a word, his fingers joined hers on the buttons, and then the garment slid off his shoulders and hit the floor.

"Thank you." She smoothed her fingertips over his naked torso. "That's much better."

He groaned, his muscles tensing under her fingers and his heart thudding louder.

When she dragged her forefingers across his nipples, he hissed her name.

"What's the matter?" She feigned innocence. "Don't you like my touch?"

His hands captured hers, stilling her progress.

"I like it too much."

"Then don't fight me." She dipped her head and kissed the underside of his jaw. "Let me explore."

"You are playing with fire," he growled but released her hands.

His body certainly felt like it was burning under her touch, and the scent he was emitting was intoxicating.

Was that the smell of his pheromones?

It must be, because any hesitation she'd felt evaporated, and she was ready to climb him like a tree and have her way with him.

Her nipples hardened to such a degree that even the silky fabric of her nightgown felt abrasive, and in a brazen moment, she pushed the straps down her shoulders and just let it slide down to the floor.

Brandon hissed but didn't reach for her like she'd hoped. He just stood there with an inferno burning in his eyes, still determined to let her explore and dictate the tone.

It was so frustrating. What did she have to do to make him react?

She was completely nude before him, her body bathing in the moonlight. Why wasn't he lifting her into his arms and throwing her on his bed?

If he needed a stronger hint, she was going to give it to him. Grasping his hands, she pulled them over her breasts and caged them with hers so he wouldn't be able to refuse her.

16

BRANDON

The contact electrified Brandon.

"You are so beautiful," he whispered as he rubbed his thumbs over her erect nipples.

The moonlight painted silvery patterns across Morelle's skin, making her seem almost ethereal despite the very real warmth of her beneath his hands.

"Tell me if I should slow down," he murmured against her throat, though restraint was becoming increasingly difficult.

"I want you to hurry up. If you go any slower, we'll be going backward."

He chuckled, the sound turning to a groan as her fingers returned to circle his nipples. "You're sure about this?"

Instead of answering, she pulled him down for another kiss, fierce and demanding. She might be inexperienced, but her enthusiasm more than made up for it.

"I want you," she whispered against his mouth.

The words sent heat coursing through him, and as his fangs lengthened, he had to fight the urge to bite her.

It was too soon for that.

He leaned away, watching her face in the moonlight. "You are absolutely stunning."

"And so are you." Her hands swept down his sides, her nails grazing his skin as she circled to his belly and then moved lower to where his shaft was peeking over the waistband of his pajama pants.

He remembered the feel of her lush lips on his cock, and the thought of her doing that again elicited a shiver.

She stilled and tilted her head. "Am I doing something wrong?"

"You are doing everything right." He put his hands on her waist, lifted her, and covered the distance to the bed in one step.

Laying her on top of the covers, he took a moment to admire her beauty.

"Perfect."

He leaned over her and returned his attention to her breasts, circling her turgid peaks before giving each one a light pinch.

"Oh, dear Mother above." Morelle arched her back, jutting her breasts up.

Brandon lowered his head, slanting his mouth

over hers, and slipped his tongue between her pillowy lips. Kissing her, he kept playing with her nipples until she was undulating beneath him.

He craved her so badly that it hurt, but he had to be patient and follow her cues.

"Take your pants off," she commanded as if she could read his thoughts.

How could he say no?

But he had to refuse and hold on for just a little longer. Before daring to remove the last barrier between them, he had to bring her to a climax in case things got out of hand.

"Patience, Princess." He dipped his head and started kissing all around one nipple.

"Yes!" She sank her nails into his back. "More!"

That he could do, and he eagerly obeyed her command, closing his lips over one peak and gently sucking it in.

Morelle gasped, and when he flicked it with the tip of his tongue, she moaned.

Brandon had a feeling that he could make her come just by teasing her nipples, but that wasn't what he had in mind.

When she threaded her fingers through his hair, he didn't expect her to grip his head and move it to her other breast in a blatant demand to give it the same treatment as he had given its twin.

Fates, that was sexy as hell.

He loved her assertiveness, the way she knew

what she needed despite her inexperience and wasn't shy about expressing her demands.

The rising scent of her arousal was scrambling his brain, and he couldn't decide if he wanted to keep teasing her breasts, move down to lap at the fountain of her nectar, feed her his shaft, or just go for the ultimate prize and bury himself in her heat.

Drawing back, he looked at his beautiful princess and waited for her to tell him what she wanted, but she just looked up at him as if stunned, undecided, or just unsure about what to ask for.

He dipped one hand, smoothing his palm up her thigh. "Tell me what you want, gorgeous."

Her knees fell wide open, spreading her slick folds. "Touch me, Brandon."

Fates, how he wanted to just push his pajama pants down and ram his shaft into that slick, welcoming heat, and if she weren't a virgin, he wouldn't have hesitated even for a moment. But she was, and he had to go slow despite her impatience and her exploring hands.

Her fingers skimmed across his waist, back and forth, before sliding lower and rubbing him over the thin fabric, and he nearly came just from that. "I want this inside of me."

He groaned. "Fates. You are killing me."

Then, when she reached into his pants, he gritted his teeth and somehow stopped himself from ejaculating all over her hand. Instead, he reached between her legs and cupped her hot, virgin sex.

She was so wet, so ready for him, that his addled brain couldn't understand what he was waiting for, and when she started rubbing his shaft from hilt to tip and back again, he knew that he was a goner and was about to come in her hand.

That was what she wanted, right? What she'd asked him for the other night?

He could give it to her.

Letting go, he started thrusting his shaft into her hand while his finger slid in and out of her sheath. With the heel of his palm pressing on her clitoris, he pumped into her hand until his erection swelled, and he knew that he had about two seconds before he ejaculated.

17

MORELLE

Morelle was lost in the pleasure, awash in the sensations and the power she wielded over Brandon. Even in her inexperience, she knew that the desperate tone of his groans and the way his shaft was swelling in her hand as his thrusts became frenzied signaled that he was nearing his climax, but then he pulled back and dove between her thighs.

Oh, no, he didn't.

She reached for him and tried to pull him back up. "Brandon!"

He was insufferable. He'd been so close, and he'd pulled back because his male ego couldn't tolerate him reaching climax before her.

He didn't budge, looking up at her with glowing eyes and elongated fangs. "I need to do this, Princess. I promise that I will let you do whatever you want to me after I wring a climax out of you."

They would need to talk about his silly male pride, but not right now.

Letting out a breath, she closed her eyes and lay back.

"Thank you, sweetheart." He planted a soft kiss on her inner thigh. "I promise you will get your turn."

He hooked his arms behind her thighs and widened her knees, further exposing her to him, and lowered his mouth to her sex. She'd known what to expect, and yet the sensation of his lips on her was a jolt, and then he sealed his mouth over her and gave her a hard suck.

He was being much less gentle with her than he had been the other day, and she had no problem with that. Her body was humming with need, and she was impatient.

The pleasure was intense. Too intense.

Holding on to his head, she panted while he licked, kissed, and sucked. The pressure mounted rapidly, and in seconds, she was moaning and groaning, her hips bucking against his mouth.

She was so close, but the edge eluded her, and she groaned half in pleasure and half in frustration, needing him to help her topple over.

When he pulled his mouth away and rose over her body, she thought he would finally penetrate her, and she was more than fine with that, but instead, he looked into her eyes while pressing his fingers against her clit and rubbing it hard.

It bordered on painful, and she didn't know whether she wanted him to continue or stop, but as she stared into his glowing eyes, she couldn't find the right words to express what she felt. His face looked demonic above her, with glowing eyes and long, gleaming fangs, and she was enthralled by his beauty.

Morelle was on fire.

Pain mingled with pleasure, and then she toppled over with a scream, her sheath spasming with a powerful climax that felt incomplete because she needed him to fill her, and he hadn't.

Leaning back, he watched her fall apart with an infuriatingly satisfied smile, then he slipped his fingers into his mouth and licked them.

Slowly.

Why was that so arousing?

"My turn." She rose to a sitting position, gripped his pajama pants, and pulled them down his hips.

Brandon's shaft sprang free, pointing up like an arrow, and its size was intimidating. How was it going to fit inside of her?

Brandon reached with his hand and cupped her cheek, his thumb teasing the corner of her mouth. "Do you want to taste me?"

Morelle nodded.

The glow in his eyes intensified as he gripped

himself with his other hand and brought the tip to her lips. "You can start with a little kiss."

She teased him, kissing his shaft as if she was kissing his cheek, and looked up at him. "Was that good?"

He chuckled. "Open your mouth."

She closed her lips over the head and gave it a lick. This was the second time she had done this, which didn't make her an expert, but she felt confident in her ability to bring him pleasure. This time, though, she hoped he would be inside of her when he bit her.

No rush, though.

His shaft was really big, and she had no idea how it was going to fit in her tight sheath, but she knew she could bring him to completion with her mouth.

When she took him deeper, he groaned, and his fingers closed over her chin while his other hand clamped on the back of her neck. "Yes. Just like that. It's so good, baby."

Baby?

Was that a term of endearment appropriate in intimate moments?

It had to be or Brandon wouldn't have used it.

He thrust into her mouth at a slow and steady pace, careful not to overwhelm her but still going a little bit deeper with every thrust until she relaxed enough to take him all the way to the back of her throat.

It was an amazing feeling to have him at her mercy like this, and she felt that he was close, but then he suddenly pulled out of her mouth altogether and did something she hadn't expected. He lay down on the bed, lifted her by her waist as if she weighed nothing, and flipped her around so her ass was in his face, and his shaft was in hers.

His hands landed on her ass with a playful slap, and then he lifted her bottom, arranging her in a way that gave him access to her drenched center.

It was such a deliciously wicked arrangement.

Bracing one hand on his thigh, she gripped his length with the other and gave him a long lick that started at the bottom of his shaft and ended at the tip.

When his tongue speared into her entrance, her eyes nearly rolled back in her head, and she lost her concentration, but she forced herself to focus and started bobbing her head up and down his erection, following the beat of his tongue's thrusts.

When he started to buck up, going deeper, it became a struggle, and her eyes watered, but she powered through it and kept going.

18

BRANDON

Brandon had wanted to climax the second her lips had touched his shaft, but he held on because he wanted to enjoy this for as long as he could. To feel her lips around his length while his tongue was deep inside where his cock was going to be soon, was as close as a male got to experiencing bliss.

He thrust his hips up while his fingers dug into the softness of her bottom, holding her in place so she wouldn't gyrate off him.

They were both close, and he needed to decide where he was going to bite her.

He could bite her inner thigh, but if he could hold off until he flipped her around, he could bite her neck, which he preferred.

Pleasure throbbed in every part of his body, and searing heat rose in his shaft, but he didn't release until Morelle's sheath fluttered over his tongue, and she lifted her head off his cock to shout her release.

The cool air was just what he needed to stop himself from coming in her mouth. Instead, he flipped her around, banded his arms around her, and thrust between her thighs while licking and sucking the spot on her neck he was about to bite.

Morelle might have been too dazed to realize what was happening, but she kept her thighs closed tight around his shaft so that he got the friction he needed, and when his seed rose again, he moved one hand to the back of her head to hold her in place, hissed, and struck with his fangs.

The climax was like a volcanic explosion of pleasure, even though he had basically dry-humped Morelle. To have his fangs inside of her once more, pumping her full of his venom, was making him delirious.

With the venom triggering a series of climaxes, she kept shuddering on top of him, and he held on to her until his seed and his venom were spent.

Retracting his fangs, he licked the puncture holes closed, but other than that, he didn't move a muscle. Morelle lay limply over him, his arms encircling her and keeping her from rolling off him, and his shaft was still cocooned between her thighs.

He knew he had to get up and clean them both up and to cover Morelle so she could sleep comfortably during her venom trip, but he didn't want to move. It just felt too good to hold her like that.

The sticky residue trapped between her thighs and his shaft was the only reason he eventually decided to let go of the little piece of heaven he clung to.

Shifting them both to their sides, he slowly untangled himself from Morelle's arms and then lifted her leg to release his still hard-as-a-rock shaft. He could keep going for round two and three and four, and so could Morelle once she got used to the effects of the venom, but he wasn't in a rush for her to do so. The best venom trips were the first ones, and this was only her second. She might spend several hours soaring on the clouds of euphoria, and he didn't want to rob her of even a minute of that pleasure.

After washing quickly in the bathroom, he wetted several washcloths in warm water and went back to Morelle to clean her up. She didn't stir as he wiped gently between her thighs or when he crawled into bed and covered them both with the comforter.

It was a pity that immortal females got used to the effects of venom, and their fun time got shorter and shorter. Perhaps it was possible to mimic the venom trip without the venom?

What if they could collect the experiences of all the village females who had immortal lovers, feed the data into the Perfect Match algorithm, and create an adventure just for them that mimicked the hallucinogenic trip?

It could also be such a boon to all the immortal females who didn't have the benefit of an immortal lover and who craved the experience of it.

The irony of that wasn't lost on him.

Here he was, the guy who didn't want to go on a virtual reality adventure because he didn't want to grant the computer access to his mind, thinking about designing an adventure for others.

Come to think of it, it wasn't only the females who would want to find out what a venom trip felt like. The males would want to know as well. What they experienced during their induction ceremony, which for the vast majority of them was the only venom bite ever, was very different from what the females experienced. All that hovering on a cloud and watching psychedelic landscapes and translucent aliens wasn't there. Different formulations of venom provided different experiences.

On the other hand, perhaps it was better that the males didn't know what it felt like. In a way, it was like going into a virtual adventure and choosing a female avatar for himself just so he could experience sex as a woman.

Brandon opened his eyes and looked at Morelle's peaceful face. He had a feeling that she would jump at the opportunity to have a male avatar and experience what sex was like for a male.

In that, she seemed much more adventurous than he was.

Hell, they could go into the virtual world in flipped roles.

Talk about kinky.

He was surprised no one had thought about creating an adventure like that. It wouldn't even be difficult. The algorithm didn't care if the chosen avatar was not the same sex as the participant.

Morelle would love the idea, but the problem was that she would expect him to do it with her. He wasn't sure he would actually have the guts to choose to experience sex as a female, but even if he could do that, he still had to get past his aversion to the idea of granting a computer access to his mind and the havoc it could potentially cause.

Brandon could not imagine anything worse than losing control of his faculties to someone or something else.

19

ROB

Rob woke up with a headache, and for a moment, he was confused about where he was. As things came into focus, he recognized Gertrude's room, but his foggy mind couldn't piece together how he'd gotten there.

She wasn't in bed with him, and given the sunlight streaming through the gauzy curtains, it was late morning. He should get up and get some coffee in him to chase that headache away.

In the bathroom, he examined his body in the mirror and was glad to find minimal bruising. Arwel had gone easy on him. In fact, he was surprised the Guardian had managed to get aggressive enough to produce venom. Perhaps he'd recited vile verses in his own head to spur himself on.

Rob chuckled and pulled out the toothbrush he kept at Gertrude's place. They were definitely getting serious about each other, and they needed to discuss living arrangements. Margo had offered him a room in her and Negal's house, and he'd told her that he would give her an answer after talking with Gertrude, but he'd been too chicken to bring it up.

Besides, there hadn't been time or, rather, the right time.

When he was done in the bathroom, he returned to the bedroom and pulled on the change of clothes that he kept in her closet. Opening the door, he smelled coffee, and his eyes nearly rolled back from imagining taking that first sip.

The simple pleasures were what made life worth living. People thought that they had to achieve great things or look like movie stars to be happy, but the truth was that it took much less. To have a partner who cared about them, a good family and friends, a great cup of coffee or tea, a tasty meal, a comfortable bed, and a job that was at least tolerable but preferably challenging and exciting.

In his previous life, Rob had all those things except for the care of a partner, and it was the lack of that one missing piece that made his life feel mediocre instead of wonderful.

He found Gertrude in the kitchen, kneading dough on the counter, her hands and her apron covered in flour.

"You're awake!" She looked surprised. "How are you feeling? Sit down before you fall down."

"I'm fine." He crossed to her and pressed a kiss to her cheek, careful to avoid the flour. "I don't remember much about last night. How did I get here?"

"You were pretty out of it after the ceremony," she said as he poured himself coffee from the carafe. "Margo helped me get you here." She smiled. "It's the job of the mother or the girlfriend to take care of the Dormant after his induction ceremony. It wouldn't have been right to bring you to Toven and Mia's house."

Now would have been the perfect time to bring up their living arrangement, but as usual, he chickened out, excusing it by the sense of lethargy that still lingered in his limbs after the match.

It shouldn't affect his mouth or vocal cords, but he felt like he needed to be in perfect shape to start that conversation.

"I had the strangest dreams," he said as he sat down and put his coffee cup on the table.

The memories were becoming foggy, and he rubbed his temples, trying to sort through the haze.

"Oh, yeah? What were they about?"

"Dragons," he snorted. "I was riding a dragon into battle. That's all I remember. It's probably the result of watching *Game of Thrones* with Toven the other evening."

Gertrude nodded sagely as she shaped the dough into a loaf. "The venom can cause vivid dreams. Not that I've experienced it, but that's what I've heard."

On the one hand, he was glad that she had never hooked up with immortals so she couldn't compare his performance to theirs and find it lacking, but on the other hand, he felt bad for her that she hadn't had the chance to experience what Margo described as an out-of-body, out-of-this-world trip.

Thankfully, his sister hadn't delved into the particulars because even hearing about that part of immortal sex had been too much information for him. No one wanted to hear about their sister's coital details.

According to Bridget, even if he started transitioning right away, it would take between six months to a year for his fangs and venom glands to become functional, so he wouldn't be pleasuring Gertrude that way anytime soon.

"What are you making?" he asked, to pull his thoughts out of that spiral.

"Bread. I don't like making frequent trips to the supermarket, so I buy flour and ingredients in bulk and bake my own bread. That's how things were done when I was young, and I also like knowing what goes into the things I eat. You have no idea what junk they put into commercially made food products."

Rob studied her face, wondering just how old she was that her early years predated not only supermarkets but also bakeries. He'd promised himself not to ask, and he convinced himself that it didn't matter, but things were getting serious between them, and it seemed wrong not to know such a basic thing about her.

"Now I know why everything in your house tastes so good. You make it all from scratch."

She seemed pleased by his compliment. "Not only that, I also use herbs that I grow in my garden. It doesn't get any fresher than that." She cast him a smile and then frowned. "You look pale. Are you sure you are feeling alright?"

"I feel strange," he admitted finally. "Not loopy anymore, but a little iffy. What are the first signs of transition?"

Gertrude wiped her hands on a dishtowel and turned to face him fully. "Usually fever or flu-like symptoms. Some males start growing their venom glands right away, so you might feel like you have an inflamed throat. If your gums hurt, it could be fangs starting to grow and push out your canines."

Rob ran his tongue over his teeth experimentally. "None of that. Just a general feeling of lethargy."

"Lethargy is a flu symptom," she said, crossing to him and pressing her hand to his forehead. "But you don't feel warm."

Her touch lingered, gentle and comforting. "Hungry?" she asked. "I could make you an omelet."

Before he could answer, his phone buzzed, and Margo's face lit up the screen.

"Yes, please," he said to Gertrude before accepting the call.

"Good morning, Margo."

"How are you feeling?" his sister demanded without preamble.

"Tired but okay." He watched as Gertrude began gathering ingredients for breakfast. "No definite signs of transition yet."

There was a moment of silence and then a disappointed sigh. "Well, look on the bright side. If your transition doesn't start today, you can attend the wedding."

"If nothing changes between now and then, I'll definitely come." He smiled as Gertrude cracked eggs into a bowl with practiced efficiency. "Right now, I'm about to eat breakfast using my old canines."

She laughed. "Soon, you'll have fangs. You are a confirmed Dormant. There is no question of you transitioning. The only question is when."

"I know. Love you."

"Love you too."

After ending the call, Rob watched Gertrude cook, and he had to admit that everything about this moment felt right—waking up in her house, watching her cook, and sharing a quiet morning together.

Which reminded him. "Where is Hildegard?"

Gertrude turned to look at him over her shoulder. "She stayed the night at her guy's place. It's the second time she's done that with the same male, so maybe she's developing feelings for him."

"Who is he? One of Kalugal's men or a Kra-ell?"

"Kalugal's. She refuses to tell me who he is, though. She's so weird."

It was now or never. "Is there a chance she will move in with him?"

That got Gertrude's attention, and she turned to him fully. "It's too early to know, but why are you asking?"

He swallowed. "Margo invited me to move in with her and Negal because I've already overstayed my welcome at Toven and Mia's, but I told her that I would discuss it with you first."

20

GERTRUDE

Gertrude nearly dropped the spatula she was using to fold the omelet. The implication in his words was clear—he wanted them to move in together.

How should she respond?

She wanted to say yes, that there was nothing she would love more than waking next to him each morning and seeing his smile when she opened her eyes, but her practical mind was throwing up warning flags.

They hadn't even said 'I love you' yet. What if their relationship failed?

It would be heart-wrenching having to untangle their lives with him living in the village, but if they'd also moved in together, it would be a nightmare.

Then again, nothing good came without effort

or risk, and fear shouldn't stop her from reaching for what she wanted.

Taking a deep breath, Gertrude turned off the stove and transferred the omelet to a plate. She brought it to the table, then poured herself a fresh cup of coffee before sitting down across from Rob.

"You gave me the impression that you wanted to wait until after your transition before making major decisions," she said.

"I did, but I find it significant that you brought me here after the ceremony and not to Toven and Mia's house. You felt like I was your responsibility and not theirs."

"Well, yeah. You are my...what?" Gertrude wrapped her hands around her coffee cup, using the warmth to steady herself. "Boyfriend? Significant other? What are we to each other?"

He swallowed. "Mates?"

"Are we? I'm not saying that we aren't. We might be. I just feel like we are rushing in headfirst, and we might regret it later."

He nodded. "I know, and I'd rather we weighed every decision carefully. Forget that I brought it up. We should wait until after my transition."

They were both cowards, hiding behind excuses to protect their fragile hearts. They had both been hurt, and both had been left for others, but Rob had had it much worse than she had, and if he was brave enough to even hint at taking their relationship to the next step, she should encourage him and not put up roadblocks.

Gertrude took a sip of coffee, giving herself a moment longer to think. "We haven't even said those three important words to each other yet, and here we are discussing moving in together. I think things need to be done in order."

He reached across the table, covering her hand with his. "I love you, Gertrude. I wish I was more romantic and had gotten you roses and chocolates, but knowing myself, I would have probably obsessed over it forever until it became such a huge mountain to scale that I would have given up on it altogether. So, maybe it's better that I said it now, spontaneously, over breakfast, with this beautiful omelet we can share instead of a box of chocolates."

She just gaped at him, not knowing whether she should laugh or cry or pick him up and carry him to the bedroom. Well, maybe she should let him carry her because his masculinity might be threatened by her doing that.

He squeezed her hand. "Say something. You are freaking me out."

"I love you too."

A bright smile spread over his face. "See? That wasn't so hard, was it?"

"It was," she whispered. "I've never said that to a man before."

"Oh, Gertrude." He rose to his feet, lifted her up, and sat back down with her in his arms.

It felt so good, so right, that tears prickled the back of her eyes. "I love you. I've known that for a while now, but I was afraid to say it."

"Same here." He rubbed soothing circles on her back. "I fell in love with you by the second time I met you."

She lifted her head and pouted. "Why not the first?"

"Because I wasn't ready yet. If I hadn't felt so ruined, I would have fallen in love with you at first sight. I'm sure of that."

Her heart squeezed. "Oh, Rob."

"I know it's fast, but being with you feels right in a way nothing else ever has."

She took a deep breath. "It's easy to get swept away in the moment, but things might not work out between us, and separating after moving in together is going to be hell."

"We are not going to separate," he said almost vehemently. "The only way you'll get rid of me is if you tell me to leave, cheat on me, or lie to me, and I know that you won't do any of those things because that's not who you are."

"What if you are the one who wants to get rid of me for some reason?"

The possible reason being his truelove mate suddenly appearing out of nowhere, like Margo had appeared for Negal. It hurt when Negal dumped her without looking back, but it would slay her if Rob did that as well.

Then again, it wouldn't matter if they lived together or not when it happened. It would be devastating in either case.

No, that wasn't true. It would be much worse if they shared a house.

"We're perfect for each other, and we're wasting time being afraid." He squeezed her hand. "Let's take a chance on each other."

She met his eyes. "I've lived a long time, Rob. Long enough to know that nothing worth having comes without risk and that it's important to weigh those risks against the benefits."

"Now, you are talking my language." His thumb traced patterns on her palm. "In this case, the benefits far outweigh the risks, and I'm willing to bet everything on you."

"That's so sweet of you to say." She chuckled. "You make it sound so simple."

"Because it is." He smiled. "We love each other. We want to be together. And the odds are in our favor."

Gertrude shook her head, but she couldn't stop smiling. "We should at least wait until after the wedding. I need to talk to Hildegard and ask her if it's okay with her for you to move in with us."

He tilted his head. "Shouldn't we just take the plunge and request a house of our own?"

Her heart skipped a beat at his suggestion. He

was even more serious about this than she'd thought. "Perhaps after your transition, we will do that. I'm not a big risk taker, and I prefer small steps."

"Fair enough." He lifted her hand to his lips. "But as soon as I'm past the initial stage of my transition, we are moving in together one way or another. I don't care if it's with Hildegard remaining as our roommate, her moving out to room with someone else, or us marching into Ingrid's office and asking her for a house."

"Deal." She cupped his cheeks and sealed the deal with a kiss.

21

MORELLE

Morelle felt the sun on her face, a feeling of warmth and contentment spreading through her. Then again, that pleasant feeling might have come from the inside rather than the sun because she was still basking in the afterglow of the venom trip.

She was no longer dazed, and the euphoria had subsided to manageable levels, but it was still there long hours after it should have completely dissipated. Still, she wasn't overly worried about her mind feeling like it was stuffed with fluffy, colorful clouds or about smiling like a fool.

Brandon said that some reacted to the venom more strongly than others and that the first few times were the most potent.

It would pass, and when it did, she was going to miss it.

She felt relaxed, happy, and loving toward everyone around her.

It would be nice if that was the new her. It felt good to radiate love instead of mistrust, suspicion, and nihilism. Although to be honest, she hadn't felt nihilistic since she'd made the choice to wake up and join the world of the living, and it was all thanks to Brandon.

Well, her mother had been the catalyst, but that wouldn't have been enough to wake her if Brandon hadn't been there to tell her stories and make her curious enough to listen and want to hear more.

He was holding her hand in his lap as he sipped on his coffee, and she gave his hand a little squeeze accompanied by a loving smile.

Naturally, he smiled back, his blue eyes crinkling at the corners and his lush lips curving up. He was such an incredibly handsome male.

All over.

Morelle felt a blush creeping up her cheeks at the memory of what they had done last night. It had been so wicked. She could never have imagined such a thing. Humans had a special name for that particular arrangement, a number, but Morelle hadn't understood why until Brandon wrote it on a piece of paper and then added embellishments to the digits to clarify the symbolism.

She'd laughed so hard that her sides had ached.

"I was so happy to see so many people show up

for Rob's ceremony," Jasmine said, gesturing with her fork. "The energy in that room when everyone started singing was magical." She sighed. "I had forgotten how good it felt to perform. I need to do it more often."

Morelle nodded, only half listening. She was too focused on the way Brandon's fingers intertwined with hers and how his knee pressed against her thigh under the table. The contact points felt electric.

"You were amazing," Ell-rom told his mate. "You enthralled the audience, my love."

"Thank you." Jasmine beamed at him. "I hadn't realized how much I missed it until I was up there." She turned to Brandon. "I'm also going to sing at the wedding, and Jackson and Vlad are going to accompany me on guitar."

"That's wonderful." Brandon squeezed Morelle's hand. "What songs are you planning for the event?"

"Just a couple. 'Can't Help Falling in Love' for their first dance, and 'Make You Feel My Love' during the ceremony." Jasmine's eyes sparkled with enthusiasm. "The rest will be broadcast through the loudspeakers from Peter's playlist—it was literally his only contribution to the planning, but at least he has good taste. He included classics like 'All of Me' and 'Perfect,' plus some more upbeat numbers for dancing."

"Amanda must be pleased to have such a hands-off groom," Brandon said with a chuckle.

"Oh, I don't think she would have minded some additional input, but I suspect that she prefers to have total control. The less the bride and groom interfere with her plans, the better. She has a certain vision for the party and she's having a blast planning everything down to the last detail." Jasmine took a sip of her coffee. "She loved that Marina left everything to her. The poor girl feels overwhelmed, so having Amanda do it for her relieves a lot of the pressure."

Morelle barely registered their words. The venom's incredible effects were still coursing through her, but the deep sense of connection she felt with Brandon was even better. Every time she looked at him, her heart swelled with emotion.

They hadn't completed their bond last night, but she wasn't disappointed. It would happen soon, and in the meantime, Brandon was teaching her all these wonderful ways to enjoy each other.

"Speaking of planning," Ell-rom said, drawing Morelle's attention back to the conversation even though he was addressing Jasmine, "you should call your father and find out when he's going hunting next. Catching him alone at the cabin is our best option."

Jasmine's smile faded. "I know I need to do that, but I'm deliberately avoiding it because I hate talking to him." She pushed her food around her plate. "He manages to turn every conversation into a confrontation. Nothing I do is worthwhile. I'm wasting my time on pursuing a career in acting, I'm getting too old to be given any good roles, and I only date losers instead of finding a man to settle down with and start a family. After talking to him, I always feel depressed."

"Not this time." Ell-rom clasped her hand. "None of that is even remotely true."

His words didn't seem to have an effect on her. "Yeah, but I can't tell him that, now, can I?"

"You can when we are alone with him in the cabin," Ell-rom said. "You can throw in his face that you will never be too old for anything and that you are mated to a demigod." He chuckled. "Never mind that said demigod has no job, so he is technically a loser, but your father doesn't need to know that. We are going to thrall him to forget that anyway."

That seemed to do the trick and improve Jasmine's mood.

She smiled brightly. "Now you've given me an incentive to call him. I can't wait to see his face when we tell him that."

"Can Brandon and I come?" Morelle asked. "I would love to see more of this world and leave the village for a day—"

She cut herself off as Jasmine winced, and understanding dawned. Of course, Jasmine wouldn't want an audience for what was likely to be an emotional and potentially devastating confrontation with her father. The reason she needed to talk to him was to find out what he knew about her mother, and she wouldn't want witnesses for that.

To cover the awkward moment, Morelle turned to Brandon. "Speaking of seeing the world, have you reconsidered joining me for a Perfect Match world tour adventure?"

His eyes met hers, and something in his expression made her heart skip. "Actually, I've been thinking about it, especially last night."

She arched a brow. "Really? What were you thinking?"

22

BRANDON

Brandon reached for his coffee cup and took a sip to give himself time to collect his thoughts. "I've had some interesting ideas about potential new applications for the technology."

"Such as?" Morelle leaned closer, seeming to be intrigued by the shift in his attitude.

After he'd told her that he didn't want anything to do with Perfect Match, she was naturally surprised.

He still didn't want to participate, though, just to offer an idea, and he didn't want to give her the wrong impression by telling her about it, but he'd backed himself into a corner by blurting it out.

"I was thinking about how immortal females eventually build up tolerance to the venom effects and how that experience becomes harder to achieve over time."

Jasmine perked up. "Oh! I know what you're thinking, and it's brilliant."

He smiled. "I didn't tell you my idea yet, so hold your accolades."

"Okay, I'm holding them." Jasmine lifted her hands in a gesture that suggested she was holding the reins. "Go ahead."

"I was thinking the Perfect Match team could create an adventure that mimics the venom trip experience. They could collect data from willing participants about their experiences and use it to program something similar."

"That's precisely what I thought your idea was, and it's brilliant!" Jasmine clapped her hands. "And not just for those who would love to experience that initial intensity again but also for those who never have. There are so many clan females who have never been with an immortal male. This could be a game changer for them." Her eyes brightened. "I have an even better idea. Why not recreate the whole experience? There will be a line of immortal females waiting their turn."

Brandon hadn't thought that far, but she was right. Could an algorithm really replicate something that intense?

He wouldn't know since he hadn't experienced any virtual adventures yet, but others had sung its praises and gushed over how it was indistinguishable from reality.

"It would be great if it could work," Morelle

said as a blush colored her cheeks a fetching shade of pink. "I'm still all warm and fuzzy from the venom's effects, and I would love to experience it many times over, but as everyone tells me, diminishing results are to be expected."

Brandon couldn't believe she'd just shared such an intimate thing with her brother. He could have understood if she confided in Jasmine in private, because females were open with each other about things like that, but to say it in front of Ell-rom just didn't seem right.

Jasmine beamed. "I had a feeling that was what had put that relaxed, dreamy expression on your face."

Morelle shifted her gaze to him. "It was only my second time, so it was still as powerful as the first. I hope it won't shrink significantly with repetition. It doesn't seem fair."

Jasmine waved a dismissive hand. "It might not last as long in the real world as it did originally, but I don't feel a significant difference while I'm experiencing it now. It feels like it's much longer while I'm venom-tripping than the actual passage of time in the real world. It's probably like the Perfect Match adventures in that three hours in the machine can translate to weeks or even months of virtual fantasy. A lot gets crammed into the experience. Not that I've gotten to try it yet, but that's what I've been told. Anyway, I think it will be difficult to break the experience up into bits and pieces for the computer to emulate, but it's worth a try."

That was an interesting observation that Brandon hadn't considered, but then his knowledge was superficial and anecdotal. In the past, he'd only been with human females and rarely more than once with the same one, so he hadn't seen firsthand the diminishing effects of his venom, and it wasn't like the mated immortals were freely sharing details with him.

He was also not familiar with the Perfect Match experience. The fact that time moved differently inside the virtual world was a good thing. It meant that there was no time limit on the venom trip, and the only difficulty would be recreating the visuals and sensations.

"I don't know much about the technology, but I know that it is incredibly sophisticated. With enough data, the AI should be able to create a very close approximation." Brandon paused, meeting Morelle's eyes. "But that's just the tip of the iceberg. There is more that I'm surprised no one has considered yet."

Morelle's eyes were wide with intrigue. "I can't imagine anything more wondrous than the venom-induced euphoria."

"Well, maybe not, but here is an idea. What if couples could experience things from each other's perspectives? The technology allows users to choose any avatar, regardless of gender. Couples could literally walk in each other's shoes and experience physical intimacy from the other's point of view. It's not for everyone, but I'm sure some would find it fascinating."

Color flooded Morelle's cheeks. "You mean we could trade places."

"In some things." He couldn't imagine taking on the female's role in sex, not even in the virtual world. "I'm not as adventurous as other males might be, but I would love to experience the venom trip from a female's perspective."

Ell-rom cleared his throat. "Maybe we should give you two some privacy."

Brandon had almost forgotten Morelle's brother and Jasmine were still at the table. "Sorry," he said, though he wasn't. "You don't have to leave. I'm sure you find the possibility as intriguing as I do, or maybe not. Not everyone is adventurous that way or curious."

"I am curious," Jasmine said. "But it's a bit uncomfortable to discuss with family present." She shifted her eyes to Ell-rom. "Right?"

He shrugged. "I wouldn't know. I'm new to all this, and I'm not embarrassed to discuss anything in front of Morelle." He smiled at his sister. "I don't remember our lives from before, and I don't think my memories of that time are ever coming back, but since we only had each other, I assume that we didn't shy away from discussing intimate topics."

"We didn't," Morelle confirmed. "But as our

knowledge was limited to what the head priestess told us, we only knew about the Kra-ell's savage customs, and we used to make fun of them. We both knew instinctively that this was not how we were meant to be intimate if we ever got to have partners. But since we were resigned to a celibate life, we didn't dedicate much thought to those matters."

Brandon found it hard to believe that two young half-gods could just accept life without sex and hadn't found alternative methods to scratch the itch. He hadn't asked Morelle if she had ever indulged in self-pleasuring, but he should when they were alone.

"I'm grateful to your mother for whisking you away," Jasmine said. "She saved you from a very sad and desolate life." She stood and started gathering plates. "It's wonderful to see you so happy." She turned to Brandon. "Your idea is fascinating, and you should definitely talk to William about it."

William wasn't the one in charge of new content for Perfect Match adventures, and Brandon wasn't sure who was. Syssi, perhaps? Or Toven? He shook his head. "It's just the germ of an idea right now. I need to think it through and jot down some concrete proposals before approaching whoever is in charge of crafting new adventures for Perfect Match."

23

MORELLE

To say that Morelle was surprised about Brandon's change of heart in regard to Perfect Match was an understatement. Only a few days ago, he had been adamant about never trying a virtual adventure, and she'd accepted that. He didn't have to like everything she did, and she didn't have to enjoy all the things he did, although she hadn't found any examples of that.

Well, not yet anyway.

They hadn't been together long enough for her to even know what things he enjoyed so she could decide which ones she didn't want to partake in.

"Are you seriously considering joining me in a virtual adventure?" she asked as soon as they were alone in their room.

He took a deep breath. "I know that it's hypocritical of me to offer ideas about a technology I have no experience with and have reservations about."

"Oh." Feeling deflated, Morelle sat down on the couch. "I thought you'd changed your mind."

He sat next to her and took her hand. "I don't know why I have such a strong aversion to letting a computer hijack my mind. Maybe it's my ignorance that is fueling my fears. I'm not tech-savvy, and it's even a struggle for me to read an operation manual on a new appliance. I always ask someone to just show me what to do so I won't have to read and understand it."

His admission melted away the tendrils of resentment that had taken hold of her heart despite her efforts not to allow them entry.

"We all have irrational fears. But maybe you are right about being wary of artificial intelligence, at least until someone who is an expert in the field can allay your fears. Perhaps my lack of concern is actually the wrong approach since I know even less about this technology than you do. Is it smart of me to blindly trust those who I consider experts and who are telling me that it's perfectly safe? Or should I do my own research before I give the machine license to enter my mind and plant false memories in there to create a fabricated personal history?"

He regarded her for a long moment and then took her hand. "You are a very wise lady, my princess, and you are a born politician. You should become a council member."

Morelle frowned. "I don't know what you are referring to. None of what I said could be considered political. I was talking about personal experiences and individual approaches to risk-taking."

"You did." He lifted her hand to his lips and brushed them over her knuckles. "But you also phrased your philosophical musings in a way that validated my reservations and offered an alternative approach without belittling me in the slightest. That's diplomacy at its best. But I shouldn't be surprised that a daughter of two monarchs has it in her blood."

"I was just trying to see things from your perspective and explain mine. I also realized that I was too trusting of the people running the program and that I should learn more about it. I thought that I would learn about the process from the questionnaires and brochures, but I didn't stop to think about the technical and neurological aspects, maybe because, like you, I don't know much about them."

Brandon put his arm around her shoulders and gently tugged her toward him. "We both need someone to explain to us how these things work, and William might not be the best person to do it. I would love to get us an audience with the people who actually invented this. The two human founders."

Morelle leaned away. "Perfect Match is a human invention?"

He smiled. "Humans are just as smart as gods and immortals, and since there are many more of them than there are of us, it shouldn't surprise you that they come up with a lot of innovation."

"There are trillions of gods, Brandon. Just not on Earth."

"Right." He ran his fingers through his hair. "I keep forgetting that. In my mind, Anumati is like Earth, just instead of humans and immortals, it is populated by gods and Kra-ell. I can't imagine how giant your planet is to accommodate so many people, or how it is possible to feed everyone."

She chuckled. "Is this your way of distracting me from talking about Perfect Match?"

"Not at all. It's just genuine curiosity. But back to that, the first step will be to talk with William and ask him who the best person is to explain how the brain and machine interface works. If the answer puts my mind at ease, I will at least feel less concerned about you going on an adventure on your own."

That was disappointing, but it was progress. "Will you at least consider joining me?"

"I would fight dragons for you, my sweet princess, but in this case, the monster I need to conquer is made from ones and zeros, and I don't know how to fight it. I'm willing to explore the possibility, but I can't promise you anything." He took her hand again and kissed the inside of her palm.

It might not be the answer she was hoping for, but it was a huge concession for him.

"Did what I say change your mind?" she asked.

His eyes held hers. "I just want to do everything in my power to make you happy, and that includes finding a way for you to keep enjoying the venom trip with the same intensity as the first time. I also want to have peace of mind while you explore the world in an expedited manner through the various Perfect Match adventures, but the truth is that I would love to take you exploring in the real world. There is no substitute for that."

"But you promised to consider joining me in the virtual fantasy."

He swallowed. "I did, and I will. I will go to great lengths to make you happy."

What he was actually saying was that he loved her and would do his best to get over his phobia for her, and she loved him for it.

Should she tell him?

If he was willing to overcome his fears for her, she should do no less for him.

"I love you, Brandon." She cupped his cheeks. "I don't care that we have known each other for only a short time and that I have nothing to compare this feeling to. I know what's in my heart."

Instead of saying something back to her, he just gazed into her eyes, seemingly too stunned to talk.

"It's okay." She chuckled. "You can say it back to me. It's not that hard. Say Morelle, I love you."

A smile bloomed on his face. "You are so sure of my love for you."

"Of course I am, but it would be nice to hear it."

"I love you, Princess Morelle. With all my heart and soul." He closed the distance between their mouths and sealed his lips over hers.

24

MARINA

Marina's bedroom was a hive of activity, with dresses draped over every surface and the air thick with the mingled scents of hairspray, cosmetics, and perfume.

Her heart fluttered with excitement and nerves as Larissa worked on her hair with a curling iron while Lusha carefully applied makeup to her mother's face.

She'd already done Marina's, and it was a work of art. The woman was really talented, and she claimed to have learned all the tricks from watching countless instructional videos on YouTube.

Marina had watched quite a few herself and still didn't know how to make her eyeliner stay in place all day without smudging and giving her raccoon eyes.

Peter had often commented that she shouldn't bother because she was beautiful as she was and didn't need cosmetics to enhance her appearance, but Marina knew better. In a place where every female looked like a supermodel, she needed all the help she could get just to blend in.

Thankfully, nearly half of the females in the room right now were human, so she felt more at home. It was good that the master suite was spacious, with a seating area separate from the bed, so there was enough space for all of her bridesmaids and her mother. Catrina remained in the living room, and Marina felt a pang of guilt for excluding her.

Then again, she hadn't told the woman to stay out there, and besides, Peter's mother could have spent the morning visiting her many friends and relatives in the village instead of sitting on the living room couch and making everyone uncomfortable.

Yesterday over dinner, it had seemed like she was warming up to Marina and her parents, but it must have been the vodka or maybe her own wishful thinking, because this morning Catrina was back to being her old standoffish self who treated everyone like they were beneath her.

Still, a small voice in the back of Marina's head whispered that she was misinterpreting the woman's behavior. Peter's mom was uncomfortable around her and her gaggle of bridesmaids, most of whom she knew only by name. She wasn't the friendly type, and maybe she needed a drink in her to loosen up.

"Stop fidgeting," Lusha commanded Marina's mother, wielding the makeup brush like a weapon. "I can't get this highlight perfect if you keep bouncing your knee."

"Sorry." Her mother tried to still her restless movements. "I'm just so excited. My baby girl is getting married."

Marina stifled an eye roll.

She was a twenty-seven-year-old woman, not a baby, and her mother hadn't babied her since she'd been twelve and started working in the compound, cleaning up after the Kra-ell, but Marina was in a forgiving mood today and let it pass.

"What about you?" Wonder asked her from her perch on the bed. "Are you nervous? Excited? Or about to explode?"

Marina stuck out her tongue at her friend, earning a reproachful tug on her hair from Larissa.

Working with Wonder at the café had been a blessing—the immortal's endless patience and kindness had helped Marina adjust to life in the village. Thanks to her, she knew almost every resident not only by name but also their backstories, provided that Wonder knew them.

"I'm still mad at you for refusing to have a proper bachelorette party," Aliya said, sorting through a collection of nail polish bottles that

Lusha had brought over. "We could have had so much fun!"

"We are having fun." Marina gestured at the comfortable chaos around her. "This is perfect. We are spending the morning together getting ready, reminiscing, and drinking."

As if on cue, Wendy appeared in the doorway with another round of mimosas balanced on a tray. She only worked part-time at the café, but she was part of Marina's inner circle of friends. "Speaking of perfect, wait until you see the village green. The flowers just arrived and—"

"No spoilers!" Eleanor called from her spot by the window. "Amanda wants it to be a surprise."

Marina had been instructed to avoid the area and, if she happened to walk by, to look in the other direction.

Her mother took a glass from the tray and raised it in a toast. "To my beautiful daughter on her wedding day."

"To Marina!" the others echoed, raising their glasses.

Marina's gaze drifted to the closed bedroom door, beyond which Catrina was sitting alone in the living room.

Guilt gnawed at her stomach.

"I should invite her in," she murmured.

Larissa's hand stilled with the curler. "Who?"

"Peter's mother. I don't want her to feel excluded."

"No one told her to stay out there. She could have walked in and joined us. It's her choice."

"Friendliness doesn't come naturally to everyone. Maybe she is waiting for someone to invite her, meaning me." Marina waited until Larissa proclaimed her hair ready before getting to her feet. "I'm going to ask her to join us."

She found Catrina perched on the edge of the couch, looking perfectly put together as always but somehow also slightly lost. Her eyes widened in surprise when Marina appeared.

"Why are you sitting all alone out here? You should join us." Marina gestured toward the bedroom. "You don't need any help with hair or makeup, but you can enjoy mimosas and gossip with us."

Catrina's smile was slightly strained. "I wouldn't want to intrude on your special time with your friends and family."

"You're family too," Marina said, though the words felt a bit forced.

"That's very kind of you." Catrina stood and smoothed her skirt. "But I think I'll stay out here. Too many people in one room makes me anxious." Her smile turned more genuine. "But thank you for asking. It means a lot to me that you made the effort to come out here and check on me."

Marina nodded, relieved but also feeling a bit guilty about that relief. "Are you sure?"

"I am." Catrina reached out and squeezed her hand. "You look beautiful. Go and enjoy yourself."

When Marina returned to the bedroom, her mother's makeup was complete, and Larissa was working on her hair.

"You look amazing, Mama."

Her mother beamed. "Thank you, baby."

"Time for the main event!" Lusha announced, clapping her hands. "Everyone out while the bride gets dressed!"

"But we want to see the dress!" Wendy protested.

Marina shook her head. "Not until it's on. I want the full effect to be a surprise." She shooed them toward the door. "Go get dressed yourselves in the other room. Only my mom stays here to help me."

Lusha must have thought that she would be allowed to stay because she cast Marina an accusing look before closing the procession out of the room.

When her mother shut the door behind Lusha, Marina retrieved the garment bag from its hiding place in the back of the closet.

When she unzipped it, revealing the masterpiece within, her mother gasped.

"Oh, sweetheart." Her mother's eyes filled with tears. "You're going to take everyone's breath away."

Marina touched the delicate fabric reverently.

"I still can't believe it's mine. I've never even dreamt about wearing a one-of-a-kind masterpiece that was created just for me."

"You deserve it and much more." Her mother helped her step into the dress, so as not to disturb her hair and makeup, and then gave her a hand as she stepped into a pair of white pumps.

"There." She turned Marina toward the full-length mirror. "Look at yourself."

Marina had seen herself in the dress before during fittings, but now, with her hair and makeup done, she looked like a fairy-tale princess.

"Ready to show the others?" her mother asked.

Marina nodded and reluctantly turned away from the mirror.

Her mother opened the door, and as Marina stepped out, a chorus of gasps and squeals filled the air.

"Oh my goddess!" Larissa waved a hand in front of her face to stave off tears. "You look like a princess!"

"Marina! You look stunning," Wonder said.

Even Catrina, who had drifted closer to take a look, seemed impressed. "You look spectacular, Marina."

"Peter's going to lose his mind when he sees you." Lusha snorted. "If he can still form coherent thoughts."

Marina spun slowly, letting the skirt swirl around her.

For the first time that morning, her nerves settled. This was right.

This was perfect. In a few hours, she would walk down the aisle to the man she loved, and nothing else mattered.

"Okay," Larissa said, her voice thick with emotion. "Final touches. Something old?"

"Wonder's earrings." Marina touched the pearl drops that her friend had given her for the occasion.

"Something new?"

"Here." Wendy handed her a blue butterfly-shaped clip for her hair, and Marina transferred it to Larissa, who clipped it in place.

"Something borrowed?"

Aliya took off a gold anklet. "You can wear this."

"And something blue?" Lusha asked with a wink.

Marina patted her hair. "Check!"

"Naha." Wendy produced another tiny blue butterfly clip, and Larissa added it to Marina's hair.

The women burst into cheers and applause, and even Catrina joined in.

Marina felt tears threatening to spill from the corners of her eyes.

"Don't you dare cry and ruin my masterpiece!" Lusha wagged a finger at her. "Happy thoughts and not the mushy kind."

"Yes, ma'am." Marina saluted.

Wonder appeared at her side with a fresh mimosa. "Liquid courage. You can always reapply the lipstick."

"To love." Larissa lifted her glass.

"To new beginnings," said her mother.

"To family," Catrina said.

25

PETER

Peter adjusted his bowtie and studied his reflection in Jay's guest room mirror. In a couple of hours, he would be standing before the clan, pledging his life and love to Marina, and he couldn't wait.

Some grooms might be nervous or anxious, but all he felt was giddy excitement. Perhaps Kagra had been right, and he was in love with being in love, but what did it matter what path his mind took to get to this point and make him a happy male?

Fates knew that he faced enough crap in his work to suck the joy out of him, but thankfully, he had Marina to replenish his stores of happiness.

"You messed it up again," Jay said, appearing behind him. "Why do you keep touching it?"

Peter frowned. "I don't see anything wrong with it."

"That's because you're blind. It's crooked." Jay reached from behind him and adjusted the bowtie. "There. Perfect. Now leave it alone, and don't touch it again."

Peter was certain that the thing had been straight before, and Jay had made it crooked, but he decided not to argue and turned around to face his friends.

His other groomsmen were lounging around the room in various states of readiness. Theo and Bowen were still wrestling with their cummerbunds, while Leon and Anandur were already fully dressed and sharing a drink on the couch in the seating area by the window.

"Speaking of perfect," Theo said with a grin, "I notice Emmett isn't here. Didn't want your old friend as a groomsman?"

Peter's jaw tightened. "I might have forgiven him for what he did to me, but we are not friends."

The guy had kidnapped him, kept him enslaved under compulsion, and threatened to gift him to his mistress as a breeding bull for the hybrids. Not that it would have ever happened, even if Emmett hadn't been captured by the clan.

His former mistress had been abducted by Igor and his minions a long time ago, and the Fates had manipulated events so now she and her people were part of the clan.

"Fair enough." Jay handed him a glass of scotch. "But Marina invited Eleanor."

"That's different." Peter took a sip, mindful of his white shirt. "Eleanor is a friend to both of us. She was my friend first, and then when Marina needed a transfer to the village, Eleanor helped."

Leon was sprawling in an armchair, looking dashing in his black tuxedo. "I'm disappointed that Marina didn't invite Anastasia. My mate feels left out."

Peter snorted. "Marina barely knows Anastasia. I don't think they've ever exchanged a single word."

"True." Leon's grin widened. "Actually, Ana's thrilled to have the house to herself. She's probably neck-deep in a bubble bath right now, enjoying a glass of white wine and the peace and quiet."

Leon and his mate were sharing a guest house with Emmett and Eleanor during their visit to the village. Since Leon was permanently posted in Safe Haven, he had given up his old place in the village.

"Thanks for making the trip," Peter said. "I know it's not exactly convenient."

Safe Haven was several hours away from the nearest airport and even further away from the one that had flights to Los Angeles.

Leon waved a dismissive hand. "Are you kidding? Of course I'd be here. After all we went through together at Safe Haven, you, Eleanor, and I changed the course of history. I found my Ana there, Eleanor found Emmett, and you..." He trailed off, something flickering in his eyes.

Peter frowned. "And I what?"

"And you got this incredible promotion." Leon raised his glass. "Head of the new Avengers division. That's huge, brother."

Peter hadn't missed the slight hesitation, and he knew what Leon wanted to say before he changed directions. His friend thought that he'd gotten the short end of the stick—a human mate instead of an immortal one—and the thinly veiled pity in his friends' eyes made Peter's stomach turn.

He understood their concern. He'd even shared it himself in dark moments. The thought of watching Marina age and die while he remained forever young was like a knife in his gut. But he refused to let that fear taint today.

Marina was the best thing that had ever happened to him, and he didn't care what anyone thought.

"I'm the luckiest male ever for finding a wonderful mate like Marina. She makes me happier than I've ever been."

Theo cleared his throat. "No one's saying she isn't wonderful—"

"But she's human," Peter finished for him. "Yes, I'm aware of that. I'm also aware that Kaia is working on a solution." He set his glass down, perhaps a bit harder than necessary. "And even if she never finds one, I'd rather have sixty years with Marina than an eternity with anyone else."

Jay lifted his hand. "Hey, it's your wedding day. No heavy discussions allowed." He walked over to Peter and clapped him on the shoulder. "As my mother always says, prepare for the worst and hope for the best."

"Isn't that the other way around?" Anandur asked. "Hope for the best and prepare for the worst?"

Jay shrugged. "Same difference. Anyway, if anyone can crack the code of immortality, it's Kaia. Besides, Bridget confirmed that frequent venom injections prolong a woman's life, so there is that."

Peter appreciated their attempt to lighten the mood, but he knew they were all convinced that he was making a mistake.

Even if they didn't say it, he could see it in their careful glances and too-bright smiles.

"I think you're all missing the point," Alfie said. "Peter isn't settling or making some noble sacrifice. He's choosing love." He met Peter's eyes. "Real, messy, complicated love. The kind that makes you brave enough to face whatever comes."

Good old Alfie, who'd watched Marina and Peter's relationship develop from the beginning, understood exactly what he needed to hear.

"To love," Jay said, raising his glass. "And to Peter and Marina."

The others echoed the toast, and Peter felt some of the tension ease from his shoulders. His friends might not fully understand his choice, but they supported him, and that was good enough.

"Now," Bowen said, "can someone please help me with this damn cummerbund? I swear it's trying to strangle me."

26

ANNANI

Annani smoothed the fabric of her flowing silver gown, one of the three she used when presiding over weddings. Unlike her day gowns, which were sleeveless, her ceremonial gowns had long sleeves that added drama to the ceremony when she lifted her arms.

Presentation was no less important than the emotions and words spoken to unite a couple forever. It all had to come together in one beautiful package to leave a lasting and cherished memory.

Today would be a first for her, though, officiating at a marriage between an immortal and a human who was not a Dormant and whose hope of ever becoming immortal did not lie in her genetics but rather in the hands of science. Hopefully, Kaia would come up with a solution for Marina before her time on this plane of existence came to an end.

Closing her eyes, Annani lifted her face toward the ceiling. "Merciful Fates," she whispered, "Peter deserves a miracle. He has served the clan faithfully, endured humiliation and pain, yet emerged stronger and more dedicated than ever. Please grant him this boon—a way for his chosen mate, the one who his heart beats for, to share his immortal life."

The prayer felt inadequate, but she hoped the Fates would understand the depth of feeling behind it. They had been generous lately, bringing her siblings to her and blessing the clan with new additions. Perhaps they would extend their generosity to Peter and Marina as well.

As the sound of wheels on gravel drew her attention, she glanced out the window. As promised, Kian pulled up in a golf cart, Syssi beside him with Allegra on her lap and Brundar at the wheel.

Ogidu bowed. "Your transport is here, Clan Mother." He walked over to the front door and opened it for her.

"Thank you, Ogidu." She put on her sunglasses before stepping outside.

Kian jumped down and offered her a hand up. "The stage is shaded, so you might be able to perform the ceremony without the sunglasses."

"I will manage." She took his hand.

"Nana!" Allegra bounced happily on Syssi's knees.

"Nana is coming." She sat next to Syssi and transferred her granddaughter to her lap. "You look so pretty. Is that a new dress?"

Allegra nodded and lifted her foot to show Annani her new shoes. "Pink."

"Of course." Annani laughed. "To match your new dress."

As Kian joined Brundar at the front, the cart lurched forward.

"What about Ell-rom and Morelle and their mates?" Annani asked.

"Already there," Syssi said. "Everyone is already gathered at the village square, or most of them are. It looks beautiful. Amanda's outdone herself with the decorations for this one."

Annani smiled. "I am sure she has. This wedding was important to her."

"I know." Syssi sighed. "It's the first of its kind. We are all praying for a happy ending to this story."

Annani patted her knee. "Good. The more of us who pray for Marina and Peter, the more chance there is that the Fates will listen."

"Why would they do this to him?" Syssi asked quietly. "Why match him to a wonderful girl who cannot be his lifelong partner?"

Annani had pondered the same question. "I do not have all the answers, child. Sometimes, the Fates sacrifice the happiness of one individual to teach the rest of us to be grateful for what we have.

I hope that is not what they are doing with Peter and Marina. I hope for a miracle."

As Brundar navigated through the village paths, Annani felt the familiar surge of pride and joy at seeing her thriving community. Immortals and gods, Kra-ell and hybrids, all living together in harmony. Even if Marina never transitioned, she would still be part of this tapestry for as long as she lived.

The crowd parted as their cart approached the village green, and Annani admired the decorations. Amanda had indeed outdone herself. Flowers cascaded from archways and twined around pillars that had not been there the day before. Where had she gotten them?

Rows of white chairs fanned out before an elevated stage, and small lights twinkled in the trees despite the early afternoon hour.

"Beautiful," she murmured as Brundar brought the cart to a stop right in front of the stage.

The gathered crowd watched expectantly as she climbed the steps all the way to the dais that had been decorated with more flowers—white roses and blue delphiniums that matched the wedding party's theme.

As Annani took her place at the top of the dais, a cheer went up from the assembled guests. She lifted her arms and dipped her head in greeting but refrained from addressing the crowd. Today, there would be a slight deviation from the tradition they had been crafting since the first wedding of Kian and Syssi.

Jackson and Vlad walked up to the foot of the stage with guitars in hand and plugged them into big amplifiers that had been placed there ahead of time. Jasmine stood between them, radiant in a flowing yellow dress, her smile bright as she looked up at Annani and nodded.

Then, with another slight nod to her accompanists, she lifted a microphone to her mouth and began to sing. Her voice soared pure and strong over the gathering, filling the air with promise and joy.

Under the music's cover, Peter and his groomsmen approached from the side.

Annani's heart warmed at the sight of him. He looked so handsome in his tuxedo, but more than that, he seemed to glow with happiness, and as he climbed the steps to stand before her, she saw no trace of doubt in his eyes.

The groomsmen arranged themselves at the foot of the stage and then came Marina's bridesmaids, a parade of blue dresses and bright smiles.

Finally, Marina herself appeared, and a collective gasp rose from the crowd.

She was stunning. The mermaid-shaped dress seemed to float around her as she moved, and the blue gems sewn into the white fabric reflected the afternoon light. But it was her face that truly captured attention—the pure joy and love radiating from her expression as she looked at Peter.

As Marina climbed the steps to join them, Annani felt her earlier prayer echo in her heart. Surely, the Fates could see what she saw—two souls perfectly matched despite the barriers between them.

Surely, they would find a way to keep them together.

Marina reached Peter's side, and as he took her hand, their fingers instantly intertwined. The love between them was almost tangible, a golden thread binding their hearts together.

Annani looked out over the assembled crowd—her family, her clan, each face holding the same hope she felt, the same wish for this couple's happiness.

Jasmine's song drew to a close, the final notes hanging in the air like crystals, and in the silence that followed, Annani drew herself up, ready to begin the ceremony that would bind these two lives together for however long the Fates allowed.

27

MARINA

Marina's heart thundered in her chest as she walked toward Peter, her dress whispering against the wooden steps of the stage. His eyes shone with such love and joy that she almost forgot to breathe. When their gazes met, his face split into a broad, beautiful grin that made her weak at the knees.

"Beautiful," he mouthed as she reached him. "So worth the wait."

She wanted to tell him that he looked incredibly handsome in his tuxedo, that her heart felt like it might burst from happiness, but she held her tongue. With the Clan Mother standing before them on her raised dais, it didn't seem appropriate to speak, even in whispers.

Marina had seen the goddess several times by now, but her presence still took her breath away. The otherworldly beauty, the glowing skin, and the raw power emanating from her elicited awe and the kindness and love radiating from her inspired adoration.

Annani was a real goddess, or as real as it got, but regrettably, she didn't have the power to grant immortality. That particular miracle, if it came at all, would have to come through Kaia's and Bridget's research.

The crowd's cheers and whistles felt like a precious gift, the warmth of their support washing over her. This was the community that had taken her in, accepted her, and made her one of their own despite her humanness. Wonder and Wendy were grinning as if their own sister was getting married, Lusha was beaming with pride, either at Marina or at her handiwork with her makeup, and in the crowd, Marina's mother dabbed at her eyes while her father held her hand.

Even Peter's mother was smiling and clapping.

Everyone knew the challenges that lay ahead, but today wasn't about that. Today was about love, hope, and new beginnings.

Annani waited for the crowd to settle, her presence commanding silence without the need for words. When she finally lifted her hands, the air itself seemed to still.

"Beloved family," she began, her voice carrying effortlessly across the gathering without the help of a microphone, "we are here today to witness the joining of two hearts, two lives, two souls who have chosen each other despite all obstacles."

Marina felt Peter's fingers tighten around hers.

"Some might say their path will not be easy," Annani continued. "That the differences between them are too great to overcome. But love—true love—has never concerned itself with such worldly limitations."

Tears pricked at Marina's eyes. She blinked them back carefully, remembering Lusha's warnings about her makeup.

"I have watched Peter grow in the Guardian force to become a leader." Annani's gaze shifted to Marina. "And I have watched Marina brave a new world with grace and courage, earning her place in our community through her strength of character and the purity of her heart."

A murmur of agreement rippled through the crowd. Marina's vision blurred despite her best efforts to hold the tears at bay. Lusha's stern words echoed in her mind, commanding her to focus on happy, non-mushy thoughts.

"Together," Annani said, "they remind us that love is not about what we are but who we choose to be. That the bonds of the heart transcend all other considerations."

She turned to face them fully now, her otherworldly beauty softened by genuine warmth. "Peter and Marina, you stand before your community today to pledge your lives and your love to each other. Are you ready to recite your vows to each other?"

"We are," they answered in unison.

Peter's voice rang strong and sure to Marina's near whisper, and his fingers tightened around hers. She drew strength from his steady presence beside her.

"Then let us begin." Annani raised her hands again, and Marina felt something shift in the air—like electricity but softer, warmer. "Before the gathered witnesses, before the Fates themselves, speak your vows to each other."

Peter turned to face Marina, his eyes bright with emotion. She could hardly believe this was real—that she was here, marrying this incredible male, with a goddess presiding over their union. But Peter's hands were warm and solid in hers, anchoring her to this perfect moment.

She might not have forever, but she had this man who looked at her like she was his whole world, and for now, that was enough.

More than enough.

It was everything.

28

PETER

Peter faced Marina and took both of her hands. "Marina, my love. Today, in front of the Clan Mother and all of our community, I choose you. I promise to love you completely and without reservation, to support your dreams and share your burdens, and to face whatever challenges life presents, standing firmly by your side." His voice was steady despite the emotion threatening to overwhelm him.

He'd rehearsed this speech so many times in front of the bathroom mirror that he was sure it was embedded forever in its walls. If Mey ever came to their house and entered their bathroom, she would for sure hear the echoes of his declaration of love to Marina without even having to concentrate or put any effort into it.

He squeezed Marina's hands gently. "You make me stronger and better, and I feel more alive with you than I've ever been before. I promise to cherish every moment we have together, to fill our life with laughter and joy, to be your partner, your protector, your best friend, and your most devoted admirer."

He let go of one of her hands to pull out the ring he had in his pocket. It was a simple gold band with an inscription engraved on its inner side, and Marina had an identical one for him.

"With this ring, I thee wed," he said simply as he slid it over her finger.

He'd written so many alternatives to this traditional declaration, but they had all spoken of forever and eternity, and he knew that would only upset Marina, so he'd decided to stick to these simple words that did the job just as well, albeit with less fanfare.

Marina's answering smile was radiant as she put her hand back in his. "Peter, my love, you showed me what real love feels like. I promise to love you wholly and completely, to stand beside you through whatever life brings, to be your safe harbor and your greatest champion." Her voice grew stronger with every word, as if she was gaining momentum. "I promise to face our future together with courage and hope and to fill our days with wonder and joy. You are my heart's choice, my soul's match, and I will love you with everything I am for as long as I live."

She reached down and plucked the ring from

where it had been cleverly attached to the fabric of her dress.

He'd wondered where she could have possibly hidden it, hoping she would pull it out from between her breasts, but his guess had been totally off.

She took his hand. "With this ring, I thee wed." She slid the ring on his finger.

As the crowd erupted in cheers and applause, the Clan Mother waited patiently and then lifted her hand, and the crowd fell silent all at once.

"Before the gathered witnesses and the Fates themselves, I seal your union with my blessings and that of our entire community. From this moment forward, your lives are intertwined—two hearts beating as one, two souls joined in perfect harmony. May your love grow stronger with each passing day and your bond deepen with every shared moment." Annani raised both her hands. "I declare you joined in love and bound together in body and spirit. From this day forward, you are partners in all things. Let your first kiss as a mated pair seal your bond."

As their guests once again cheered and clapped and Peter's fellow Guardians hooted and whistled, he pulled Marina close, pouring all his love and joy into their first wedded kiss.

When they finally separated, both breathless and grinning, a commotion started below that drew their attention.

At least ten Guardians had formed lines on either side of the wooden dance floor, and to Peter's amazement, they'd produced ceremonial swords.

"Oh no," he laughed, recognizing the set-up for the Scottish sword dance. "You can't do that without kilts."

Jay grinned at him. "Oh yes we can."

As the music started playing through the loudspeakers, his friends began the intricate footwork of the dance, stepping carefully between and over the crossed swords while maintaining perfect formation.

Marina squeezed his hand. "Go on," she urged, eyes sparkling. "I know you want to join them."

Peter didn't need to be told twice. Jumping off the stage, he crossed over to the dance floor and joined his fellow Guardians, falling easily into the familiar steps, though it had been years since he'd performed the dance.

Marina's delighted laughter rang out over the music, spurring him on to add an extra flourish to his steps. The other guests had gathered around the dance floor, clapping in time with the music. Even his mother looked impressed, clapping along and grinning.

When the dance ended, Peter returned to Marina's side, slightly out of breath but full of joy. "Did you enjoy the show?"

"Very much." She stretched up to kiss his cheek.

"You were the best one there. I just regret that you weren't wearing a kilt." She winked.

"Next time," he promised in a low voice.

As Jasmine stepped onto the small stage with Jackson and Vlad and the opening notes of 'Can't Help Falling in Love' filled the air, Peter led Marina to the center of the dance floor for their first dance as a wedded couple.

The setting sun painted the sky in brilliant oranges and pinks while thousands of tiny lights twinkled in the surrounding trees, transforming the village green into an enchanted garden.

Peter drew Marina into his arms, one hand settling on her waist while the other clasped hers. "You look absolutely stunning," he murmured as they began to move together. "It was smart of you to hide this dress from me until now. If I'd seen you in it before, it wouldn't have made it to the wedding in one piece."

She laughed. "You look very handsome yourself, but I would very much like to keep this dress in pristine condition. Who knows, maybe one day our daughter will get married wearing it."

Peter swallowed, overwhelmed with emotion. "I'll do my best to preserve it as I peel it off your exquisite body later tonight."

Marina rested her head on his shoulder, and the rest of the world seemed to fade away until there was nothing but this—the music, the lights, and his mate in his arms.

29

MORELLE

Morelle held a hand over her heart as she listened to Peter and Marina exchange their heartfelt vows. The depth of their love was evident in every word, every gesture, every shared look. Despite the obstacles they faced—Marina's mortality chief among them—they chose to embrace their love fully and without reservation.

Their courage made Morelle's own fears seem almost insignificant in comparison.

"Dance with me?" Brandon held out his hand as other couples joined Marina and Peter on the dance floor.

She took it, letting him guide her onto the wooden platform. "I don't know the steps," she said as he drew her into his arms.

"Just follow my lead." His hand settled warm and steady on her waist. "Like this."

Morelle let Brandon guide her through the movements while watching others and trying to emulate them. As they found their rhythm together, she leaned into his solid warmth and breathed in his familiar scent.

The fairy lights twinkled overhead like stars, the music wrapped around them like silk, and the moment could have been perfect if not for the guilt gnawing at her conscience.

She should have told him the real secret behind her telekinetic power right after they'd confessed their love to each other, but she'd been too overwhelmed with emotion to even remember that she was still hiding her vampiric nature from him.

There shouldn't be secrets between mates, especially not something this important, and Brandon deserved the truth. They all did—Annani, Kian, Amanda, this entire community that had welcomed her and Ell-rom with open arms and open hearts.

Not only that, she also needed help to master her power.

Absorbing energy from others happened without her intending to do it. It was instinctual, which made it worse because she didn't have a mechanism to prevent it from happening.

What if she drained too much from someone right when they needed their power for an important task and didn't have time to recuperate from the drain? What if she used too much of her own reserves and perished?

The thought wouldn't have bothered her in her previous life, but now that she had so much to live for, Morelle didn't want to die.

She had to tell Amanda the truth. Perhaps she would not only help her control the ability but also find practical applications for it. After all, as important as her talent had been to avert a disaster, it wasn't something that happened often, thank the Mother of All Life.

"You seem preoccupied." Brandon's voice cut through her spiraling thoughts. "What's wrong?"

She looked up into his concerned blue eyes. "We need to talk."

As his body tensed against hers, and his steps nearly faltered, she realized how he could have misinterpreted her words and quickly added, "I love you, and I always will. It's not about that."

The tension in his back eased. "I love you too." His thumb caressed her waist. "What do you want to talk about?"

Morelle glanced around at the other couples dancing on the tightly packed dance floor. "Later," she said. "When we're in our room with the door closed."

A smile tugged at his lips. "Anything that involves you and me behind closed doors sounds good."

She pressed closer to him. "I agree, but that's

not why I want to talk to you in private. I just need to tell you something important."

Brandon studied her face for a long moment. "I don't think I can wait that long. Would you like to take a walk with me?"

Morelle would have preferred to have more time to think about the best way to tell him, but he was right about it causing tension that would prevent them from enjoying the rest of the evening. It was better to get it over with sooner rather than later.

"The village walkways are abandoned," he added. "Almost everyone is here."

"Won't we be missed?"

His hand on her waist tightened. "We can say that you needed a breather from being surrounded by so many people."

She chuckled. "And it wouldn't even be a lie. I'm not used to so many bodies so close to me. It's overwhelming."

He took her hand. "Let's go. Just a short walk." He led her off the dance floor, through the sprawling lawn, all the way to the walkway.

Morelle took a deep breath. "I didn't realize how anxious it made me to have so many people surrounding me. I love this community and I'm grateful for how welcoming everyone is, but I need more time to adjust to the hive."

"So, what is this about?" Brandon asked.

She hesitated.

What if he was frightened by the parasitic nature of her power? What if he thought that she was dangerous and should be kept away from Annani and anyone else who had a paranormal talent?

"You can tell me anything, Morelle. I won't judge, and I won't criticize, and I will keep on loving you no matter what."

She wanted desperately to believe that, but the fear still coiled in her gut.

"Hey." Brandon stopped, turned to her, and cupped her cheek. "I'm sure that you're working yourself up over nothing."

She snorted. "Oh, it's definitely something. I'm just trying to figure out a way to say it the right way."

"Don't overthink it. I promise that there is no wrong way for you to say whatever it is that you are obsessing about."

"Okay. Here it goes. I'm a vampire."

30

BRANDON

A vampire?

She didn't even have fangs.

What had gotten into her?

Was it a faulty translation?

Yeah, that must be the issue. There was no way Anumati had vampire mythology like Earth, given that a large portion of its population was the Kra-ell, who actually were vampires.

Was that what she was trying to tell him?

"I know that you are half Kra-ell, but you don't drink blood, so I assume something has gone wrong with the translation, and you meant something different. Can you tell me what you mean by a vampire?"

"A soul-sucker," she said, in a tone that implied he should have known that. "People that suck the life energy from others."

Well, that was more or less what vampires were, except instead of energy, they sucked blood.

Evidently, Anumati had its own vampire mythology with a different twist.

"So, let me get this clear. You think that you are able to suck out the souls of others? Which souls have you devoured lately?"

He could barely say that without laughing or at least smiling, but it seemed that Morelle was dead serious about her ridiculous claim, so he had to tread carefully not to offend her.

She shook her head. "I don't suck souls. I suck out paranormal energy, which is how I power my telekinetic ability and probably my nullification ability as well. I draw power from others to fuel it. I'm a parasite." Her voice cracked on the last word.

Understanding dawned. This was what had been weighing on her, why she'd been evasive whenever anyone mentioned her incredible power. He'd thought it had been the trauma of Darius's near-death event, but it was for an entirely different reason.

"First of all, you need to stop thinking of yourself as a parasite. Secondly, how do you know that you sucked the energy from others? Did you feel it?"

Morelle wrapped her arms around herself, looking fragile and uncertain in the gathering darkness. "I'm not sure. Even before I realized what was about to happen, I felt like I was drawing on everyone's energy, but I hoped I was imagining it. But I must have felt that something terrible was about to happen and that's why I was doing it, or at least I hope that's the reason. It is better than the alternative of me just stealing energy from others for the fun of it. Then, when the crack became visible, and I could see what was coming, I pulled even harder on all those tendrils of energy, and I harnessed them all to fuel the telekinesis. Only later did it occur to me that I might have nullified the power of others, not by blocking it but by taking their energy away. The scariest part is that I don't know how I'm doing that or when. It just happens."

Brandon frowned. "You must have felt something when you thought you were blocking their talents from manifesting."

She'd blocked Toven, a god, and if she was correct about the siphoning of energy, that was a concern, but then if she had drawn on Annani's power to save Darius it was a good thing, and no one would object to that.

"I thought about blocking them or just making their abilities inactive, but I didn't feel like I was doing anything. It's a good thing that the effect was temporary, or I would be really panicking."

"Why panicking? It's not as big of a deal as you are making it out to be. There are much worse powers out there, compulsion being chief among them. A command issued with compulsion can block an immortal's paranormal ability even more effectively than your drain. You don't know to what extent it drains and for how long." He led Morelle to a bench and sat down with her. "I think in your mind you've built it up into a monster when it's just a small poltergeist."

She let out a breath. "Thank you for making me feel better about it, but I don't think it's such a minor thing. What if I drain Annani? Imagine the amount of power I could take from her and then channel it into something else." She snorted. "I might be able to lift the entire village and move it to a new location of Kian's choosing. At least that could be useful."

She was wandering into the absurd, which was fine if it helped her deal with this scary newfound ability.

"I should have told you sooner, but I was afraid." She avoided his eyes.

He took her hand. "Afraid of what?"

"That you would think I was a monster, a parasite, someone who should be locked up so she couldn't harm others."

Brandon understood why Morelle would think that, and he could even see some reacting to her power exactly as she'd described, but the facts were that she hadn't harmed anyone yet, and the only time she'd used a significant store of energy was to save the life of a child. She'd also depleted her own reserves to do that and was nearly comatose afterward.

Leaning over, he lifted her onto his lap and wrapped her in his arms. "You are a good person, Morelle. You used your ability for good and not for harm. You just need to figure out how to control it."

"What if I harmed someone in the process?" she murmured.

"Have you?" He stroked her back. "Has anyone shown signs of being harmed by the energy drain?"

She looked at him. "I don't know. Did you feel anything?"

"I was a little shaken, but that was because of the adrenaline rush."

"It could also have been because of the drain." She sighed. "Tomorrow, I'm supposed to meet with Amanda again, and I think that I should tell her."

"You should." He pulled back just enough to look into her eyes. "You have an extraordinary gift, Morelle, and like any powerful ability, it needs to be understood and mastered. That's all."

"So, you are not afraid to be with me?"

The genuine anxiety in her voice tugged at his heartstrings. "Of course not. I'm impressed, and I'm honored to have such a powerful mate. Do you realize what potential applications this talent could have?"

She blinked up at him. "What?"

"Think about it." He kept stroking her back. "In a crisis situation, you could potentially redirect power where it's needed most. I don't know that you could, but it's a possibility. Imagine pulling some of Annani's power to fuel Cassandra so she could blow up an attacking aircraft. Your power is not parasitic—it's complimentary. You're a conduit and an enhancer and maybe even a little bit of a seer."

That was a stretch, and he didn't know whether Morelle could redirect the energy or just absorb it into herself, but she needed encouragement and a new way to think about her ability.

"I hadn't thought of it that way."

"Of course you haven't. You've been too busy catastrophizing." He smiled to soften the words. "Amanda can help you understand and develop this ability properly."

"I know, but I'm scared. What if she's not as understanding and supportive as you are?" She smiled, which was a great improvement over the worried looks she'd given him so far. "You are a little biased."

"So are Amanda, Annani, Kian, and the rest of your family. They all want what's best for you, and they will accept you the way you are. All of you—including the power-borrowing ability that you've dramatically labeled vampirism."

Another reluctant smile tugged at her lips. "You're making fun of me."

"Only a little." He pressed a kiss to her forehead. "Please don't ever think that you have to hide parts of yourself from me. I want all of you—the good, the bad, and the complicated."

She chuckled. "You are too good to me."

"Not at all. I'm just the right amount of goodness."

As music from the wedding celebration drifted toward them on the evening breeze, Morelle leaned her head on his chest and sighed. "We should head back," she said, though she made no move to leave his embrace.

"In a minute." Brandon tightened his grip on her. "This feels too good to stop."

"I know. But we will be missed, and Annani might send a search party after us."

He took her hand and pressed a kiss to her palm. "I'll just have to explain that I stole you away because I'm a selfish male and wanted you all to myself."

"That's a good explanation. I think she'll be okay with that."

"I'm sure she will." He pressed another kiss to her forehead. "You are absolutely adorable when you work yourself up over nothing."

"It wasn't over nothing, and I am not adorable," she protested. "I'm fierce and dangerous."

"Mmhmm." He pulled her close again. "Terrifying. A real monster. But you are my monster, and I'm not sharing."

She melted against him, and he felt the last of her tension drain away. "You are terrible."

"I know."

31

GERTRUDE

The music swelled around Gertrude and Rob as they swayed on the dance floor. It had been a wonderful ceremony, unique in that the Clan Mother had united a mortal and an immortal, something that was unheard of in the clan.

Watching Marina and Peter together, it was easy to see that they were meant for each other, and Gertrude had to wonder why the Fates were being so cruel to Peter.

Why had they found him a truelove mate who couldn't be his lifelong companion?

She consoled herself that the Fates worked in mysterious ways and that they might have a plan for Marina that no one could even guess at the moment.

As Rob once again tried to steer them toward where Margo was dancing with Negal, Gertrude shifted her attention to doing the opposite and pulling in another direction.

It wasn't that she harbored any lingering romantic feelings for Negal, but being around him still made her uncomfortable, stirring up old memories of being cast aside the moment he'd found his true mate in Margo.

She would have to get over that discomfort, though.

Now that she and Rob were talking about moving in together, family gatherings would be inevitable. Rob would want to host his sister and her mate for dinner or movie nights, and Gertrude would have to find a way to enjoy Negal's company without letting her resentment ruin the family dynamic.

Family.

It was strange to even think in those terms. For the longest time, the only ones she'd considered family were her mother and her best friend, Hildegard. Now that things were getting serious between her and Rob, his sister and her mate would become her family as well.

In a way, they already had, but she'd kept an emotional barrier between herself and Negal that would have to come down at some point.

As Rob's steps began to falter, guilt washed over her. She'd been so caught up in her own thoughts that she'd forgotten he was still human and couldn't keep up with her immortal stamina.

Worry niggled at her that he would need another induction because he wasn't showing signs of transition, and even though they still might start manifesting later today or tomorrow, she was already thinking of who should be his next inducer.

She might ask Dagor.

As a full-blooded god, his venom was potent, and he was more approachable than Aru or Toven. Negal would no doubt say yes to her request out of sheer guilt, but she didn't want him to be Rob's inducer. It might be petty of her, and if he were the best option out there or the only one, she would swallow her pride and ask him, but as long as there were other alternatives that were just as good or better, she didn't have to.

"Let's take a break," Gertrude suggested, squeezing Rob's hand. "We should get something to eat. Have you seen what the Odus have prepared? There are like twenty different dishes for every taste and preference possible."

"I could use a rest," Rob admitted.

He let her lead him off the dance floor, practically collapsing into one of the chairs arranged around the tables near the buffet. "But I'm not really hungry."

"You should eat something." She frowned at the sheen of sweat on his forehead. "I'll fix you a plate."

"Okay." He reached for the pitcher of water on

the table with a slightly trembling hand. "Can you bring me some water?"

She frowned at the odd request. "There's water right here," she pointed to the pitcher in his hand. "But I can get you something stronger if you'd like."

"No, water's fine." He poured himself a glass, some of it sloshing over the side.

Could it be that he was starting to transition?

She pressed her palm to his forehead. "You don't have a fever, but the rest of your symptoms might indicate the start of your transition."

Rob crossed his fingers. "I hope so. I definitely feel off, and it's not just from the dancing, so you might be right."

"Maybe we should get you to the clinic—"

"Not yet. Even if you are right and I'm transitioning, there's plenty of time." He smiled. "Go get something to eat. I'm not about to faint or anything."

She wasn't entirely convinced of that, but the buffet line was close enough that she could keep an eye on him. "Promise you'll tell me if you start feeling worse?"

"Promise." He lifted his water glass in a mock toast. "I'll just sit here and take it easy."

As Gertrude joined the buffet line, she glanced back at Rob every few seconds, and each time, he waved and smiled, so the urgency started to wane. Not every Dormant lost consciousness, and those who didn't also didn't require much care. Perhaps

Rob was one of the lucky ones who would transition easily.

When it was finally her turn, she loaded two plates with an assortment of dishes, making sure to include things she knew Rob liked. When she turned back toward their table, though, Rob wasn't in his chair.

Her eyes scanned the crowd, thinking he might have gotten up to speak with someone. Then she spotted him—sprawled on the grass beside his abandoned chair, unnoticed by the celebrating guests around him.

The plates clattered onto the table as she rushed to his side. His chest rose and fell steadily, but when she tried to wake him, he didn't respond. He was unconscious, and his skin felt hot to the touch.

Without hesitation, she gathered him into her arms and started toward the clinic, but then Bowen rushed to her.

"Let me," he said, already reaching for Rob.

She wanted to refuse—her immortal strength more than adequate to carry Rob—but there were other considerations, with Rob's pride being one of them.

He wouldn't like his transition story to start with his mate carrying him to the clinic.

His mate.

Was she? Was he hers?

As Bowen took Rob from her arms, Margo finally noticed the commotion and ran over, her face pale with concern. "What's wrong? Is Rob transitioning?"

"That's what it looks like," Gertrude said. "Go get Bridget."

Margo nodded and sprinted to look for the doctor.

Thankfully, the clinic was a short walking distance away, and since the door was never locked, Gertrude just pushed it open and held it for Bowen. "This way." She pointed him toward the first patient room.

"It's a good sign that he's transitioning so soon after the induction," Bowen said as he laid him on the bed. "Am I right?"

"I hope you are. Every transitioning Dormant is different." She sighed. "On the one hand, I'm glad that it's happening and he doesn't have to be induced again, but on the other hand, I'm terrified."

Bowen nodded. "I know how you feel. But as you and all the docs have kept telling everyone, we haven't lost a single Dormant yet, so we shouldn't worry, right?"

She chuckled. "It's much easier to say when it's not the one you love who is transitioning."

The Guardian's eyes widened. "Love, eh? You two moved fast."

She shrugged. "When it's right, it's right."

Bowen chuckled. "I won't argue with that."

Rob's breathing remained steady, but his temperature seemed to be climbing with every passing second, and his skin felt like it was on fire.

"Do you need my help to undress him?" Bowen offered.

"Thank you, but I can do that." She smiled at him. "I've been a nurse for a very long time."

He nodded. "Do you need me for anything else, or can I go back to the party?"

"Go. You were a great help. Thank you."

After Bowen left, Gertrude undressed Rob, put a hospital gown on him, and covered him with a sheet. She was about to duck into the back room and exchange her party dress for some scrubs when the clinic door opened, and Bridget walked in with Margo and Negal.

"How long has he been unconscious?" the doctor asked, already checking Rob's vital signs.

"About ten minutes," Gertrude said. "He only started manifesting symptoms less than half an hour before that—fatigue, tremors, fever."

"Pulse is rapid but strong," Bridget murmured, more to herself than her audience. "Breathing regularly. Classic onset pattern."

"It happened so fast," Margo said. "Is that normal?"

"For males, it usually happens faster than for females." Bridget pulled out a stethoscope from the drawer and started listening to Rob's chest. "The speed of onset doesn't necessarily indicate anything about how the transition itself will progress, but it is a good sign."

Bridget was being cautious, but Gertrude knew from experience that the faster the onset, the faster the change was going to happen. For males, it meant that their venom glands and fangs grew more rapidly, which was more painful.

"You should wait in the waiting room," Bridget told Margo and Negal. "Gertrude needs to connect Rob to the monitoring equipment." She shooed them out.

As Gertrude moved to comply, Rob's eyes fluttered open. "What happened?" he slurred.

The fact that he woke up was another good sign. Dormants who slipped in and out of consciousness had an easier time transitioning than those who were fully unconscious for the entire time.

"You're transitioning." She cupped his cheek and smiled. "Everything's going to be okay."

He managed a weak smile. "Told you I wasn't about to faint."

"Technically, you did faint." She couldn't help but smile back, relief making her a bit giddy.

"Oh, bummer." His eyes slipped closed again.

Gertrude pressed a kiss to his burning forehead. "Rest now. I'll be right here when you wake up."

"Love you," he mumbled before unconsciousness claimed him again.

"I love you too," she whispered, though he couldn't hear her.

32

MORELLE

Morelle and Brandon were on their way home when Annani's front door opened, and one of her Odus stepped out and bowed. "The Clan Mother would like to invite you for a cup of tea."

It wasn't an invitation either of them could refuse, especially since they had promised Annani to visit her every day.

"Of course," Brandon said, leading Morelle up the steps. "We would love to have tea with the Clan Mother."

"You're glowing," Annani said as Morelle sat beside her. "Did you enjoy the wedding?"

"Very much so."

Morelle's feet ached in the most wonderful way as she settled onto the couch in Annani's living room. She'd never danced before tonight, but her body had taken to it naturally, following Brandon's lead until she could anticipate the steps herself. By the end of the evening, she'd been spinning and swaying as if she'd been doing it her entire life.

She patted her cheeks, which felt warm. "Peter and Marina are a lovely couple, and the ceremony was beautiful. You were amazing."

"Thank you." Annani beamed. "I love weddings. Each one is as unique as the people I am joining." She took a deep breath. "I feel like a real goddess when I preside over weddings. That and bringing babies into the world is truly divine." She smiled and patted Morelle's knee. "But enough about me. Did you get to dance?"

"A lot. I had no idea dancing could be so much fun. The way the music flows through you, how your body just knows what to do..." She trailed off, still caught up in the magic of it. "When I was growing up, only males danced, and those were warrior dances that were performed to commemorate important battles. I never imagined dancing just for the pleasure of it."

"Your brother seemed to have taken to it as well," Brandon said. "I don't think I've ever seen him smiling so much."

That was true. Ell-rom had always been a pensive boy who had grown up into a pensive adult. There hadn't been much in their circumstances to smile about.

Annani's eyes sparkled. "You know what we should do? We should start a dance class in the gym. Not everyone enjoys running on machines or lifting weights, but dancing—that's exercise disguised as pure joy."

The idea sent a thrill through Morelle. "Really? You'd actually consider joining a class like that?"

Her sister was very involved with the community, but she also kept a distance as necessary, given her station. Morelle couldn't see Annani frolicking on the dance floor with a bunch of clan members.

"We could keep it small." Annani's smile widened. "It would be wonderful to have an activity we could share. Something just for the ladies of the close family to enjoy together."

That made more sense, and it could actually be fun if Syssi, Amanda, and Alena joined them.

"Who would teach the class?" Morelle asked.

"Oh, that is simple enough." Annani waved a hand. "We can follow instructional videos. There are exercise programs on the internet that we can watch on the television. The steps are quite easy to follow. We can do it right here."

"That could be fun." Morelle accepted a teacup from Ogidu. "Thank you."

She glanced at Brandon, who also got a cup and immediately started sipping on it. He seemed deep in thought, but when he felt her gaze on him, he turned to look at her and smiled.

Morelle wanted to ask him if he thought that it was a good idea to tell Annani about her ability now, but she didn't know how to ask that discreetly.

He must have understood what she was trying to convey with her eyes because he gave a subtle shake of his head.

The weight of her secret felt heavier suddenly, especially since she was going to tell Amanda tomorrow. Then again, Brandon's reasoning was probably that it made sense to tell everyone together rather than to have the story spread piecemeal through the family.

She needed a moment alone to think.

Putting the teacup on the coffee table, Morelle rose to her feet. "If you will excuse me for a moment, I need to use the restroom."

"Of course, my dear," Annani said. "You can use the one in your old bedroom."

"I'll go with you." Brandon stood as well. "I need to go too."

If Annani thought it strange, she didn't say anything.

When they closed the door of their old room behind them, Brandon wrapped his arms around Morelle's waist. "I know that you want to tell Annani, but I think it's better to do this once, with everyone present."

She turned in his embrace. "I'm meeting Amanda tomorrow to continue testing my ability, and I need to tell her the truth about how it works so she can help me. Shouldn't I tell Annani first?"

Brandon studied her face for a long moment. "You're right," he said finally. "Annani should hear it first. She's not just the Clan Mother—she's your sister."

When they returned to the living room, they found Kian and Syssi sitting on the couch with the sleepy-looking Allegra cuddled in her mother's arms.

Morelle's steps faltered. Having Kian there made everything more intimidating, but then she felt Brandon's steady presence beside her, his quiet strength bolstering her own.

A sudden thought struck her, and she grabbed his arm. "Do you feel weak?" she whispered in his ear. "Am I drawing energy from you without meaning to?"

"Not at all." He covered her hand with his. "I feel perfectly normal."

The relief that flooded through her nearly made her knees buckle. At least she wasn't unconsciously draining him.

"Oh, here you are." Annani waved them over. "I caught Syssi and Kian on the way home the same way I caught you. It is a great advantage that we all live in such proximity to each other."

"You could've called me," Kian said. "There is no need to have your Odu stand by the window and wait for us to pass by."

Annani laughed, the beautiful sound sending chills up Morelle's arms. "But this is much more fun, and you cannot come up with an excuse and say that you need to go home because Allegra is tired or something of that nature."

"I would never." Kian feigned offense.

Taking a deep breath, Morelle cleared her throat. "Actually, it's good that you are here because I need to tell you all something important, and it will save me having to say it twice." She ran her fingers through her short hair. "Three times, in fact, because I will have to tell Amanda about it tomorrow."

"Would you like me to call her?" Annani asked. "She could come over and save you the need to repeat your story."

"That's okay." Morelle cast her a nervous smile. "I'd rather just get it off my chest now."

Annani's expression turned serious while Kian straightened in his seat. Even little Allegra seemed to sense the shift in mood, lifting her head from Syssi's shoulder to look at Morelle with curious eyes. "Illy?"

"What is it, dear?" Annani asked.

Morelle's throat felt dry. Where should she begin?

How could she explain without making herself sound like an energy thief? Or worse, a parasite?

She felt Brandon's hand settle, warm and reassuring, on her lower back and drew strength from his touch.

"It's about my ability. The telekinesis and the

nullifying power are connected, but not in the way we thought. I draw power from others to fuel both of these actions. I'm not blocking others' abilities, I'm preventing them from using them by draining their powers, and to move things with my mind, I have to draw energy from everyone around me." She looked at Annani. "If you hadn't been there to supply me with a potent boost in energy, I don't know if I could have swatted that stone aside. Everyone else's power together might not have been enough for me to move such a heavy object. I didn't mean to do that. I didn't even know that I could. I reacted on instinct."

"Then I am glad I was there," Annani said. "I thank the merciful Fates for putting us both in the room so we could save Darius."

Morelle felt like hugging Annani for the heartfelt response. She would have said the exact same thing if she were in Annani's place, and it was good to know that she and her sister thought alike.

"That makes a great deal of sense," Kian said. "It would explain why you were so exhausted afterward—you were processing and channeling an enormous amount of energy."

"You're not concerned by what I can do?" Morelle asked.

"Why would I be?" Kian frowned. "You saved a child's life, and you were the only one in that room who could have done that. I'm grateful for your ability."

"But I'm like a parasite, sucking the life energy from others."

Kian chuckled and shook his head. "That's a bit dramatic, don't you think?"

"I do not want to hear you referring to yourself as a parasite." Annani's voice was firm. "You are channeling energy to where it is needed most. That is not parasitic—it is symbiotic. Think of how useful such an ability could be in a crisis."

Morelle blinked in surprise. It was almost exactly what Brandon had said.

Kian lifted his hand. "Nevertheless, we should work on helping you control your power. Amanda will probably know what to do."

"I'm going to tell her tomorrow," Morelle said. "But I wanted you all to know first. Especially you." She walked over to Annani, crouched in front of her, and took hold of her sister's hands. "I've been so afraid of what you'd think of me."

"Never be afraid to tell me anything." Annani gave her hands a light squeeze. "You are my sister. I love you, and nothing will change that. Come, give me a hug."

As Morelle sat beside Annani and the two of them embraced, the sound of small feet pattering across the floor drew their attention. Allegra had wiggled down from Syssi's lap and now stood in front of them, arms raised in a clear demand to be included in the hug.

Morelle laughed and scooped her up, sandwiching the little girl between herself and her sister. The simple acceptance of a child—who didn't care about powers or abilities, who just wanted to be part of the love being shared—was perhaps the most healing of all.

33

BRANDON

Brandon leaned against the doorframe of his and Morelle's bathroom, watching as she sank deeper into the bubble bath with a contented sigh. The tension that had been evident in her shoulders all evening seemed to melt away in the warm water.

As her phone buzzed with an incoming message, he handed it to her, but she shook her head. "Tell me what it says. My hands are covered in soap bubbles."

"It's from Ell-rom. Rob's transitioning, and Ell-rom and Jasmine are heading to the clinic to sit with Margo and the others. They'll be home late."

"That's wonderful news." Morelle smiled, trailing her fingers through the foam. "I hope the transition goes smoothly for Rob."

"From what I hear, the faster it starts, the better the chances of a smooth transition." Brandon settled onto the edge of the tub. "And his started very quickly."

Morelle nodded, then let out another deep sigh. "I still can't believe how well everyone took my news. I was so terrified of their reactions, especially Annani's. But they were all so accepting."

"Of course, they were." Brandon extended his hand to gently sweep a cluster of bubbles from her forehead. "They love you. And your ability isn't nearly as frightening as you'd built it up to be in your mind."

"I'm not sure you are right about that." She caught his hand and pressed a kiss to his palm. "But thank you for helping me shrink the big monster into a little one."

"Your ability could never be monstrous," he said softly. "You're one of the most compassionate people I know. The only reason your ability even manifested was because you needed it to save a child."

"True." She smiled up at him, her blue eyes sparkling. "There's one more secret I need to tell you, and then there will be no more secrets between us."

"What's that?"

"It's about Ell-rom's power—"

"Stop." Brandon held up a hand. "As much as I appreciate you wanting to share everything with me, Kian doesn't want the council to know about that yet. And I don't want to put myself in a position where I'm defying him. I can wait to learn that particular secret," he assured her. "When Kian decides it's time, I'll hear it along with everyone else."

To his relief, Morelle didn't seem hurt by his interruption. If anything, her smile grew warmer. "You're a good man, Brandon. Loyal. I value that a great deal."

"I aim to please." He leaned down and kissed her forehead.

Morelle's eyes took on a mischievous glint as she gestured at the spacious tub. "Well, if you really aim to please, you should get undressed and join me. There's plenty of room for two in this huge tub."

Brandon didn't need to be asked twice. He stood and began unbuttoning his shirt, watching as Morelle's eyes followed his movements with clear appreciation. The heat in her gaze sent warmth spreading through his body that had nothing to do with the steamy air.

"You know," he said as he shrugged off his shirt, "I never actually used this tub before you moved in. I always preferred quick showers."

"What a waste of a perfectly good bathtub." Morelle shifted to make room for him. "Though I suppose that means we get to break it in together."

His pants joined his shirt on the floor, and he couldn't help but notice how Morelle's gaze dropped to admire his naked form.

As he stepped into the tub behind her, the warm water enveloped him like a caress, and as Morelle settled back against his chest, he wrapped his arms around her, pulling her close.

"This is nice," she murmured, laying her head back on his shoulder.

"Very nice," he agreed, pressing a kiss to her temple. The sweet scent of her shampoo mingled with the steam rising from the water, creating an intimate cocoon around them.

He ran his hands up and down her arms, marveling at the silky texture of her skin. He was hard, and he knew she could feel his erection poking her bottom, but he didn't intend to start anything unless she initiated it. Morelle needed his support tonight, and that's what he was doing. If she needed anything else from him, all she had to do was ask or just throw a hint.

He was easy.

"I love you," Morelle said suddenly, turning her head to look up at him. "I like saying that."

Brandon tightened his arms around her. "And I love hearing that. I love you too, my princess." He kissed her shoulder. "You've completely changed my life."

She shifted in his arms to face him more fully. "Changed in what way? For the better, I hope?"

"Infinitely better." He traced a droplet of water down her cheek. "You've brought light and joy and wonder into my world. And yes, some complications, too—but that just makes things more interesting. I wouldn't change a single thing about you."

"Even my questionable abilities?"

"Especially those." He grinned. "They're part of what makes you uniquely you. Besides, I meant what I said earlier—your ability could be incredibly useful in the right circumstances."

"I'm starting to believe that," she admitted. "Especially after seeing how everyone reacted. Even Kian seemed more interested than concerned. I dreaded his reaction the most. He's so protective of his mother and his whole community."

"He was intrigued because he saw the potential." Brandon ran his fingers through her wet hair, loving how it was growing out. "And he trusts you to use your gift responsibly."

"I just hope I can learn to control it." She closed her eyes. "I don't want to accidentally drain someone's power when they need their energy, or to expend too much of my own and harm myself."

"Amanda will figure it out." He caught her hand and brought it to his lips. "After you explain to her what you are really dealing with, she will know how to approach it. She might not look it, but she's a very smart lady."

Morelle's eyes popped open. "Why do you say she doesn't look smart?"

"The first impression people have of her is that of a frivolous socialite, but that's just the façade she wears for whatever reason, and you wouldn't know what that means, so forget I said it. The important thing is that she can help you develop proper control."

Morelle nodded, and then a small smile curved her lips. "You know what else I need to learn better control of?"

"What's that?"

Instead of answering, she straddled his lap, sending water sloshing against the sides of the tub. Her hands came up to frame his face as she leaned in to kiss him.

Brandon groaned into the kiss, his hands sliding down to grip her hips. The warm water made her skin impossibly silky under his palms, and the way she moved against him was rapidly driving coherent thought from his mind.

When she finally pulled back, they were both breathing heavily. "That," she said with a grin. "Though I think I'm getting better with practice."

"Much better," he agreed, his voice rough. "Though I think you might need more practice just to be sure."

As he pulled her down for another kiss, her delighted laugh echoed off the bathroom tiles. The water splashed around them, but Brandon couldn't have cared less about the mess they were making.

34

MORELLE

As their bodies started to slide against each other, the heat turned into an inferno, but fire and water didn't go well together, and the bathtub wasn't where Morelle wanted her first time to happen.

"I think we should get out." She put her hands on Brandon's chest and pushed back. "We can continue this dance in bed."

His eyes were glowing like a pair of stars, and his fangs were almost fully elongated.

Tonight, he wasn't going to resist her.

Tonight, they were going to complete their bond.

"You seem like a female on a mission." He rose to his feet and stepped out of the tub, soap bubbles and water sluicing off his magnificent naked body.

While clothed, Brandon was handsome, and when he wore a suit he looked elegant and sophisticated, but he was absolutely breathtaking in the nude. Lean muscles covered his tall body, creating a physique that was utter perfection.

He reached for a large towel and spread his arms to unfurl it. "Come on, Princess. Let's get you dry."

"What about you?" She stepped out of the tub and let him wrap her in the towel.

"I'll use your towel after you are done with it." He swung her cocooned body into his arms and carried her to the bedroom.

After laying her down on the bed, he took the towel from her and dried himself off while giving her a very clear frontal view of his maleness.

The thing was huge, and she didn't know how he was going to fit it inside of her, but she wasn't going to back out just because she was a little apprehensive. Her new lady friends had told her that the first time was often miserable, and it hurt and that the best way to handle it was to get it out of the way and get to the third one, which was usually when things started to get pleasurable.

It didn't make sense to her.

Why would nature design a female body to suffer through the first two times? In preparation for childbearing, perhaps?

Morelle had a feeling that her first time with Brandon was going to be wonderful. She wasn't willing to accept any other outcome.

When he joined her on the bed, he lay on his

side without touching her and just looked at her for a long moment with hooded eyes that were so full of passion that his gaze felt like a caress.

"Why are you looking at me like that?" she murmured.

"I'm just admiring your beauty and thinking that I'm incredibly lucky. I want to always remember you like this."

She wasn't sure what he meant by that. The only thing that was going to change about her was the length of her hair, but if he was so enamored with how it looked now, she could keep it short. The look was growing on her.

"Can I kiss you now?" he asked.

"Yes, please."

He smiled with a mouth full of fangs. "So polite." He dipped his head and kissed her gently as if it was their first kiss, but as he wrapped his arm around her and pulled her closer, the length of his erection pressing against her belly told a different story.

There was no way he was going to fit, width or lengthwise.

Pulling back, Brandon looked into her eyes. "What's the matter? You tensed on me all of a sudden."

She chewed on her lower lip, embarrassed to ask the question and reveal that she wasn't as confident and ferocious as she wanted him to believe she was.

He smiled. "Come on, Morelle, my fearless warrior. Tell me what got you tensing."

"You're too big."

He actually looked down at his erection. "Thank you. It's usually considered a compliment, but that wasn't your intent. I don't think that I'm exceptionally well endowed, but I can understand how it might seem a little scary to a virgin." He cupped her cheek. "I promise that we are going to fit despite how it looks, and I also promise to make it pleasurable for you."

"It's not scary at all." She reached with her hand and took hold of the smooth length. "It feels very nice in my hand, and I'm sure that you didn't have any problems fitting it inside your other partners, but..." she hesitated. "I seem to be built differently than your human paramours. You were barely able to fit your finger inside of me."

There, she'd said it.

He looked at her for a long time as if trying to figure out how to assuage her fears, or maybe he was just lost for words because she was caressing his erection, and it was growing even larger in her hand, which meant that he was enjoying it.

"I don't think that your Kra-ell heritage makes you any different. You felt just right on my finger and on my tongue, but we will go slow, and if at any moment you want to stop, we will stop. Nothing has to happen tonight. We are not in a rush."

Morelle kind of was, even though she'd gotten to experience the venom bite without fully joining with Brandon. It had been wonderful, the best experience of her life, but she knew it would be even better once they were fully joined and bonded.

According to her new friends, the bond wasn't going to snap into place until she and Brandon made love, and she wanted that to happen sooner rather than later.

35

BRANDON

Morelle seemed so confident, so assertive, that her hesitancy had taken him by surprise. It wasn't that he'd allowed himself to forget even for a moment how inexperienced she was, but he hadn't expected her to be apprehensive about the fit after all they had already done together.

He'd thought that he'd prepared her as well as he could, but since he'd never bedded a virgin, he couldn't have realized that no amount of prep would have been enough.

Right now, she seemed fascinated by his cock, stroking it gently while pressing her breasts against his chest. The scent of her arousal was intensifying, which he hoped meant she was over her initial hesitancy.

He closed his hand over hers and halted her up-

and-down strokes. "As good as this feels, you need to stop."

She lifted her gaze to his. "Why?"

"Because I want to be patient with you, and it's going to be difficult if I'm racing toward a climax." He gave her shoulders a little push, helping her to her back. "Allow me to be in charge of our pleasure tonight. Can you do that?"

Chewing on her lower lip, she nodded.

"Put your hands over your head and keep them there."

She did as he asked but narrowed her eyes at him. "For how long?"

He stifled a chuckle. "Until I tell you that you can put them down."

There was a moment of hesitation in her eyes, but then she nodded. "I trust you."

"Excellent." He palmed her breast, thumbing the nipple, and then leaned and fastened his lips around it, sucking it in and flicking his tongue over the tip.

When she arched her back, bringing more of her breast into his mouth, he rewarded her with a hand on her other breast, kneading and plucking in sync with what he was doing with his mouth.

Small moans escaped Morelle's throat, her hips gyrating on the mattress, seeking friction, and he knew that if he touched her opening he would find her soaking wet, but that didn't mean she was ready for him.

Releasing one breast, he slowly trailed his hand over her flat belly down to the junction of her hips.

She groaned, and the glow in her eyes intensified along with the scent of her desire.

"You have the most incredible eyes, Princess." He kept trailing his hand over her outer and inner thighs, teasing her, making her pant for more.

When his finger finally reached her wet folds, she hissed, and when he gathered her moisture and pressed his thumb to her clit, she groaned and spread her legs apart.

He was going to make her come at least twice before he penetrated her, and even though they had progressed beyond just touching, the first time was going to be with his fingers. She'd said that he'd barely been able to fit one finger inside of her, and he wanted to show her that she could take two and even three, and it would still feel great.

At first, he just circled her opening, keeping his thumb gently pressed to her clit, and then he slipped his finger inside her wet, hot sheath, just up to the first knuckle.

Her breaths were coming out in rapid puffs, and she wiggled her hips, trying to get more of it.

"You want more, baby?"

"Yes. More," she confirmed.

With his thumb still pressed over her clit, he pushed his finger all the way in and then started moving it in and out of her until she was so soaking wet that adding another finger to the play didn't cause her discomfort.

"Does it still feel good, baby?" he whispered in her ear, then licked into it.

She shivered. "Yes."

"Do you want more?" he asked while pumping in and out of her with two digits.

When she nodded, he pulled back and returned with three. She was tight, and at first she winced, but when her hips started gyrating again, he knew she was close.

"Do you want to come, Princess?"

She moaned and arched her back. "I'm burning."

That wasn't a yes, but it was good enough.

Three more pumps and a slight pinch to her nipple, and she exploded, coating his fingers in the sweetest of nectars.

Watching her fall apart was enough to make him come, and he had to grit his teeth to stop himself. He had to wring one more climax out of Morelle before he could satiate his hunger.

When her quaking subsided, he couldn't help himself and lifted his fingers to his mouth, sucking them dry, and then he kissed her, sharing her own taste with her.

When he rolled on top of her, his shaft nudging her wet entrance, Morelle stiffened.

"Don't worry. We are not there yet." He kissed her neck, then trailed his lips down to her breast.

"Why?"

"Because I need to make you come one more time."

36

MORELLE

Brandon slid further down Morelle's body, kissing her sternum, her abdomen, and then the top of her mound.

"You know one of the things I love about you?"

She lifted her head off the pillow to look at him. "The way I taste?"

He was obsessed with what he called her nectar, licking his fingers clean every time after he'd had them inside of her, his eyes nearly rolling back in his head.

Brandon chuckled. "Yes, that's one. But I also love that your stamina can match mine. I've never had that before."

It took her a moment to process what he'd meant, and when she realized he'd been referring to his countless human lovers, it was like a bucket of cold water on the embers of her desire.

How could he have mentioned his prior

encounters while his mouth was hovering above her entrance, and they were about to make love for the first time?

"Please, don't ever mention your former lovers to me."

He blanched, and the smile slid off his face. "I'm sorry. I shouldn't have said that. Can you forgive me?" He made a pouty face.

How could she stay angry at him when he was so adorable? Besides, she'd done that first, mentioning his prior paramours at the start of their lovemaking.

Somehow, though, it was worse when he did it.

"You're forgiven." She waved a hand. "Carry on."

Brandon laughed. "Yes, Your Majesty. Your obedient servant is at your service." He gave her a long lick starting from the top of her slit all the way to the bottom.

Smiling and moaning at the same time, she closed her eyes, lay back, and gave herself over to the pleasure. Perhaps Brandon was right, and orgasming twice before the main act would make it pleasurable instead of painful. He was the experienced one between them, and she had to trust him.

Using his thumbs, he spread her wide and lapped at her gently at first, just a few soft up-and-down swipes, then penetrated her with his tongue, slowly thrusting in and out.

It felt so good, and her hips churned under him uncontrollably.

He put his hands on her belly, pressing her down as he went deeper, thrusting with his tongue the same way he was soon about to thrust with his shaft.

The thought was both scary and exhilarating.

Keeping her pinned down, he licked the top of her slit where she was most sensitive and then penetrated her with one thick finger, then two, and then three, stretching her, preparing her for his much larger erection.

Pumping in and out of her with those thick fingers, he added a twist to his thrusts, stretching her even wider, and as he touched a magical spot inside her and closed his lips over her throbbing nub, she erupted.

He kept licking and sucking and pumping until the last of her quakes subsided, and when he withdrew his fingers, a stream of wetness followed, running down her inner thighs.

It was time.

"I need you." She threaded her fingers in his hair and pulled him up.

Gripping himself, he guided his shaft to her entrance.

"Relax," he whispered as she tensed under him. He rubbed his erection against her wet folds, gathering her moisture and coating it with her juices. "You are half goddess and half Kra-ell. The stories you heard from former humans don't apply to you."

Was he right about that?

The priestess had never mentioned the first time being painful or uncomfortable for the female, but given that she had been teaching her and Ell-rom at the same time, she might have glossed over the details. Besides, everything about Kra-ell coupling was savage and meant to cause pain, so mentioning that the first time was even more traumatic might have seemed superfluous to her.

Then he pushed, wedging just the tip of the broad head inside, and halted.

Despite all the prep, the stretch burned, and Morelle felt tears gather at the corners of her eyes, not because it hurt but because her dream of this being a perfectly wonderful experience wasn't coming true.

Refusing to surrender to the momentary ennui, she wrapped her arms around Brandon's broad back and concentrated on all the other sensations. The way his body felt good on top of hers, his hard chest pressing on her soft breasts, and his cheek pressed against hers.

In mere seconds, the burning subsided, and the emptiness inside her demanded to be filled. She moved, taking in another fraction of his length, and it hurt, but it was also pleasurable in a strange way.

"A little more," she whispered, bracing against the pain and willing her body to accept the intrusion.

As he lifted his head to look at her, his expression was tormented. "You have tears in your eyes."

"It hurts a little, but it also feels good, and in a moment, it will feel much better."

"Are you sure? We can stop. We don't have to finish it tonight."

She dug her fingers into the tight muscles of his buttocks. "Just go slow."

He lifted his hand and cupped her cheek, and when he kissed her, her own taste on his tongue was incredibly erotic. He kept kissing her until the pain ebbed, turning from a burning sensation into a dull echo of an ache.

Brandon didn't move. Holding still above her, he brought his finger to her mouth and pushed it inside, and when she sucked on it, she remembered doing the same to his shaft, and it was so arousing that the pain dissipated.

He pulled his finger out of her mouth and brought it down between their bodies, pressing it to her clit and gently rubbing it as he pushed another inch inside.

He stilled and looked into her eyes. "Are you okay?"

She nodded.

"I can bite you now, and it will ease the pain. Do you want me to do that?"

Was he offering that now?

Not that she would have agreed, even if he had asked her ahead of time.

Morelle didn't want to miss out on her first time with her mate only because it was a little uncomfortable and didn't meet her expectations of perfection. She wanted to remember every moment of it, including the imperfect ones.

"No. I want the whole experience. No cheating."

A smile bloomed on his face. "I thought you would say that, but I had to make sure."

He kissed her again, deeply, passionately, and as she melted into the kiss, he drew back and, with one forceful thrust, plunged all the way in.

For a split second, the pain was almost blinding in its intensity, and Morelle cried out, but then the pain was gone, and only a stretching sensation remained.

They were finally joined, and it felt incredible.

"Are you okay?" he whispered in her ear.

"Yes. Just give me a moment."

She counted to ten in her head, and when she reached the last digit, the discomfort was gone, replaced by an almost frantic need to have him move inside of her.

She wrapped her arms around him and bucked up slightly, letting him know that she was ready.

He lifted his head and looked at her, and when he was satisfied that she was fine, he withdrew and thrust again, and this time, there was no pain, only pleasure.

She moaned and lifted her hips to meet the next thrust and the next, and the one after that.

"It feels so good," she murmured in his ear, giving him permission to let go.

Her words snapped Brandon's restraint, and he turned rougher. Grabbing her bottom in both hands, he lifted her and held her in place as he drove harder and deeper with every stroke.

It was glorious, and soon she was racing toward another climax.

When she screamed his name, he hissed and clamped his hand over her head, twisting it sideways. He swiped his tongue over the spot he was about to bite, and he struck, sinking his fangs into her flesh.

She didn't even feel the incisions, and as the venom hit her body, she climaxed again and again, and then she soared.

37

JASMINE

Jasmine paced the length of her and Ell-rom's bedroom, her phone clutched in her sweaty hand. The number was already pulled up on the screen—she just needed to press the call button. Simple as that.

Except it wasn't simple at all.

She hadn't spoken to her father in over a year, and their last conversation had been...well, typical. He'd criticized her career choices, her lifestyle, the men she dated, and her entire existence, really. And now she needed to call him and ask about using his hunting cabin in hopes of getting him there alone so she could interrogate him about her mother with the help of a Guardian.

"Just call him," Ell-rom said softly from the couch. "What can he do to you over the phone?

She shot him a look. "Make me feel worthless, stupid, a colossal disappointment."

He rose to his feet and pulled her into his arms. "He can say whatever he wants, but none of that is true, and you know it. You are a wonderful and incredibly gifted person, both paranormally and normally. You are also gorgeous, kind, and loving, and you make everyone around you feel good, unlike your father, who seems to thrive on making everyone around him miserable."

"Thank you." She kissed his cheek. "You always know the right things to say."

"I only say the truth." He let her pull out of his arms. "Anything else I can do to help?"

Jasmine shook her head, running her fingers through her hair. "Unless you can magically make my father less judgmental or give me ideas for what I'm going to tell him about my life. I'm no longer acting and working in customer service, and I'm no longer living in the apartment I've been renting for years."

"Actually..." Ell-rom rubbed a hand over his jaw. "I have an idea." He took her hand and led her to the couch. "How about working for Perfect Match? They're known for their secrecy, right? You could say you're training in their secret location."

The idea appealed to her. "That's perfect. I can evade all his questions by saying that I signed a nondisclosure agreement and I can't tell him anything. Then I can say that I'm about to finish the training program and would like to spend a weekend in the cabin with a great guy I met there. A software engineer. He's going to love that."

Ell-rom chuckled. "What's this special someone's name?"

"Eli." The name slipped out without conscious thought. "Eli Romulus. It's close enough to Ell-rom that I won't slip up but common enough not to raise questions."

"I like it." He wrapped an arm around her. "See? You've got this. A perfectly reasonable cover story that explains everything without revealing anything."

Jasmine leaned into his embrace. "I just hope he won't make me so nervous that I forget the cover story. I always get so anxious when I talk to him."

Ell-rom pressed a kiss to her temple. "You'll do fine. We need answers about your mother, and he's the only one who might have them. There is no way around this."

The mention of her mother sent a familiar ache through Jasmine's chest. "I think that's what makes me the most anxious. I'm afraid to find out that he had something to do with her disappearance. I'm not close to him, but he's my only remaining family, and I don't want to lose him."

"I understand." He put a hand on her shoulder. "No one wants to find out that their parent is a monster."

She nodded, twisting the phone in her hands. "If it were just about me, I might have given up on ever finding out, but this involves Annani and Khiann. If her mate is out there somewhere and my mother is the key to finding him, I have to find her. I need to stop being such a chicken about this."

"You're not being a chicken." Ell-rom's voice was gentle. "You're brave to face this head-on."

She leaned her head on his shoulder. "How do you always know exactly what to say to me?"

"I don't. I just want to tell you the truth as I see it. And the truth is, you're one of the strongest people I know."

She snorted. "Now you're just flattering me."

He caught her hand and squeezed it. "You've built a life for yourself despite your father's disapproval. You've pursued your dreams even when everyone said that they were impossible. And now you're willing to face painful truths for the sake of others." His eyes held hers. "That's strength, Jasmine."

Tears pricked at her eyes, but she blinked them back. "I love you," she whispered.

"I love you too." He brushed his thumb across her cheek. "And I'll be right here, holding your hand while you make this call."

Jasmine nodded, straightening her spine. "Okay. I can do this." She looked down at the device clutched in her hand. "But I need to pace while I'm talking with him, so I can't hold your hand."

"Do you want me to give you privacy?"

"No." She patted his shoulder. "Stay right here. Please."

"Of course." He settled on the couch while she rose to her feet and started pacing again.

She took another deep breath, mentally reviewing her cover story one more time. She worked for Perfect Match. She was in their training program. She'd met a software engineer named Eli. Simple. Believable. Close enough to the truth that she wouldn't trip over the lies.

Her thumb hovered over the call button. "What if he asks for details about the program?"

"It's classified," Ell-rom reminded her. "Perfect Match is famous for its secrecy. He'll expect that, and if not, he can look it up."

"Right." She nodded. "And if he asks about Eli?"

Ell-rom smiled. "Say that he's handsome, irresistible, and a god in bed."

When she laughed, he added, "Eli is also kind and smart, and you're serious about him."

"Right. I'll also tell him that you are rich. He always says that I'm dating losers."

"Well, that's not true, but since you are already making up a story, go for it."

She shrugged. "I could tell him that you are a prince, which is true, and that I'm immortal now, which is also true and much more impressive than anything else I could tell him, but he won't believe that."

"You don't need his approval, Jasmine."

She knew he was right. She'd built a life she was proud of, found love she never expected, and discovered a community that accepted her completely. Her father's opinion shouldn't matter anymore.

Jasmine nodded, and before she could talk herself out of it again, she pressed the call button.

The line connected, and after two rings, her father's gruff voice came through. "Who is this?"

"It's me, Dad." Jasmine winced at how small her voice sounded. "I got a new phone number."

A pause. "Well, this is unexpected."

She forced brightness into her tone. "I know, it's been a while. How is the family?"

"Since when do you care about them?" His disdain was clear even through the phone. "Last I checked, you and Matthew weren't speaking, and Kevin blocked you on Facebook."

Jasmine kept her voice steady. "I'm trying to be better about family connections. How are they?"

"Fine." Another pause. "Matthew's made junior partner at his firm. Kevin's engaged."

Of course, he'd brag about her stepbrothers' achievements. He always did, even though they weren't even his sons.

"That's...nice."

"What about you? Are you still waiting for that big role that will never come?"

"Actually, I got hired by Perfect Match. Have you heard about them?"

"The dating company?" His tone dripped with disdain. "Is this another one of your acting schemes?"

"They are not just a dating company. They provide virtual experiences for people with mobility issues, training for pilots, skydiving, skiing, and whatever you can just imagine. They are growing at a rapid rate, and the pay is exceptional."

She knew he would react to the last part.

"I'm glad that you've finally come to your senses. What exactly do you do there?"

"I can't discuss the details. They had me sign a very restrictive NDA. They are very secretive and protective about their software and hardware."

"Yeah, I've heard that about them."

This was good. It made things easier.

"I've also met someone—"

"Of course you have." The sigh that followed carried the weight of years of disappointment. "And let me guess, he's another loser with no income?"

Jasmine gritted her teeth. "His name is Eli, and he holds a very important position in the organization. It's serious between us."

Jasmine was proud of the way she'd phrased it. She'd managed not to lie but still make Ell-rom sound like the type of guy her father wanted her to date.

"Hmm." The sound managed to convey complete skepticism. "And what's that position?"

She rolled her eyes. "All I can tell you is that he's related to the owners. I can't discuss what he does for the company."

"Aha. A loser whose parents are supporting him by giving him a job in their company. Nothing new there."

Jasmine gritted her teeth. "Dad, I didn't call to debate my life choices." She cast Ell-rom an apologetic smile. "I wanted to ask about using your hunting cabin."

That got his attention. "The cabin? You've never shown an interest in it before."

"Eli and I would like some time away. Somewhere quiet." She forced herself to add, "If that's okay with you."

"When?"

"My training program ends next week. Any weekend after that is good."

"Hmm." Papers shuffled in the background. "I'm going hunting with the guys the first week of next month. Just Ray is staying with me this year. Greg's knee is acting up, and Mike's wife won't let him come. Joe and his usual gang are staying in his cabin."

Jasmine's heart quickened. This was the opening she needed. "Oh? So, you are not taking in some of his crew?"

"No." More shuffling. "Just me and Ray. You can use it after that if you want. Just leave it clean."

"Will you be staying the whole week?" she asked.

"What's with all the questions?" His voice sharpened. "Since when do you care about my hunting trips?"

"I just want to make sure we don't overlap," she said quickly. "And you know, catch up. We haven't talked in so long..."

"You're the one who stopped coming for the holidays."

Why come when everyone was going to treat her like an unwanted orphan girl?

She decided to change the subject. "How's Ray doing? Still with the same insurance company?"

"Retired last year." His tone suggested she should have known this. "Listen, Jasmine, I have a client calling on the other line. The cabin's yours any weekend except the first week of next month. Just text me when you're heading out there."

"Thanks, Dad." She hesitated. "It was good talking to you."

"Mmhmm." The line went dead.

Jasmine let the phone drop and fell back on the bed, throwing an arm over her eyes. "Well, that was awful."

Ell-rom joined her. "You did great. You got the information we needed." He brushed her hair back from her face. "Are you okay?"

"No." She let out a shaky laugh. "But I will be. That was actually one of our better conversations. At least he didn't bring up how I'm wasting my life or compare me to his precious boys who aren't even his."

"He doesn't deserve you," Ell-rom said.

Jasmine curled into his side, letting his warmth chase away the chill of the conversation. "Jasmine, the greatest disappointment of his life, who chose to become an actress instead of getting a broker's license and working in insurance."

"His loss." Ell-rom pressed a kiss to her forehead. "You made the call, got the information, and managed to keep your cover story intact. I'm proud of you."

38

KIAN

Monday mornings were usually busy at the office and taking even a few hours off was a bad idea. Kian didn't want to think about the pile of work waiting for him when he accompanied Amanda and Syssi to Brandon's house. But he wanted to witness the testing and see what Morelle could do when she was not reacting to an emergency.

Syssi and Amanda had taken a day off from the university to conduct Morelle's testing in the village, so he could sacrifice a few hours as well to satisfy his curiosity.

He'd spent half the night awake thinking about the broader implications of what Morelle could do, and it was quite unsettling, but at the same time the possibilities were exciting.

The Eternal King had been right to fear the twins, even without knowing their specific powers. Kian's mother had mentioned a prophecy her grandfather received about his own blood bringing him down, which had led him to fear all of his children and their descendants.

His one legitimate heir had rebelled and lost, but his children still posed a risk. El didn't know about Annani's existence, but the truth was that she couldn't topple him from his throne even if there was a way to get her to Anumati. The twins, on the other hand, possessed abilities that should terrify any tyrant who feared for his throne.

Hell, they should terrify any reasonable person as well.

Ell-rom could potentially kill the Eternal King just by willing it, and now they knew that Morelle could theoretically drain power from a large group of immortals or gods and possibly channel it to boost her brother's abilities or to do some serious damage of her own, like send a spear flying into the king's heart.

Had their mother known how dangerous they were?

Had she hidden them away not just to protect them but to protect others from what they could do?

"You're thinking very loudly." Syssi squeezed his hand. "What's on your mind?"

Kian pulled himself from his dark thoughts and smiled at his mate. "Just thinking about Morelle's power and its potential applications."

"Oh, I have several ideas about that," Amanda said over her shoulder as she approached Brandon's front door and rang the bell.

Jasmine opened the door with a bright, welcoming smile. "Good morning. Please, come in." She led them to the living room where Ell-rom and Brandon were seated on the couch with a laptop open in front of them, and Morelle was curled on an armchair with hers. "Before you begin the testing," Jasmine said. "I just wanted to tell you that I spoke with my father, and he will be at his cabin for the first week of next month. I will need a Guardian who is very good at thralling to accompany Ell-rom and me."

Kian was glad that she had finally contacted her father, but now was not the time to talk about that. "Remind me about this later. We should schedule a meeting to discuss the arrangements."

"Of course." Jasmine dipped her head.

Morelle put her laptop on the side table and rose to her feet to greet them. "Good morning." She looked at Kian. "I didn't expect you to come. Am I in trouble?"

He smiled. "Why do you assume that my presence here means you are in trouble?"

She shrugged. "Why else would you want to spend time watching Amanda and Syssi test me?"

He put a hand on her shoulder. "I've had a lot of time to think about your talent, and I think that it has tremendous potential. I want to check a couple of theories I have."

"I see." She looked nervous. "Makes sense."

"Should Ell-rom and I clear out?" Jasmine asked.

"Stay," Morelle said, turning to Jasmine. "I want you to see what I can do."

Amanda nodded. "The more, the better, actually. We need you both for the experiments I have in mind."

The more people with paranormal powers in the room, the more energy Morelle could draw on to fuel her telekinesis.

That was also another reason why Kian had wanted to be present. If Morelle drew power from him, he wanted to know if he could feel it—and more importantly, how it would affect him.

"In that case, I'm going to make coffee." Brandon rose to his feet. "I assume that everyone wants a cup?"

"Definitely," Syssi said. "I've only had two this morning, and I need at least three to function."

Brandon chuckled. "I apologize in advance. My coffee-making skills are nowhere near your level. All I know is how to use the drip machine."

"I could teach you to make cappuccinos," Syssi offered. "It's all in the equipment. When you have the right stuff, it's not as complicated as it seems."

Morelle tilted her head. "What is that specialized coffee drink?"

There was no word in the Kra-ell language for a cappuccino, and although the translation earpieces were getting better at inserting names and words that couldn't be translated directly, they were still far from perfect.

"It's coffee with steamed milk and foam," Syssi explained. "The milk makes it creamy, and the foam gives it a luxurious texture."

While Syssi explained the mechanics, Brandon ducked into the kitchen, and soon the sounds and smells of brewing coffee filled the air.

Morelle settled onto the couch beside her brother. "That sounds interesting. I would like to taste it."

Syssi's eyes widened. "I forgot that you didn't get to taste my cappuccino when you were in our house. You were so tired after performing that miracle that Brandon had to take you home. You have to come over again."

Kian crossed his legs at his ankles. "We have a very ugly fireplace for now, but I'm sure you won't mind."

"I won't," Morelle said. "I assume the workers removed the stone that surrounded the fireplace." She glanced at the intact mantel in Brandon's living room. "I guess that's why you didn't bring the little ones with you. Ours is still here."

"That's not the reason," Amanda said. "Dalhu is watching the girls so we can work." She grinned.

"I'm telling you. Having a work-from-home husband is very convenient."

"What does he do?" Morelle asked.

"He's a talented artist." Amanda gave her a thorough once-over. "He should draw a portrait of you." She pulled out her phone and snapped a picture of Morelle. "Your hair is growing out nicely. I should take you to my stylist to give it some shape."

Morelle's eyes brightened. "I would be so grateful. I was just thinking yesterday that your hairstyle would look good on me."

Kian stifled a chuckle. Some things were just universal, and females were always concerned with their looks, with their hair being the priority.

Brandon smiled as he returned with a tray of coffee cups. "I hope it's passable."

"I'm sure it's great," Syssi said as she accepted a cup.

After Brandon distributed the cups to the rest of them and everyone prepared their own drink to their liking, Kian decided that they had spent enough time socializing and it was okay to get down to business.

"Have you tried using your telekinesis again since the other night?" he asked Morelle.

The glow in her eyes dimmed. "No. I didn't want to risk drawing power from anyone without their knowledge or consent. I don't like doing that, but it just happens, and it doesn't feel right to me."

"That's the wrong way to think about it," Syssi said.

Kian chuckled. "Well, not necessarily. If you think about leeches, they have medicinal usages, like drawing poison from an organism, so leaching away excess power might be a good thing in some situations."

"What do you mean?" Morelle asked. "And what are leeches?"

"Medicinal leeches are a type of worm, and they have been used for thousands of years," Kian explained. "They can help remove contaminated blood from wounds, improve circulation, and even help with certain medical conditions. Something that seems parasitic at first glance can actually be beneficial in the right context."

"That's fascinating." Morelle leaned forward. "We had nothing like that back home. Our parasites are mostly just opportunistic without providing any benefits."

"The point is," Amanda interjected, "your ability isn't inherently good or bad. It's a tool, and its value depends on how it's used."

Kian nodded. "Exactly. And that's why we're here—to help you understand and control it."

"I just don't want to accidentally hurt anyone," Morelle said softly. "Including myself."

"None of us reported feeling hurt or drained after you used your ability. The only one who was drained was you," Kian said.

"Hold on." Jasmine held up her hand. "I'm feeling like the kid who's not part of the clique. What are you all talking about?"

When Morelle was done explaining, Jasmine rubbed her temples between her thumb and forefinger. "Oh, wow. Now it all makes sense. I wonder how much you can draw and channel. I bet there is a limit to how much you can hold."

"Good observation." Amanda waved with her stylus. "That's easier to check than to measure how much power you can expel."

Brandon shook his head. "It should be done gradually. I don't think Morelle feels the power, so she might draw too much without realizing it."

Amanda turned to Morelle. "Is that true?"

"I didn't feel anything when I drew energy from Jin, Arwel, Cassandra, and even Toven, but I felt it when I drew it from everyone at dinner. It felt good, like an inflow of positive charge. There was nothing uncomfortable about it, but then I didn't know I was doing it."

"We need to test it," Amanda said. "Can you draw from all of us?"

Morelle swallowed. "I'm not sure I know how."

Kian had a feeling that she was blocking herself from accessing the power because she viewed her ability in a negative light.

Leaning forward, he braced his elbows on his knees. "You shouldn't think of what you do in terms of taking or drawing. Think of it as redirecting or channeling. You're not depleting anyone's power permanently—you're redirecting it temporarily for a specific purpose."

"Like a conductor leading an orchestra," Syssi suggested, catching his line of thought. "Each musician still plays their own instrument, but the conductor helps direct their combined effort into something greater."

Morelle seemed to consider this. "I know that you are just trying to make me feel good about my ability, and I'm grateful, but the meaning attached to it has to come from me."

Kian could respect that, but he didn't have all day, and Morelle was being stubborn. "You saved a precious life, and you were the only one who could have done it. I would have gladly parted with as much of my life energy as I could give to help you do that. But I cannot channel it into you unless you make the request. Make the request, Morelle. There might be more at stake here than your sensibilities."

39

MORELLE

Ouch. Kian was pulling no punches, but that approach resonated with Morelle.

"You are right, but I'm still not sure that I can just will it. I can try."

"That's all I'm asking."

"We'll start small." Amanda tapped the tablet with her stylus. "For starters, I just want to see if you can consciously detect when you're drawing power and from whom. Then we can work on controlling the flow."

Kian set his coffee cup down. "I volunteer to be the first test subject."

"Are you sure?" Morelle asked. He was the last person she wanted to test her power on.

"Absolutely." He smiled reassuringly. "I'm curious to see how it feels, and I have a lot of power to spare. After all, I'm Annani's son."

"And I'm her daughter," Amanda said. "And Ell-rom is a demigod as well. We should have plenty of energy for you to siphon."

Jasmine snorted. "Thanks for making Brandon and me feel insignificant. Just to remind you, I might not be a demigoddess or even a quarter of one, but I have a significant paranormal ability. I bet there is a lot of energy Morelle can draw from me as well."

It was ridiculous to hear them fighting over who was the best candidate for her to steal energy from, but it was definitely better than them shying away from her or giving her funny looks.

Ell-rom patted his mate's back. "We are all going to contribute to the effort."

"Perfect," Amanda said. "We will try to establish a baseline, and what we need for that is someone who is very sensitive to power fluctuations." She looked at Syssi. "I think that's you, darling, and I'm not saying that to make fun of you."

"I don't mind." Syssi flung a strand of her long hair behind her shoulder. "Do you want me to summon a vision after Morelle's siphoned my energy?"

"No way," Kian barked. "That's the last thing you should do. Summoning visions drain you even when you are fully charged. You should never attempt that when you are depleted."

Chuckling, Syssi leaned her head on his shoulder. "You make me sound like a cellphone, telling me that I shouldn't place calls unless my battery is fully charged." She lifted her face to look at him. "You know that calls can be placed even when the battery is almost empty. They just need to be kept short."

Kian frowned. "You are not a phone, and you are not going to summon a vision with less than a hundred percent capacity."

Morelle would have bristled if Brandon had ever used that kind of tone with her, but Syssi only smiled and patted Kian's cheek. "It's okay, my love. I was just teasing. I know better than to attempt it when I'm low on energy."

The relief on Kian's face was precious, and Morelle couldn't help but glance at Brandon for his response to the scene developing in front of them. Did he wish that she was as sweet and accommodating as Syssi?

She hoped he didn't because there was no way she could be so patient and understanding. She could learn to be more mellow, though.

Amanda bit her lower lip. "On second thought, perhaps you should start with Kian. I'm afraid he's going to pop a vein if you siphon energy from Syssi."

That was probably a good idea. "What should I direct that energy onto? Not that I know I can do that, and I also don't know if I can hold it inside of me."

Amanda took out one of the artificial flowers from the arrangement decorating the coffee table and placed it some way from the vase. "Move this. If it flies at someone, it's not going to do any damage."

Morelle glanced at Brandon, who gave her an encouraging nod. "I'm not sure how to do it consciously. Before, it just happened."

"That's okay," Amanda said. "Start by focusing on Kian and see if you can sense his energy the way you might sense a warm presence in a room."

Everyone fell silent.

Morelle closed her eyes, scrunching her forehead in concentration and imagining the energy flowing in the room like golden streams of sunlight that zoomed from person to person, creating an energy field that hovered over the group.

The problem was untangling a specific thread. It was all or nothing.

She opened her eyes. "I don't think I can separate one string of power from the field. I can only draw from the field as a whole."

"That's easy to fix." Amanda pushed to her feet. "Everyone other than Kian, please come with me. We need to step outside."

Morelle really didn't want to be left alone with her nephew, but that was silly. He was Annani's son, a good leader of his community, and a very gracious host to her and Ell-rom. She had only good things to say about him. He was just a little too intense, which could be intimidating.

After the others left, Morelle closed her eyes and imagined a single string of energy. She tugged on it, absorbing it into her body, and then pushed it out to direct the energy at the artificial flower.

It moved, but barely so.

Kian chuckled. "You need to take more, Morelle. Don't be afraid. If I feel faint, I'll tell you to stop."

She cast him a hard look. "What if you are too weak to verbalize what you are feeling?"

"I won't let you take too much. Don't worry. Just do it."

"As you wish. Don't blame me if things go south, as they say."

She closed her eyes again, and this time, when she saw the golden ribbon of light, she didn't merely tug at it. She sucked it in, filling herself to the brim with power before expelling it to move the flower.

Everything cluttered to the floor, including the half-empty coffee cups that broke apart.

Gasping, Morelle shifted her gaze to Kian, terrified of what she would see, but he seemed fine, and when he turned to look at her, he seemed more amused than tired or angry or any of the other emotions she'd expected to see.

"That was one hell of a telekinetic display."

She jumped to her feet. "I need to clean up the mess."

"I'll help you." He stood up and then swayed a little. "Now I feel it. You did take a lot out of me."

As the door opened and the others returned, Jasmine gasped. "What happened?"

"Kian had a lot of energy," Morelle said apologetically. "I took too much."

Syssi rushed to her mate's side. "How are you feeling?"

"Like I had too much to drink or have done something strenuous." He wrapped an arm around her shoulders. "I'd better sit back down."

"And I'd better bring the broom," Brandon said.

"I'll get the vacuum cleaner." Jasmine rushed after him.

Looking satisfied, Amanda sat down, pulled out her tablet, and snapped a picture of the mess on the floor. "You did it all with your mind," she said.

"I did."

"Did you feel how much you drew from Kian?"

Morelle shook her head. "I just imagined inhaling his energy until my lungs were full and then expelling it at the flower, but I must have taken more than I realized, and everything went flying."

Amanda shifted on the couch to face Kian. "What did you feel?"

"Nothing until I tried to stand up. I would have

never suspected that anyone had done anything to me."

"Interesting." Amanda tapped her finger over her lower lip. "The stealth nature of this power has a lot of potential."

Kian nodded. "I agree. It's one hell of a powerful ability."

40

ROB

Rob drifted back to consciousness gradually, awareness returning in fragments. The steady beep of monitoring equipment. The slight scratch of sheets. The warm pressure of Gertrude's hand in his.

He opened his eyes to find both Gertrude and Margo sitting by his bed and watching him anxiously.

"Welcome back," Gertrude said, squeezing his hand.

"How long was I out this time?" His voice came out raspy.

Margo checked her phone. "A little over an hour. How are you feeling?"

Rob took mental stock of his body. "Not too bad, actually. My transition seems pretty easy so far. I'm glad that I'm waking up from time to time and not staying under."

"Any headache? Nausea?" Margo leaned forward in her chair.

He remembered her asking that before, but he wasn't sure whether it was a real memory or a memory of a dream.

"A little of both," he admitted. "But nothing too bad."

"Those were my main symptoms." Margo smiled. "My transition was super easy because my inducer was a god. Having Negal's venom helped smooth things along."

Rob squeezed Gertrude's hand, noting how she tensed at the mention of Negal. He knew she didn't harbor any romantic feelings for the god, but no one had fond memories of being dumped for another—especially not when that "another" eventually turned out to be your mate's sister.

He could hardly imagine having to be friendly with Lynda or her new/old boyfriend if the situations were reversed. The thought of watching them together, having to smile and make nice, made his stomach turn. Yet here was Gertrude, forced to be friendly with Margo and Negal because of him.

They were going to be a family, and they needed to learn not just to coexist but to actually enjoy each other's company.

The thought reminded him of his parents and their self-imposed isolation. They'd cut ties with most of their extended family over various slights, some real and some imagined. Looking back, it seemed so pointless—wasting precious years of their short human lives nursing petty grievances.

Human lives.

The thought sparked something in his mind. "Hey, Margo?"

"Hmm?"

"Do you think we should tell Mom she's a Dormant?"

Margo winced. "I've thought about it a lot, but it's complicated."

"I know. I've been too busy with my own problems to even think about it, but now I am." Rob shifted to face her better, still holding on to Gertrude's hand. "We should tell her."

"She's in her early sixties," Margo said. "It might already be too late. And even if it's not..." She grimaced. "What about Dad? She'd have to have sex with an immortal, and if it worked and she turned immortal, that would also be heartbreaking for both of them. With all their faults, the one thing that's always been evident is their love for each other."

Rob shuddered, thinking about his mother doing the deed with anyone, whether it was his father or someone else.

"I don't know about you, but I prefer to think that our parents have a purely platonic relationship," Margo echoed his thoughts.

Gertrude laughed. "Humans and their hang-ups

about sex. Your parents have clearly done it at least twice—you're both here, aren't you?"

"That's different," Rob protested jokingly. "That was necessary procreation."

"Right." Gertrude rolled her eyes. "Because people only have sex to make babies."

"Can we please change the subject?" Margo pleaded.

"Actually, no." Gertrude sat up straighter. "This is important. I think you should meet with your parents and take Negal along. After you explain the situation, and they give you their answers, Negal can thrall them later to forget the conversation. It's not fair for you two to make the choice for them. You need to let them decide for themselves."

Margo winced. "But who would want to...you know...with Mom? She's not like Ronja—she's not some gorgeous older woman who looks twenty years younger than she is. She's just an average woman who looks her age, saggy boobs and all."

"There has to be another way," Rob said. "What about donated venom and the other necessary ingredient for transition?"

"Venom can't be harvested," Gertrude said. "But semen might be." A smile played on her lips. "I'm sure you two can figure out the mechanics of how the encounter can be arranged. I don't need to explain the birds and bees to you."

Rob felt his face heat. "I don't want to think about it."

"You don't need to," Gertrude said. "Your mother deserves to know her options, and if she decides to pursue them, I'll gladly explain the birds and the bees. The thing is that it's not guaranteed to work when it's done that way. I would need to consult with Bridget."

Rob closed his eyes as another wave of dizziness washed over him. "Can we table this discussion until after I'm done transitioning? My brain feels like it's trying to escape through my ears."

"Of course." Gertrude's cool hand pressed against his forehead. "You're running a fever again. Try to rest."

He nodded, already feeling consciousness slipping away again. The last thing he heard was Margo and Gertrude's quiet voices discussing the venom bite and whether it was dangerous for an older human, but he was too far gone to follow the conversation.

His dreams were strange, filled with medical diagrams and ravens wearing lab coats. At one point, he thought he heard Bridget's voice discussing something about artificial insemination, but that had to be his fevered brain playing tricks on him.

When he surfaced again, Margo was gone, but Gertrude was still beside him, reading something on her phone.

"Hey," he said softly.

Gertrude looked up and smiled. "How are you feeling?"

He felt worse than before, but he didn't want to worry her. Then again, she was not only his mate but also his nurse, and she needed to hear the truth.

"Like I've been hit by a truck. Everything hurts. Is this normal?"

"It is." She set her phone aside. "Your body is going through major changes, and the fact that you're conscious at all is actually a good sign. I should probably measure you to see if you've grown."

He'd heard about Jasmine, who had grown taller during her transition, but that had happened over many days. His transition started yesterday. "Isn't it too early for that? You took my original measurements, and it's not likely that they have changed in less than twenty-four hours."

"You'd be surprised. Besides, it will give me something to do."

"Where is Margo?" he asked.

"I told her to go home." Gertrude smiled sheepishly. "I told her that she needed to rest and I will call her if anything changes, but the truth is that I wanted you to myself for a bit."

He turned on his side, dragging a bunch of wires and tubes with him. "Does it bother you that you have to be friends with Margo? I mean, she stole your guy, and even though I'm your guy now, it must still be a little uncomfortable for you. Talk about awkward family dynamics."

"Oh, Rob honey, I'm fine." She lifted his hand to her lips and kissed the back of it. "Margo didn't steal Negal from me. The Fates had other plans, and I'm glad that they intervened. I'm still somewhat uncomfortable around Negal, but not around Margo. I like your sister."

The simple sincerity in her voice made his heart swell. "I love you," he whispered.

"I love you too." She leaned over to kiss his forehead. "Now rest. The sooner you get through this transition, the sooner you will grow your fangs and venom. All that talk about venom bites has made me wistful."

Chuckling, he let his eyelids drift closed. "I'm working on it, sweetheart. I'm working on it."

41

BRANDON

Brandon was filled with a mixture of pride and concern as he watched Morelle continue the experiments. She was getting better at controlling the flow of power, learning to modulate it so she didn't accidentally send anything crashing through walls, but she had a long way to go before she could use her ability with precision.

Amanda had placed several sensors around the room to collect data and transfer it to her tablet while Brandon and Jasmine cleared the living room of breakables.

Brandon had never paid attention to the decorative pieces the designer had picked out for his house and carefully placed in strategic locations to make the space look more welcoming, but now that they were no longer there, their absence was notable.

The room felt bare without them.

"I think I'm ready for another round," Kian said, rolling his shoulders. He'd spent the last hour recovering from Morelle's previous draw on his power. "I want to see if my recovery time affects the amount of energy you can pull and if your ability to channel it changes with repeated attempts."

Morelle looked around the room. "I need something hefty to channel the energy to, but it should be something that is not breakable. Any ideas?"

"I know what we can use." Brandon ducked into their bedroom and collected the overflowing laundry basket from the bathroom.

"This weighs about thirty pounds," he said, pulling the drawstring tight to keep everything contained. "Should be a good test object."

"Perfect." Amanda took a picture of the basket with her tablet. "Morelle, try to lift and throw it using only Kian's power while we are still in the room."

After several tries and guidance from Amanda, Morelle managed to pull individual strings of power from Brandon and Jasmine and used them to move small objects a short distance.

The question was whether she'd be able to isolate Kian's massive power from the grid and use only that to power a major telekinetic feat.

Brandon moved to the far corner of the room,

watching as Morelle closed her eyes in concentration.

The air seemed to thicken with potential energy, and then the laundry basket shot across the room like it had been fired from a cannon, hitting the opposite wall with enough force to make the house shudder.

"Sorry!" Morelle winced. "That was more than I meant to use."

"You're getting stronger," Brandon said. "That throw had more force behind it than all of your earlier attempts."

"I'm just more confident," Morelle admitted. "Fear was holding me back from pushing more power into the objects, and Kian's energy is particularly potent." She winced and glanced at Syssi. "Sorry. That didn't sound right. I hope you know that I didn't mean it that way."

Syssi waved a dismissive hand. "Don't worry about it. I'm not the jealous type, and I know that my Kian is exceptionally potent." Her cheeks pinked when she said that, but she didn't look shy at all when she winked at her husband.

"The readings support that," Amanda said, studying her tablet. "The energy output is increasing rather than decreasing with repeated use."

Morelle looked a little uncomfortable. "That's also because I'm not using any of my own power.

I'm just channeling what I draw from others. It's easier now that I've got a feel for it."

"Try me now," Syssi said. "I'm more sensitive to energy fluctuations than most, so I might be able to provide better feedback about how it feels."

Kian frowned. "Are you sure?"

"Absolutely." Syssi stepped forward. "Just promise to catch me if I faint."

Brandon retrieved the laundry basket while Morelle turned to face Syssi, and this time, when she channeled the power, the basket barely lifted a few inches off the ground before floating a couple of feet away.

Syssi swayed, and Kian was at her side instantly, propping her up. "I need to sit down," she murmured.

"I told you not to do it," Kian grumbled under his breath. "Why do you need to be so stubborn?"

She chuckled. "If I weren't stubborn, you would put me in bubble wrap before letting me out of the house." She leaned over to kiss his cheek. "Coffee might help, and maybe a cookie or a cracker?"

"Coming right up." Brandon hurried to the kitchen to get the coffee carafe and some energy bars he kept in the pantry. When he returned, Syssi already looked better, though Kian had his arms around her as if they could restore her depleted energy stores.

"That was fascinating," Syssi said between bites. "I could actually feel the energy being drawn out. It wasn't painful. It was just like I was a balloon, and there was a tiny hole through which my energy was draining."

Amanda scribbled on her tablet, her stylus making rather pleasant scratching sounds.

"I want to see what happens when I draw from Ell-rom." Morelle turned to her brother.

He shifted uncomfortably. "I'm not sure that's wise. We don't know what might happen if you try to channel my ability."

Brandon tensed. He still didn't know exactly what Ell-rom could do, but given everyone's careful handling of the subject, it had to be something either dangerous or very powerful.

Kian glanced his way and let out a sigh. "I guess it doesn't make sense to keep Ell-rom's ability a secret from you any longer, but what I'm about to tell you needs to stay absolutely confidential. I want to wait to inform the council until we understand more about both twins' abilities."

Brandon nodded. "Their secrets are safe with me."

"Ell-rom can kill with a thought," Kian said without much preamble for such a shocking revelation. "We don't know how he does it or what the limitations are in regards to distance, line of sight, and other factors. He just wishes someone dead, and the person drops dead with no apparent clinical cause."

The implications hit Brandon like a physical

blow. Morelle could draw and channel power from others. Ell-rom could kill with a thought. Together, they were the perfect killing machines.

A terrible suspicion began forming in his mind. These weren't random abilities. This level of destructive potential couldn't be coincidental.

Had their father and the Kra-ell queen deliberately created living weapons? Ahn had access to the best genetic labs on Anumati. Had he and the Kra-ell's royal heir apparent conspired to create offspring capable of destroying the Eternal King?

Brandon looked at the twins with new eyes.

Morelle, his compassionate mate who had been so worried about accidentally hurting someone with her power. Ell-rom, quiet and thoughtful, carrying the burden of his lethal ability. They seemed so far removed from the weapons they had been designed to be.

And yet.

Morelle could theoretically drain power from an entire army of immortals or gods, channeling that energy into her brother's death-ray thought. Together, they could potentially level cities. Take down kings. Reshape the very power structure of their world.

No wonder their mother had hidden them away. It hadn't been done just to protect their identity as half-gods. She must have known about the abilities they had been genetically engineered with and had anticipated their manifestation.

42

KIAN

Kian looked up from his paperwork, surprised to see Brandon standing at the open door. They had parted only several hours ago, and although Brandon had seemed concerned about something, he hadn't indicated that he wanted to talk.

Usually when the councilman needed to discuss his ideas for InstaTock or any other matter, he arranged a meeting in advance, and never just showed up unannounced.

"May I come in?" Brandon asked.

"Of course. What brings you to my office?"

"Morelle and Jasmine are visiting Rob and Margo at the clinic, so I took the opportunity to have a private conversation with you."

Something in Brandon's expression made Kian sit up straighter. "Please take a seat."

Instead of pulling out a chair, Brandon rubbed

the back of his neck. "Do you still have your smoking station on the roof?"

A smile tugged at Kian's lips. "You are a man after my own heart. I was just thinking about having a smoke up there." He opened his desk drawer and pulled out a bottle of fine whiskey, handing it to Brandon. Two shot glasses followed, tucked safely into his pockets, and finally, a box of cigarillos. "Shall we?"

When they emerged into the afternoon air, Brandon let out an appreciative whistle. "This is a nice setup you've got up here." He settled into one of the two comfortable lounge chairs. "An umbrella to provide shelter from both sun and rain is a lovely idea."

"I have Shai to thank for this, and probably Amanda, but she won't admit that she had a hand in it." Kian poured them each a measure of whiskey.

After Brandon accepted both the drink and a cigarillo with a nod of thanks, they sat in companionable silence as Kian lit Brandon's cigarillo first and then his own.

He waited patiently for Brandon to start talking, and after a couple of puffs, the guy seemed ready. "I have a new theory about the twins."

Kian took a slow drag, letting the smoke curl around them. "Go on."

"Their abilities are not only uncommon, they are unheard of." Brandon stared into his whiskey.

"They're too perfect, aren't they? Too complementary. Morelle can draw power from others and channel it. Ell-rom can kill with a thought. Together, they could theoretically take down any opponent, no matter how powerful."

"Including the Eternal King," Kian said. "It has occurred to me."

"I'm glad that I'm not the only one with a suspicious mind." Brandon took another puff of his cigarillo. "What are the odds that such unprecedented abilities would manifest randomly in twins? I think that they were engineered to be lethal weapons to take down their grandfather. Their father and the Kra-ell princess deliberately combined their bloodlines and enhanced them artificially to create these living weapons. Ahn had access to the best genetic engineering labs on Anumati, and the princess could hide his offspring where no one would think to look for them. But then the Eternal King started suspecting something, either because of the prophecy or spies or both."

Kian let out a long breath. He'd had similar suspicions since learning the full extent of the twins' powers, but he hadn't taken them as far as suspecting deliberate planning that involved genetic manipulation.

"Their mother hid them away not just because they looked like gods," Brandon continued. "She knew what they were created to be."

Kian took a puff of his cigarillo. "Igor was genetically engineered with enhanced abilities that even the twins don't have, but he wasn't given their kind of power. Unless their ability is the result of combining the bloodlines of the two royal houses, Ahn would have needed to have access to genetic engineering that was not available to the Eternal King, and that's not very likely."

Brandon shrugged. "Ahn was a rebel with a cause, and he wasn't the only one. Maybe one of his cohorts was an expert in genetic manipulation, someone who had also researched the Kra-ell, and Ahn and the future queen of the Kra-ell decided to experiment."

Kian arched a brow. "On their own children?"

"Rebels with a cause can be ruthless, justifying any sacrifice on the altar of their beliefs."

Kian had a hard time imagining Ahn as a fanatic. From his mother's tales, he had constructed an image of a politically savvy leader who cared about his people and tried to do the best he could for them. Still, he'd ignored his daughter Areana just because she had been born from a concubine, so he had obviously been far from a perfect father. As for the Kra-ell queen, Kian had no doubt that she'd been capable of experimenting with her own children to give them a leg up on the Eternal King.

"The question is," Kian swirled his whiskey, watching the amber liquid catch the light, "what do we do with this theory? Even if we confirm it somehow, does it change anything?"

Brandon took a long drag from his cigarillo. "That's why I wanted to talk to you. I don't want to hide my suspicions from Morelle, but telling her that she was created to be a weapon might be devastating to her. Her brother won't take it well either."

Kian topped up their glasses. "But if we're right, and we don't tell them, we leave them vulnerable. Once their abilities become known to the rest of the clan, others will probably come to the same conclusions."

"The Eternal King feared his own blood bringing him down," Brandon said. "What if he knew more than that vague prophecy? Perhaps someone betrayed Ahn and told the king what his son had done. Knowing that his grandchildren had been engineered with the clear purpose of ending his reign of power, of ending him, would explain his obsession with finding them and eliminating the threat. It would also explain the elaborate plot to have Igor befriend them, crown them, and then kill them. The king knew that they were too powerful to attack directly."

Kian chuckled. "I wonder if you see all the puzzle pieces fitting in so perfectly together because of your background in movies. Plotting a storyline is your forte."

Brandon took another sip of his whiskey.

"Maybe. The pieces only clicked for me today after you told me what Ell-rom's ability was."

Kian nodded. "Indeed. It wasn't possible to put it all together without that missing piece. Still, we might be totally off about all this, and those who could tell us are dead." He took another drag. "Their parents are both gone, and the Eternal King is not going to tell us even if we had a way to reach him."

"Here is another possible piece of the puzzle," Brandon said. "What if their mother didn't die by accident nor was she assassinated by the Eternal King's minions? What if she sacrificed herself to save them by taking their secrets to her grave?"

They sat in silence for a moment, each lost in thought. The smoke from their cigarillos mingled in the air between them, carrying the weight of their speculations.

"It's possible, although as far as I know, suicide is taboo for the Kra-ell. If she wanted to take a secret to her grave, the queen would have more likely engaged in battle to the death."

"We need safeguards," Brandon said. "Whether we tell them our suspicions or not, we need to make sure to keep their abilities in check. Ell-rom and Morelle are good people, but power corrupts, and absolute power corrupts absolutely. We need to make sure that doesn't happen to them."

Kian nodded. "I'm officially charging you with safeguarding Morelle. As her mate, you are the best qualified to do that. I'll have to talk to Jasmine about watching Ell-rom, which I'm not looking forward to."

Brandon finished his whiskey. "We should wait to reveal Ell-rom's ability until it's absolutely necessary, and since you are still planning to test him, I assume that we have plenty of time. In the interim, we should focus on helping Morelle master hers first and establish her as a protective force rather than a destructive one, especially for her sake."

"Good thinking." Kian poured them each another measure. "Naturally, I need to tell the Clan Mother our suspicions, and she might have some ideas and suggestions of her own."

He wondered if that was something his mother should share with her grandmother. Ani, queen of the gods, wanted to get rid of her husband, so she would probably be very happy to know that the twins could be the weapon she needed. The problem was that she couldn't get them to Anumati, and Kian doubted their abilities would work across the galaxy.

43

ANNANI

Annani was reclining on a lounger in her backyard with her light-filtering glasses on, even though the sunlight wasn't as harsh this late in the afternoon during the winter months. It was still warm enough for her to wear nothing more than a long-sleeved gown, and the shawl Ogidu had brought out for her was draped over the other lounger just in case it got colder when the sun set.

She had a glass of sparkling water on the side table next to her and several slices of apple on a plate, but she hadn't touched any of that yet. She was meditating, or rather trying to, and it wasn't going well.

As old as she was, Annani had not mastered the art of emptying her mind. Thoughts raced through as if she had a maze of high-speed highways in her brain, and trying to slow down the traffic only made her head ache.

When the sliding door behind her opened, she turned to look, expecting one of her Odus with yet another snack for her, but it was Kian who stepped out into her backyard.

"Good afternoon, Mother." He leaned to kiss her cheek.

"Good afternoon to you, too. To what do I owe the pleasure of your visit?"

He sat down on the other lounger, his legs spread out and his elbows resting on his knees. "I want to talk to you about something, and instead of calling, I decided to stop by on my way home. I hope it's alright and I'm not interfering with your plans."

"Not at all. My last visitor of the day departed a while ago, and I was just resting out here and enjoying the crisp winter air while trying to meditate, but I gave up on that even before you arrived."

He nodded. "I know what you mean. I've never been able to meditate, either. But it is lovely out here, and just enjoying the outdoors is nice. One of the main positives of this geographic location is the weather. Business-wise, though, it's not very hospitable."

She smiled. "My dear Kian. You should have promoted a politician who would make this beautiful state friendlier to businesses. Enterprise is the bedrock upon which all else is built. Without it, the entire community deteriorates."

Kian chuckled. "There was no one I felt comfortable backing with clan contributions, and it's not like we could have run one of our own as a candidate, although, to be frank, I was tempted to suggest it to Amanda. Imagine her running the state."

He had said it as a joke, but Annani believed that Amanda would have made a great governor. In a state that worshiped beauty, she would have been elected in a landslide, and after serving for a few years, she could have faded into obscurity by dramatically changing her looks. She had done that before quite successfully, but without holding public office.

Amanda was smart and capable, and she was not too proud to consult with others when she felt she needed help, and just that already put her ahead of others.

"At least your sister would have solved the homeless situation. It is so shameful how such a resource-rich state squanders its wealth on corruption instead of housing the homeless and providing them with the assistance they need." She tilted her head. "Is there a way for us to undertake this mission as well? Perhaps we can help these poor people."

Kian shook his head. "The problem is not the lack of money but its abundance. So much gets diverted into the pockets of those close to the power brokers that none of them is interested in actually solving the issue. They put roadblocks in front of any organization that attempts to do that and strangle them with nonsensical regulations that make it impossible to provide meaningful help to those in need. The best we can do at the moment is support soup kitchens."

"Well, at least we do that." She lifted her glass and took a sip of the cool sparkling water. "So, what did you want to tell me?"

"We continued testing Morelle's ability today. She drew on my power and used it to move objects. The drain was noticeable, but I recuperated quickly. Even Syssi, who felt the drain the most, recharged in no time."

"That is good news," Annani said. "Morelle was worried about causing harm. I hope she realizes now that she should not fear using her ability."

Kian nodded. "She gained confidence, that was evident." He rubbed a hand over his jaw. "Brandon was there, of course, and when Morelle wanted to see what would happen if she drew energy from Ell-rom, I ended up telling Brandon why Ell-rom was concerned about Morelle attempting to channel his abilities. He later came to see me alone, and he has an interesting theory about Morelle and Ell-rom's unusual powers."

Annani tensed. "Given that you are here to tell me about it, you're taking his theory seriously."

"It makes a lot of sense, and I'm surprised at myself that it didn't occur to me sooner. Brandon suggests that the twins didn't get their unique powers randomly, and that it wasn't just the result of combining the genetics of two incredibly powerful royal bloodlines. He thinks that Ahn arranged for his children to be genetically enhanced to become the perfect tools to take down the Eternal King."

Annani shook her head. "He did not know that the princess was pregnant with his children when he was exiled."

"We assumed that he didn't know, but that doesn't mean that he didn't. Besides, communication with Anumati was possible for several centuries after the gods' arrival on Earth. The Kra-ell queen could have found a way to inform him. So, the fact that he never mentioned having children back home to anyone shouldn't be taken as proof that he had no knowledge of them."

"My father never spoke of his home," Annani said. "He wanted us to believe that the gods had always been present on Earth. So, even if he knew about the twins, he would not have said anything about them." She frowned. "I am trying to remember what Morelle told me about her mother visiting her in her dream. I think the queen told her that Ahn did not know about the pregnancy and that he found out only after he died because everything is known in the afterlife, but I am not sure about that. I need to ask Morelle to tell me about that dream again."

Kian smiled. "Dreams are not reliable. Our memories of them are influenced by our thoughts, feelings, and preconceived notions, and they are also open to interpretation. Besides, it's possible that the queen preferred to tell Morelle that her father hadn't been aware of his children's existence to make her feel less abandoned."

"Our father could not have done anything for the twins even if he knew about them. He was exiled to Earth with no ability to ever visit his home."

"True," Kian said. "But do you agree that it is possible that your father not only knew about the twins but also arranged for them to be genetically enhanced?"

"I can see Ahn doing something like that." Annani put her glass back on the side table. "I would not put it past him. Combining his bloodline with that of the Kra-ell princess in order to create children with specific abilities, and then manipulating their genes to be even more than nature could have done seems fantastic, but I fear this fits his strategic and detached approach to achieving his goals." She sighed. "I prefer thinking of my father and the queen's relationship as a love story—two souls finding each other despite their differences—but knowing my father, I am afraid that Brandon's version is more likely. Ahn was always pragmatic and ruthless when he needed to be."

"Brandon called him a rebel with a cause."

Annani nodded. "I wanted to believe my father's motivation was reforming how the gods treated the Kra-ell, not merely overthrowing our grandfather, and perhaps that was true, and the twins were the backup plan."

"That sounds reasonable," Kian agreed.

"Still, the fact that Morelle and Ell-rom might be genetically capable of terrible things does not mean that they are terrible people. As I have said from the start, when we still suspected them of possessing even worse powers, we should judge them by the kind of people they are and not by what they can do. They are not a threat to us."

"That's not what I was trying to convey," Kian said quickly. "If they were designed with these abilities—and it's still just a hypothesis—it was specifically to eliminate the Eternal King. Those kinds of powers would be overkill against lesser gods, immortals, or mortals."

"True." Annani nodded. "It would seem that they were designed with one purpose in mind. If we could get them close to the Eternal King, they could fulfill their destiny and potentially save all of Earth and its inhabitants from his wrath. He is still an existential threat to us."

Kian shifted on the lounger, trying to make himself more comfortable while sitting on it sideways. "Right now, they are not powerful enough, and once they are, we have no way of getting them close to the Eternal King, so at this time it is just a hypothetical possibility."

"They could still be our salvation, though," Annani murmured. "That is how we should treat them. Not as a threat, but rather as a shield against the more severe threat we face."

"Exactly." Kian rose to his feet. "I was conflicted about what to tell the twins, but you've just given me the answer."

"They do not know yet?" She followed him as he opened the sliding door and stepped inside the house.

"They know what they can do, but they don't know that they were created as a tool against their grandfather. Not that we know that for sure, but it seems like a very likely scenario."

"Indeed." Annani removed her goggles and put them on the counter. "I wanted to invite them and their mates to dinner tonight, but let us make it a family affair. I want my brother and sister to see that none of us view them as a threat."

Kian frowned. "Are you sure that's wise? Maybe they should be told privately first."

Annani shook her head. "Telling them privately would send the wrong message. I want them surrounded by family when they learn this, so they can see immediately that nothing has changed—that we all still love and accept them regardless of what abilities they possess or why they might have them."

She pulled out her phone. "Dinner in two hours. My Odus can have everything ready by then."

"Mother—"

"No arguments. The worst thing we could do is treat this like some dark secret that needs to be whispered about behind closed doors."

Kian sighed, but she could see him fighting a smile. "You're probably right about the family, but that's as far as it goes. I don't want the entire clan to know about these special abilities, let alone how and why they have them."

Annani nodded. "I can agree to that."

44

MORELLE

Morelle watched Brandon out of the corner of her eye as his fingers flew across the keyboard. Something had been bothering him all day, but each time she asked, he deflected with explanations about Insta-Tock and the short attention spans of human teenagers.

"I need to create high-value production short clips," he'd said, his smile not quite reaching his eyes. "They'll convey the message better than anything written. These kids have the attention span of insects."

She didn't fully grasp what he meant, but she'd stopped asking. They might be a couple now, fully and blissfully joined and bonded, but they weren't one person. They each had their own interests and preoccupations, and it was okay not to understand everything about each other.

On the contrary, it added to the mystery and excitement.

Still, after last night she was walking on air, and he had seemed to feel the same in the morning before the testing ensued. But then his mood had soured for some reason, and despite his assurances that it was not about her, she had a feeling that it was.

Turning back to her own laptop, Morelle pulled up the Perfect Match questionnaire. Kaia had shown her how to set the device to translate questions into Kra-ell, and since most of the questions were multiple choice, she didn't even need to write her answers in Kra-ell first and have them translated into English.

Still, the language barrier wasn't the only challenge. The cultural differences were glaringly evident in many of the questions, and she found herself struggling with the answers and second-guessing each choice until her head throbbed.

One question asked about her ideal vacation. The options included backpacking through Europe, lounging on a tropical beach, or exploring ancient ruins. What was supposed to be exciting about carrying a pack on your back? The beach seemed nice but boring, and so did the ancient ruins.

She chose the last option, which said none of the above.

Another asked about her favorite type of

cuisine, listing options she'd never heard of. While she was learning to appreciate Earth's varied food offerings, she didn't know which country they had originated from and certainly couldn't rank them by preference yet.

She was about to close the laptop and take a break when her phone rang, displaying Annani's contact information.

"Hello, sister," she answered, eager for a break. "I'm so glad you called, so I have an excuse to stop answering the Perfect Match questionnaire. It's giving me a headache."

From across the room, Brandon lifted his head and arched a brow.

Had he forgotten that she intended to fill out the questionnaire?

He'd said he would reconsider joining her on a virtual adventure, but they hadn't discussed it since, and she hoped he hadn't changed his mind.

Still, even if he decided not to join her, she intended to go on as many solo adventures as she would be allowed on, and to experience as much as she could of Earth in a short period of time. It was unnerving to be an adult in a place she knew next to nothing about, and that was made even more evident by the questionnaire.

She had to learn fast.

Annani laughed, the sound warm and beautiful. "I am happy to provide a distraction. I am calling to invite you and Brandon for dinner tonight.

Eight o'clock at my house. I have already spoken with Ell-rom and Jasmine."

Their brother and his mate had gone for a walk around the village, so Annani must have caught them out there. "That sounds lovely. Brandon and I would love to come."

"Excellent. I have also invited my children and their mates along with their children," Annani added. "So, it will be a larger than usual midweek family meal. Or start of the week, as it may be. It is only Monday."

The prospect of seeing the little ones had Morelle's heart swelling with warmth and anticipation. "That would be wonderful. I love spending time with the children."

Annani chuckled. "Blood truly is thicker than water. I'm the same way—nothing makes me happier than being surrounded by children."

After ending the call, Morelle turned to Brandon. "Dinner at Annani's tonight. The whole family will be there."

He nodded, but something flickered in his eyes. Concern? Anticipation? She couldn't quite read his expression.

"That's nice," he said, his tone carefully neutral.

"Are you sure you're okay?" she asked. "You've seemed distracted all day."

Brandon's expression softened. "I'm fine, Princess. Just work stuff." He stood and crossed to her, pressing a kiss to her forehead. "I know it must be terribly disappointing that your storyteller sometimes gets grumpy."

She caught his hand and brought it to her cheek. "I'm not at all disappointed. I love you in all your forms, and you don't have to pretend to be upbeat for me. I get grumpy, too."

"You do?"

She laughed. "As if you haven't noticed. I'm not a ray of sunshine like Syssi."

"I'm sure she has her grumpy moments as well." He leaned and kissed her lips. "So, what questions have you answered so far? Did you get to the naughty parts yet?"

She shook her head. "I'm just on the first page, and so far, the questions are both boring and confusing because I don't know what half of the answers mean."

She glanced at her laptop screen displaying the Perfect Match questionnaire and decided that it was enough for one day. Something was clearly weighing on Brandon's mind, and perhaps talking about it would help his mood.

"Tell me about these InstaTock videos you're planning," she said instead. "Maybe I can help."

His smile this time was more genuine. "It's pretty simple, really. We need to grab their attention in the first three seconds or we will lose the audience completely. Then we have about fifteen seconds to make our point before they swipe to the next video."

"That doesn't seem like much time to convey anything."

"It isn't." He settled on the arm of her chair. "But that's the world we're dealing with. Everything has to be quick, flashy, and instantly engaging."

"Unlike the Perfect Match questionnaire. They are not catering to the same audience. Some of these questions require serious thought."

Brandon glanced at her screen, but since it was displaying the questions in Kra-ell, he couldn't read them. "What are the questions about?"

"Vacations." She closed the laptop. "It can wait. We have about two hours till dinner, and Ell-rom and Jasmine are not home."

He arched a brow. "What do you have in mind?"

She smiled up at him. "Exactly what you have in yours."

45

BRANDON

Brandon's stomach churned with anxiety as he sat beside Morelle at Annani's dining table. He knew what was coming—after all, his own suspicions had sparked this gathering—and he berated himself for not warning Morelle beforehand.

He should have told her and prepared her for this. But how do you tell someone you love that you suspect they were created to be a weapon?

Hopefully, Kian would handle the revelation diplomatically, though Brandon had his doubts. His boss, for all his leadership qualities, wasn't known for his emotional intelligence, and his delivery style left a lot to be desired.

Annani might do better, but now that they were all gathered around the table, it was too late for Brandon to make suggestions about who should break the news to the twins.

Thankfully, Morelle seemed unaware of his inner turmoil, completely absorbed in entertaining Allegra. The child had demanded her highchair be placed between Morelle and Syssi, and no one had thought to argue. The little girl was clearly taking after her father, already showing signs of Kian's assertiveness.

"More!" Allegra demanded, holding out her empty cup to Morelle.

"What do we say?" Syssi prompted from her other side.

"More! Please!"

Brandon caught Kian's eye across the table and gave a subtle shake of his head, trying to convey that he hadn't shared his suspicions with Morelle yet.

Kian's responding nod suggested he understood, and Brandon hoped they were on the same page.

"Everyone, please," Annani called for attention as her Odus began pouring wine. "We have reason to celebrate tonight."

Brandon's heart skipped. Had Annani found a way to spin this into something celebratory rather than concerning? He wouldn't put it past her—she had a gift for finding the bright side of any situation.

When everyone had full glasses, Annani lifted her glass. "To Morelle and Ell-rom, who by joining our clan have brought such joy to my heart and to our entire family, and who make us all safer by their presence."

Brandon watched as confusion flickered across both twins' faces, but they raised their glasses and drank along with everyone.

In a way, the Clan Mother was right. Having a one-of-a-kind weapon was a tactical advantage, so the twins' presence made the clan safer. The goddess was truly a master diplomat.

Throughout the meal, Allegra and Evie provided endless entertainment, keeping Morelle distracted with their antics, and Brandon managed to eat a few bites and not offend their hostess by leaving the food on his plate untouched.

"No, like this," Allegra was explaining seriously to Evie, demonstrating the 'proper' way to eat peas with a spoon. Most of them ended up on the floor, but neither child seemed concerned, and the adults just laughed, knowing the Odus would clean everything up.

When everyone was done, the dinner plates had been cleared, and the Odus began serving coffee, tea, and dessert, Brandon's anxiety spiked.

This was it.

Annani set down her coffee cup and looked at her siblings with so much love that Brandon felt his throat tighten.

"My dear sister and brother. Your extraordinary gifts didn't come to you by chance." She paused, gathering her thoughts. "They were given to you deliberately. We do not know this for certain, but it seems very likely that you were created to be Earth's shield against the Eternal King—to help rid the galaxy of a tyrant when he decides to threaten to end all life on this planet in order to get rid of the three of us—his grandchildren, his blood, the threat to his throne."

The silence that followed was deafening. Morelle's face had gone pale with shock, while Ell-rom looked like he might be sick. Brandon wanted to reach for Morelle's hand but found himself unable to move a muscle.

"Extraordinary is right," Amanda said. "What a blessing the two of you are. Naturally, it will take us decades to fully understand and hone your abilities, but you are no doubt our best defense against the king. In fact, you are the only defense. Without you, our only hope was for him to never set his sights on Earth, but we all felt like we were living on borrowed time."

Brandon couldn't have said it better even after working on it for hours, and Amanda had nailed it on the spot without any preparation, unless Kian and Annani had told her ahead of time.

"I'm so grateful you are here," Alena said. "It hadn't occurred to me that your talents were the only possible defense against the Eternal King. But now that it's spelled out, it's so obvious. Your father and mother created you for a purpose."

Ell-rom swallowed. "I don't know what's worse.

Thinking that we were the result of an illicit affair or that we were created with a deadly purpose in mind."

Jasmine took his hand. "Does it matter? You are who you are, not what your parents wanted you to be. You decide what you want to do with what they gave you."

He nodded. "I'm honored that you regard me as a shield against the Eternal King, but even if Morelle and I master our powers, we can't reach him. He's literally across the galaxy from us."

"We don't know the full scope of your abilities yet," Amanda said softly. "For all we know, distance might not matter. Your powers could potentially reach across space."

Ell-rom shook his head. "I doubt it. Besides, why do you think we were created to be weapons? It could be just the natural result of combining royal godly genes and royal Kra-ell genes. Both our parents were powerful."

Morelle regarded her brother with a pair of sad eyes. "I don't think so. When the head priestess pushed us, she knew that one of us could kill with a thought. I think that she also knew what I was supposed to do, but I just couldn't access my abilities. Maybe if she had hinted at what it was, I might have been able to do it back then."

"She might have pushed too hard," Syssi said. "Sometimes, it has the opposite effect, especially with paranormal abilities. They need to be gently coaxed to the surface."

Ell-rom snorted. "That was not my experience. My so-called talent was wrenched out of me by fear. I was afraid of that guard exposing Morelle and both of us getting…" He glanced at Allegra, who was watching him with a serious expression on her little face. "Well. You all know what would have happened. The second time I used my talent, I was terrified for Jasmine's life."

"My trigger was also fear," Morelle said.

Amanda lifted a finger. "Not true. You started using it on a small scale when you siphoned powers from Cassandra, Jin, Arwel, and Toven. Fear just triggered a massive siphoning." She leveled her eyes at Morelle. "Theoretically, you could absorb power from thousands and channel it to topple a building. I have a feeling that with training, you will one day be able to do that."

As Morelle reached for Brandon's hand under the table, seeking his comfort, he felt so guilty for not telling her sooner himself and letting others do it. He knew that he needed to confess that he'd been the one to first voice these suspicions, but he couldn't, and now it would have to wait.

"What are we supposed to do with this knowledge?" Ell-rom asked.

"Whatever you choose," Kian said. "This information doesn't change who you are or what you want to do with your life. It just explains some things about your abilities and highlights the importance of training. We are not going to force you to become our shield against the Eternal King, but if he comes for Earth, your lives will depend on your ability to utilize your gifts as much as ours will, so we hope that you will want to hone them and be prepared to save everyone."

Silence fell over the room as everyone mulled over Kian's statement.

"More cake!" Allegra's demand broke the tension, making everyone laugh.

"Just a small piece." Syssi reached for the dessert plate.

Under the table, Brandon squeezed Morelle's hand, and she squeezed back. They needed to talk, and he hoped she would not hate him once he confessed.

46

MORELLE

Morelle let the hot water cascade over her shoulders, grateful for the privacy of the shower. She needed time alone to think, to process everything she'd learned. Nothing had really changed—she was still herself, still the same person—but somehow everything felt different.

In a way, thinking of herself as a tool was better than seeing herself as a parasite, but she wasn't either of those things, was she?

She was Morelle, a complex individual with many facets who was still growing as a person and discovering not only her strange abilities but also what she liked and didn't like, what interested her and what didn't, and she still didn't know what she wanted to do with the rest of her life.

After her sheltered and secluded existence in the temple, everything was a discovery. But who was she, really? Was being Earth's shield her ultimate destiny?

Steam filled the bathroom as Morelle contemplated her place in this world.

She loved Annani and her new family fiercely and would defend them with her last breath if needed, and even the idea of eventually confronting the Eternal King didn't bother her if it meant protecting the people she'd come to care about.

So why did she feel so unsettled?

Perhaps the worst part was the realization about her mother. Had she really woken Morelle up because she wanted her daughter to find happiness and love? Or had it been purely strategic—activating a weapon when it was needed?

Then again, why couldn't both be true? Her mother could have loved her deeply while still needing her to do what she'd been created for.

The two weren't mutually exclusive.

And what about their father? Despite what her mother had told her, he must have known about them because the pregnancy hadn't been an accident.

It had been planned.

Still, Morelle remembered vividly what her mother had told her in the dream.

"He was sent into exile before I could tell him that I had conceived," her mother had said. "He died not knowing about you and Ell-rom. But since all is known here in the Fields of the Brave, he knows now."

It still bothered Morelle that her mother hadn't mentioned Ahn reincarnating like she had about the head priestess, and she hadn't said anything about him being with her in the Fields of the Brave either, but she'd said that he knew about Morelle and Ell-rom, which hinted that he was there.

Then again, her mother had said that, as a general rule, all was known in the afterlife, so perhaps she hadn't been in contact with their father since they parted on Anumati.

Another option was that her mother had lied, and still another was that the dream had been just a dream and not the spirit of her mother visiting her. But then, how could her mother have known about things that Morelle had no knowledge of at the time?

Like the fact that Ahn was dead?

After all, he had died long after her mother was no longer on this plane of existence. Could it be that Brandon had told her about the gods' history on Earth while she was in a post-stasis coma, and it had somehow registered in her mind subconsciously?

But then, what about her mother dying before her time?

Brandon could have known about that from the gods who were new arrivals on Earth, but surely he wouldn't have told Morelle about it while she was in a coma. Maybe he had, though. Maybe he had also told her about the queen of the gods delaying the ship.

Had Ahn known that his children had been sent to him?

According to Annani, their father had never mentioned that, but then he'd also kept the gods' origins a secret, so he wouldn't have told his Earthborn daughter that there was a spaceship on the way with her brother and sister on board.

Communication between their parents would have been too dangerous. Any message between them might have exposed her and Ell-rom's existence to their grandfather, so their mother couldn't have told their father that she was sending them to him.

It was very likely that he hadn't known.

As she finally turned off the water, Morelle felt the storm of emotions in her mind settling somewhat. The revelation that she and Ell-rom had been created for a specific purpose rather than being the product of an affair between star-crossed lovers was less romantic. Certainly, it was more pragmatic, but it wasn't terrible.

She could live with it.

She could even find purpose in it.

When Morelle finally emerged from the bathroom, she found Brandon in bed wearing his black silk pajamas. He had told her that he'd never worn them to bed before because he preferred to sleep in the nude, and he only put them on out of regard for her. But now that they had completed their bond, there was no reason for him to be dressed in bed.

So, what was going on with him?

Was he bothered by her being a tool? A weapon?

He was staring at his phone with an expression even more troubled than the one he'd worn all day, which reinforced her suspicion that she was right about him not being okay with the earlier revelation.

Funny how it hadn't even occurred to her that he might have an issue with it. Annani and the rest of the family were happy to have a shield, and they thought highly of her and her ability. Why would Brandon have a problem with it?

She slipped into bed beside him. "Still thinking about those InstaTock videos?" she asked, knowing that wasn't what had put those deep lines on his forehead.

"No." He set his phone aside and took her hand, his expression serious. "I have a confession to make."

Something in his tone made her stomach clench. "What is it?"

"I was the one who realized your and Ellrom's talents couldn't be random—that you must have been engineered with a specific purpose in mind."

The words hit her like a physical blow. "Why didn't you tell me?"

"I wanted to consult with Kian first—"

"Behind my back." The hurt in her voice surprised even her. "How long have you suspected this?"

"Only since this morning." He squeezed her hand, and she resisted the urge to pull away. "When you were visiting Rob, I went to talk to Kian about it. I needed someone to tell me that I wasn't creating a script in my head and that the story made sense."

"You should have told me first. We could have talked about it and then gone to Kian together."

That was what she would have done if the roles had been reversed, and the way Brandon had handled it was disappointing, to say the least.

Brandon looked tormented. "I wasn't sure about it. I needed to run it by Kian first to see if I was reaching too far." He swallowed hard. "And then, after he agreed it made sense, I was too much of a coward to tell you. I was afraid of how you'd react."

"That's not okay, Brandon." Morelle pulled her hand free. "Life is full of difficult moments, and people who care about each other shouldn't shy away from them and hide their thoughts and suspicions."

"I know." His voice was heavy with regret. "I'm sorry. Can you forgive me?"

Looking at his earnest face, Morelle knew that she had no choice but to eventually forgive him because she loved him. Not yet, though. She couldn't do it when it still stung so fiercely. It wasn't just that he'd kept this from her, but that he'd thought she couldn't handle hearing it from him and relied on others to deliver the news to her.

"You're forgiven," she said finally, but she couldn't keep the truth of her hurt feelings from her voice.

She turned away from him, pulling the covers up to her chin, and after a moment, she felt him curl around her from behind, his arm draping over her waist. She didn't push him away—his warmth was still comforting, even now—but something felt off.

The disappointment sat heavy on her chest, an unwelcome emotion when it came to Brandon. She'd never felt this way about him before, and she wasn't sure what to do with it.

It wasn't that she doubted his love for her or his intentions. She understood his impulse to protect her, to make sure he wasn't wrong before potentially hurting her with his theory. But that was part of the problem—he'd made decisions about what she could handle without giving her the chance to prove him wrong.

His breath was warm against her neck as he whispered, "I really am sorry."

"I know." She covered his hand with hers, where it rested on her stomach. "I just need time to process things. It's been a difficult day."

She did have a lot to process. Not just Brandon's actions but everything they'd learned tonight. Her very existence had been engineered for a purpose—she and her brother created to be the perfect weapon against a tyrant king.

Ironically, that was easier to accept than the knowledge that Brandon hadn't confided in her first. Genetic engineering was something that had been done to her before she was born, but his choice had been made today, and he should have known better because he knew her.

She wasn't weak, she wasn't fragile, and trust meant everything to her.

Somehow, she would move past this. She loved Brandon, and one mistake wasn't going to change that, but she needed to make it absolutely clear that trust went both ways—and that caring for someone also meant trusting them with difficult truths.

47

ROB

The smell of coffee pulled Rob from sleep, a scent so tantalizing it made his mouth water.

When he opened his eyes, he found Margo sitting in the chair beside his bed and sipping from a paper cup that bore the village café's logo.

"Can I have a sip?" His voice came out raspy but stronger than he expected.

"Good morning." Margo stood and pressed her hand to his forehead. "Your fever's down." She studied his face. "How are you feeling?"

"Great." He tracked the coffee cup with his eyes. "But I really want a sip of that coffee."

"Bridget's going to kill me," Margo muttered, but she reached for the bed controls, raising the head until he was comfortably reclined, and handed over her cup.

The first sip was heaven, and Rob's eyes nearly

rolled back in his head at the rich taste. "This is so good."

Margo laughed. "That's the best sign that you're officially past the initial stage of transition. You were always like this when you were sick—couldn't stand coffee, not even the smell, but as soon as you started getting better, you couldn't wait to have some. That's how Mom always knew you were on the mend."

"True." He took another appreciative sip. "Where's Gertrude?"

Margo pointed toward the bathroom door. "She slept on a cot next to your bed, and she waited for me to get here before grabbing a shower."

Rob had vague memories of the night—flashes of fevered dreams, Bridget instructing Gertrude about medication, but he couldn't remember if it had been pills or an injection or something added to his IV. Everything was wrapped in a haze of heat and discomfort.

The bathroom door opened, and when Gertrude stepped out wearing fresh scrubs, her hair still damp from the shower, she was the most beautiful sight he'd ever seen.

"Hello, gorgeous," he said with a grin. "Seeing you is the best medicine."

She smiled. "Good morning to you too, my love. How are you feeling?"

"Great." He held up the coffee cup

triumphantly. "This is the sign. If I can drink coffee, I'm definitely over whatever was going on with me."

One dark eyebrow arched skeptically. "Really?"

"Really." He tapped his forehead. "No fever. Come check."

As she approached to feel his forehead, Rob seized his chance, catching her hand to pull her down for a kiss and delighting in her surprised laugh.

"You are definitely feeling better," she said, pulling back with a grin. "But let me get a proper thermometer to check your temperature."

The thermometer confirmed what Rob already knew—his temperature was normal. After a quick look at the monitors, Gertrude pulled out her phone and called Bridget.

While they waited for the doctor to arrive, Rob finished Margo's coffee and tried to piece together his scattered memories. "Was I as delirious as I think I was during the night?"

Gertrude patted his hand. "You talked about coffee and coding, but I had no idea what you were saying until you switched to ninja squirrels. Was it a computer game you worked on?"

The twitching of her lip betrayed her.

"No, and I'm choosing to believe you're making that up." Rob narrowed his eyes at her. "And since you're avoiding meeting my eyes, I know that you and Margo cooked this up to make fun of me."

Margo laughed, but before Gertrude could respond, Bridget arrived without her white doctor's coat but with her trusty tablet in hand.

"Good morning, Rob. I hear that your fever has broken, and you even had coffee this morning." She cast Margo an accusing look.

"I didn't leave her a choice," Rob defended his sister. "For me, the ability to drink coffee is the best sign that I'm out of the woods."

"I won't argue with you about that, but I will just say that plain water would have been a much better choice."

Bridget checked his vitals, comparing them to the numbers on her screen.

"Looks good," she said finally. "If you maintain these levels for the next two hours without slipping back into unconsciousness, I'll release you to Gertrude's care at home."

"Perfect." Rob sat up straighter. "Can I have something to eat? I'm starving."

"You can have clear liquids for the next two hours," Bridget said. "You'll have to wait for the steak at least until tomorrow."

He frowned. "How did you know that was what I was craving?"

She patted his shoulder. "You are not my first transitioning male Dormant, Rob. Rest now." Bridget made a note on her tablet. "I'll be back to check on you in an hour." She walked out of the room.

"Do you want to have the transition test done before you leave?" Margo asked.

Rob shook his head. "I don't need one."

"It's tradition," Margo protested. "You only get to do it once, and you might regret not commemorating your transition properly later."

"I agree with Margo," Gertrude said. "You should have it like every other newly minted immortal."

He looked between their eager faces and sighed. "Fine. But only because you both seem so excited about it."

Margo's face lit up as she reached for her phone, but Rob lifted his hand to stop her. "Let's wait the two hours Bridget indicated, just to be sure."

It had suddenly dawned on him that Bridget had said she was releasing him to Gertrude's care, which meant that he was going home with her, but they hadn't decided anything in regard to their living arrangements.

He reached for her hand. "It's decision time. Are you taking me to your house, or are we getting a new place just for the two of us?"

She smiled so brightly that he was momentarily blinded by it. "First, I will take you home, and Hildegard will help me take care of you. I hope that the three of us will get along splendidly so we will all want to just continue living together."

Rob would have preferred for the two of them

to move into a new place and have a fresh start, but he knew how much Gertrude cared about Hildegard. The two had been best friends for decades.

"I would love to have you all to myself, love, but I don't want Hildegard to be lonely."

"I know you would, and so would I." Gertrude sighed. "But I don't want Hildy to feel like I'm abandoning her or kicking her out. Hildegard is seeing one of Kalugal's men, but I don't know if she's serious about him."

"You need to talk to her," Margo said. "Perhaps she's ready for a change."

48

PETER

Marina sat cross-legged at the foot of the bed. She tried for a casual expression as she watched Peter's preparations, but she couldn't quite hide her concern. She'd gotten better at masking her worry every time he left on a mission, but he could still read the tension in her shoulders, the way her fingers twisted in the fabric of her shirt.

"The surveillance equipment is already in place," he said, hoping to reassure her. "We've been monitoring the estate for days. This is just initial reconnaissance."

"With a full tactical team," Marina pointed out. "That doesn't sound like just reconnaissance to me."

He paused, checking his gear. "We need to be prepared for any contingency. If we confirm there are children on the premises—"

"You'll go in immediately." She nodded. "I know. And I support that. I just..." She trailed off, biting her lip.

"What is it, love?"

"I'm worried about what this new assignment will do to you. Seeing that kind of evil up close, day after day..."

Peter set down the earpiece he'd been checking and moved to sit beside her. "I've been doing this for a long time, and some of the girls we rescued from the traffickers were very young. Early teens, at best. So, this is more of the same for me. I can handle it."

He knew he could, but he also knew that it would leave more scars on his soul. It was difficult to accept that such evil existed in the world. It tainted the whole of existence and sucked the joy out of life.

Peter even had a hard time looking at young girls, and he was thankful there weren't many in the village. Too many times, it evoked images of other girls that he and his friends had rescued, and thoughts about all of those they hadn't and who were still suffering.

Knowing what was going on in the sewer of the human world sometimes made it hard for him to enjoy his everyday life and feel happiness. If he could, he would quit the force and beg the Clan Mother to make him forget everything he had seen, but he couldn't.

Strong males like him had to do everything in their power to fix what evil members of their gender were doing to the weak and defenseless.

It was his moral obligation.

Not that evil was exclusive to men.

As hard as it was to comprehend, there were plenty of females who either stood by and let it happen or even encouraged it, but there were fewer of them than their male counterparts. Women like that usually belonged to dark cults and were so brainwashed that they couldn't even distinguish between good and evil.

Luckily, he had Marina to replenish the joy in his life.

"I know you can handle it," Marina said. "You're the strongest person I know." She squeezed his hand. "But that doesn't mean that you have to do it alone. Promise me you'll talk to me about it. Even the hard stuff?"

"I promise," he lied, and pressed a kiss to her forehead. "Though some of it might be too disturbing to share."

"I grew up in Igor's compound, remember? I've seen some pretty bad stuff." Her eyes hardened. "I've been a victim, and I've helped other victims to heal. Don't try to protect me from the reality of what you're dealing with."

Judging by what he had seen, Igor had been a run-of-the-mill narcissistic dictator, but he hadn't been deliberately or exceptionally cruel, and he'd made rules that protected the humans in his compound, at least to some degree.

Peter didn't make light of Marina's suffering and what she'd endured and had to overcome, or the hardship everyone else living in that compound had experienced, but compared to what he had seen, they'd been lucky.

Naturally, he had no intention of sharing his observations with her, and he valued and respected her resilience and her determination to make the best out of a bad situation.

Marina was a survivor who hadn't let the miserable circumstances of her life keep her down. If anyone deserved the Fates' boon, it was her, and he was disappointed they hadn't granted her immortality.

He shouldn't be greedy and upset the capricious Fates by complaining. They had given him a truelove mate, and he was grateful for that. Perhaps Marina would be the first mortal who received the immortality gene through science and not ancestral descent.

After all, the gods hadn't always been immortal. They had found a way to modify their genes to make themselves live forever, and Kaia was working on deciphering the blueprints that had been stored in Okidu's cybertronic mind.

"Speaking of protection," Marina said, pulling open a nightstand drawer. "I have something for you."

She pressed a small object into his palm—a silver medallion on a sturdy chain.

"It's Saint Michael," she explained. "Patron saint of warriors and protectors. I found it in the gift shop in Safe Haven and just felt like I had to buy it." She smiled. "The funny thing is that I got it before I met you, and it just rested on the bottom of my jewelry bag. I found it today and thought that you should have it."

Peter didn't believe in any of the human religions, and he knew that the trinket was just something someone had manufactured for profit. It held no power, but it was an expression of Marina's love.

He ran his thumb over the raised image of the archangel. "Thank you." He slipped the chain over his head, tucking the medallion beneath his shirt where it rested cool against his skin. "I will wear it on every mission."

A knock at the bedroom door interrupted the moment. "Peter?" His mother's voice came through. "May I come in?"

His mother had decided to stay in the village, and she was looking for a place of her own, but since she didn't want to live alone, it wasn't as easy as just getting her into one of the vacant houses. Ingrid was trying to find her a roommate.

"Come in," he said.

Catrina entered, taking in the tactical vest laid out on the bed with an expression Peter couldn't quite read. "I just wanted to wish you good luck and congratulate you again on the promotion. I hope the mission tonight is a great success."

"Thank you," he said.

His mother nodded briskly, her moment of sentimentality passing. "Well. I'll let you finish preparing." She turned to go, then paused at the door. "Be careful out there."

After she left, Marina squeezed his hand. "That was unexpected."

"Yeah." He chuckled. "I wonder who she's been talking to lately. Someone is coaching her on how to be a supportive mother."

Marina laughed. "Perhaps it's the Clan Mother?"

"Perhaps. I should send her my thanks. Also, for the beautiful speech at our wedding."

Marina nodded. "Is it customary to give the Clan Mother gifts? Should we get her something?"

He snorted. "The only gift you can give the goddess is your adoration, and she will take it with open arms."

"I have no problem whatsoever with that. My adoration for her is genuine."

"So is mine." He returned to his equipment.

The tactical vest went on first, followed by various pouches and holders.

"You know what's funny?" Marina said softly. "I used to dream about being rescued when I was in the compound. Now I'm helping my warrior husband gear up to rescue others."

"Life has a way of coming full circle." He caught her hand and pressed a kiss to her palm.

When they separated, Peter refocused on the final preparations.

This mission was different from his previous ones—not just because he was in charge, but because of what they were facing. The intelligence suggested they weren't just dealing with regular criminal enterprises anymore. The possible involvement of Doomers added layers of complexity and danger.

49

DROVA

Drova studied her reflection in the full-length mirror. She didn't look all that different because she usually wore black fatigues almost identical to the uniform she'd been given.

The only significant difference was the insignia of the Avengers. It was an eagle with two swords crossing over it, and it was so small that it was not visible unless someone specifically looked for it. Onegus didn't want them to have any identifying features, which was fine for the immortals, but the Kra-ell couldn't help their alien looks. She and Pavel, the only purebloods on the team, stuck out with their height, their big eyes, and slim frames.

She adjusted the utility belt, making sure everything was secured properly. There was no gun in her holster. She either hadn't earned the right to one yet or just wasn't trusted with one, which was kind of stupid. What was she going to do with a gun? Put it to a Guardian's head and order him to drive her somewhere?

As if there was anywhere she could go.

"You're wearing it wrong."

Drova jumped at her mother's voice. She hadn't heard Jade enter her room, which was embarrassing given her training. She'd been too absorbed in her own thoughts, and because she was safe in her house, her training hadn't engaged, but that was a mistake. Her mother had told her a thousand times that safety anywhere was an illusion, and she needed to always be vigilant.

"The knife sheath goes on the left side for right-handed fighters," Jade said, moving to adjust the belt.

"I know how to position equipment," Drova said, perhaps more defensively than she'd intended.

Jade grimaced but adjusted the belt, nonetheless. "Always accept advice and corrections with an open mind, especially when they come from someone with vastly superior training and experience. Arrogance and stubbornness can and will kill you."

"I know that." Drova took a deep breath. "Thank you for the correction, Mother."

Jade nodded. "Today, your job is to listen, watch, and learn. If you respond to any of the

Guardians the way you've just responded to me, you will be dismissed and not allowed back."

"I understand."

But she didn't, not really. She was one of the best fighters among the Kra-ell—Jade had made sure of that, training her relentlessly since she could walk. It seemed wasteful to keep her on the sidelines just because she was young and the Guardians considered her inexperienced.

Something of her thoughts must have shown on her face because Jade's expression hardened. "You lack field experience, Drova. This is not like training in the compound or here, where no one is trying to kill you. The people the Avengers are going after are ruthless monsters who prey on children. It doesn't get any worse than that. Don't expect them to follow the rules or hesitate to cause you harm. The only reason I feel okay with you going out there is your ability to control their minds. The problem is that bullets are faster than spoken commands, and you might not have time to stop them. Rely on your speed and strength instead."

Drova smiled. "You worry too much. I will not be taking part in the attack. I'll be watching from the surveillance van. The worst that can happen to me is the Guardian in charge confusing me with too much technical information and causing me a headache."

That got a chuckle out of Jade. "Right. But my

advice still stands. If something goes wrong, you might need to assist, and if that happens, I want you to remember what I've told you. No one will expect your speed and strength, and that will give you an advantage."

"Got it."

Before Jade could continue her lecture, Phinas appeared in the doorway. "You look good in tactical gear." He smiled. "Fierce."

"Thank you." Drova returned his smile. He always knew how to defuse tension between her and her mother and never spoke down to her like Jade often did.

"May I offer some advice?" When she nodded, he continued, "Follow orders and trust your team leader's judgment."

"I will." She meant it, too. "I'm not stupid." Despite her pride and rebellious tendencies, she understood the importance of the chain of command.

"Never said you were, but the young are known to be impulsive, and you are still very young."

As a knock sounded at the front door, Drova's heart skipped. It was probably Pavel who had promised to collect her on his way to the training center.

"That'll be your escort," Jade said.

Her stupid heart was still thundering in her chest, and Drova assumed a blasé expression. "Yes, it will."

She walked to the front door, conscious of her mother and Phinas watching. When she opened it, Pavel stood there in his own tactical gear, looking as handsome and as confident as ever.

"Ready?" he asked.

"Yes." She turned back to her mother and Phinas. "Wish us luck."

Jade's expression softened again, pride breaking through her usual stern mask. "Good luck." She turned to Pavel. "Get the bad guys and save the children. And be careful."

"We will," Pavel said.

Drova nodded her agreement and then stepped out into the cool midday air beside Pavel without looking back. There was no need for drama. After all, she wasn't going to fight tonight, so all that pep talk had been superfluous.

"Nervous?" Pavel asked.

"No. Just excited to see some real action. Regrettably, I don't have an active role. Not this time, anyway. I hope Peter is not going to keep me on the sidelines forever."

He chuckled. "It's okay to admit that you are nervous. Everyone's nervous their first time out, even if all they do is watch from the sidelines. It's the difference between training at home and finding yourself behind enemy lines."

"I'm not everyone."

"No," he surprised her by agreeing. "You're definitely not."

Their eyes met briefly, and Drova felt that familiar flutter in her stomach that she always got around him, but she commanded her traitorous body to stand down.

This wasn't the time for such girly concerns. She couldn't let her attraction to Pavel distract her.

Still, as they walked in companionable silence she couldn't help but hope that in time, after she proved herself, maybe he would start seeing her not as Igor's daughter, not as a compeller or a troublemaker, but as a female of worth he would one day be proud to belong to.

50

GERTRUDE

Gertrude leaned over Rob and kissed his forehead. "I'm only going to make a quick phone call, and I'll be right back."

He tilted his head to look at her with curiosity in his eyes, but he didn't ask why she needed privacy for her call. "Can you get me fresh coffee from the vending machine? A big cup. Just pretend that it's yours if you bump into Bridget."

She laughed. "I'll see about that."

"Please?" He looked at her with a puppy-dog expression.

"Oh, that's not fair. Fine."

On her way out, she passed by Margo, who'd taken a seat in the waiting room to make phone calls to everyone she wanted to invite to her brother's testing ceremony.

"You seem so sure that he's not going to slip back," Gertrude said.

Margo lifted her head. "I know he won't. You should realize by now how stubborn Rob is. If he decided that he's done, he's done."

"Yeah, you're right."

In this case, Rob's stubbornness was a good thing, but it hadn't served him well in others. It was what had kept him with Lynda because he hadn't been willing to admit that he'd made a mistake in his choice of life partner and had stubbornly clung to a made-up notion of her.

Stepping outside the clinic, Gertrude headed toward the vending machines in the back of the café. She needed to talk to Hildegard about their living arrangements, and she didn't want to do that in front of Rob in case the conversation got unpleasant.

It wasn't that she really expected that from Hildy, but people often reacted in strange ways to unexpected changes, although her friend should have seen this one coming.

The vending machines stood below the canopy of a large tree, and since the small building housing the café proper was in front of them, they were always in the shade. It was nice in the summer, but quite chilly in the winter, and Gertrude had only her scrubs on. However, it was much more private in the back of the café than in the front, so it was worth the slight discomfort.

Leaning against one of the machines, she placed the call.

"Good news?" Hildegard answered right away, and given the background noises, she was driving.

"Yes. Rob is awake, and if he manages to stay that way for another hour, Bridget is going to run the test."

"Congratulations! That's wonderful! Are you bringing him home after Bridget clears him?"

Leave it to Hildegard to get straight to the point.

"Yes. That's what I wanted to talk to you about."

"No worries. I've already spoken with Ingrid about finding another place."

Gertrude felt her heart squeeze. "What? No, I don't want you to move out. I was calling to ask if you're okay with Rob moving in with us."

Hildegard laughed. "Oh, Gertie. I'm not going to stand in the way of true love. Besides, Ingrid told me that Catrina, Peter's mother, is looking for a roommate, and I've already called her. She was very excited to hear that I needed a new roommate as well, and we decided to move in together."

Despite it being good news, Gertrude felt a pang of sadness. She didn't want to part with Hildegard.

"Maybe you should meet her first?" Gertrude suggested. "Make sure you two get along?"

"Oh, I know Catrina well from back when I still lived in Scotland," Hildegard said dismissively. "We'll be fine. And you and Rob can have the house to yourselves."

Tears pricked at Gertrude's eyes. She and Hildegard had been roommates for so many years, sharing everything from late-night conversations to studying nursing together and working in the same hospital, until Bridget asked them to work in the keep's clinic and then in the village. "I'm going to miss you."

"Don't get sentimental on me." Hildegard's voice softened. "You can visit me anytime, and Catrina and I would love to be invited to dinner from time to time."

Gertrude wiped at her eyes. "Thank you for making it so easy and so hard on me at the same time."

"You're welcome." Hildegard sighed. "Change happens, Gertie, and this time it's for the better. Sooner or later, I will find my truelove mate as well, and then Catrina will have to look for a new roommate. That's how it's supposed to be."

"I guess." Gertrude shifted so she was leaning on her other side. "Where are you off to?"

"The keep. The new Avengers unit is going out tonight, and they'll be bringing prisoners back for interrogation. In case anyone needs mending, I'm stationed there today and tomorrow. Julian is on call."

It must be serious if they needed healers, but Gertrude knew better than to ask for details. "Then I guess I will see you tomorrow?"

"Of course. I need to pack my things and clean out my room."

"There really is no rush. Rob and I only need one bedroom."

"I know, darling. Give kisses to Rob from me and tell him that I will personally welcome him to the clan tomorrow."

"I will. And thank you again."

"No need to thank me. Kisses." Hildegard ended the call.

With a sigh that was bittersweet, Gertrude pulled out her charge card from her pocket, inserted it into the machine, and chose the largest coffee it offered. Rob liked it with cream and no sugar, so she selected that, and once the machine was done brewing, she collected the cup, put the lid over it, and headed back to the clinic.

When she entered Rob's room, she caught him fighting to keep his eyes open. "My savior!" He extended his arm. "Come to revive me with the heavenly brew."

Chuckling, she handed him the cup. "Careful. It's hot." She hopped up on the bed to sit next to him. "I spoke with Hildegard, and she's moving out as early as tomorrow. Tonight, she's in the keep."

He frowned. "Why? I don't want her to feel as if she has to go because I'm moving in. The two of us can look for a place of our own."

"What's the difference?" she asked.

"The difference is that she wouldn't have to pack, and we will get a fresh start."

Gertrude let out a breath. "Moving to another house would be more difficult for me because of my herb garden. Hildegard would have let me keep it, of course, but it's an added level of complexity. Besides, Hildy has already spoken with Ingrid, and she's also found a new roommate. Peter's mother decided to stay in the village, and the two of them are moving in together."

"Good news," Margo walked in. "The whole gang is coming to witness the test. Mia and Toven, Negal, Frankie, Aru, Gabi, Jasmine, and Ell-rom. They are all on their way."

Gertrude glanced at her watch. "Did you check with Bridget? It hasn't been two hours yet."

"I did, and she's ready. We are only waiting for the gang to arrive."

Gertrude turned to Rob. "Is there anyone else you would like to invite?"

"Arwel and his mate, if Jin wants to come. William and Roni, if they can take a break from work."

"Right." Margo was already typing on her screen. "I forgot about them. Shame on me. I'm texting them to ask if they can make it."

A few moments passed until the replies arrived. "Jin is on her way, and the guys will rush over, and leave as soon as the test is done. There is some big mission going on, and they are all on high alert tonight."

That was probably the Avengers mission. Perhaps they expected complications and were keeping senior Guardians on alert.

Gertrude rushed to brush Rob's hair, give him a quick shave with the electric razor, and splash him with cologne, making it just in time before his friends began filing in.

Rob managed to look both pleased and overwhelmed by the attention, welcoming his guests and thanking them for coming.

A few minutes later, when William and Roni walked in, Bridget appeared with her ceremonial tray, a small knife gleaming under the fluorescent lights.

"Alright, everyone, find a spot where you can see. Who's filming?"

"I am," Mia said, holding up her phone.

"I'll time it." Margo pulled up the stopwatch app on hers.

Gertrude squeezed Rob's hand as Bridget approached the bed, and he squeezed hers back, his grip surprisingly strong so soon out of the first stage of his transition.

"Your left hand, please," Bridget instructed.

Rob extended his hand, and Gertrude felt his slight tension as Bridget positioned his palm upward.

"This will sting a little," the doctor warned, though they all knew what to expect. "Now."

The knife's edge was sharp enough that the initial cut barely registered, but Gertrude saw Rob's jaw tighten slightly as the pain bloomed. They all watched intently as blood welled in the shallow cut.

Almost immediately, the edges began knitting together. The healing was happening quickly, and they could all track its progress. In mere seconds, the wound closed, and a few seconds later, no trace was left of the cut.

"Twenty-eight seconds total," Margo announced triumphantly. "That's a fantastic time!"

A cheer went up from their assembled friends, and Rob's face broke into a wide smile as congratulations poured in from all sides.

"Welcome to immortality," Toven said formally.

Rob's grip on Gertrude's hand tightened. "Thank you all for coming and for making me feel so welcome."

"Alright, that's enough excitement," Bridget announced. "Our new immortal needs rest. You can all celebrate properly once he's recovered."

As Rob's friends filed out with final congratulations and good wishes, Gertrude leaned down to kiss his forehead. "You can sleep now. I'll be here when you wake up to take you home."

"Love you," he murmured, already drifting off.

51

DROVA

The training center hummed with activity as Drova entered with Pavel. Unlike the other training sessions that she'd participated in since being allowed to join the Avengers, where Guardians often joked and laughed before the start, tonight's atmosphere was heavy with purpose.

Immortals in tactical gear were standing in small groups, talking in hushed voices, while Peter spoke with Onegus near the large display screen.

Drova knew everyone on the team from training. They were all experienced Guardians, chosen because this was untested territory for the clan and no place for newbies. She was grateful to be granted even an observer's spot.

Tonight, they were making history, and in a small way, she was taking part in it.

"Take a seat," Pavel said, gesturing to the chairs arranged in front of the screen.

As Drova settled in, she noticed one of the Guardians giving her a skeptical look. She lifted her chin, refusing to show any uncertainty. She belonged here, whether the others accepted it or not.

Onegus cleared his throat, and the room instantly fell silent. "Good evening." He activated the display screen, showing an aerial view of a sprawling Beverly Hills estate. "Our target has been under surveillance for over a week, mostly via drones, because there are no structures with a direct line of sight of the estate for us to mount cameras on. Given the heavy security, we had to be careful when flying the drones as well. We didn't see any children arriving at the estate or leaving it, but since the place has a large eight-car garage, it is easy to hide such an activity. We've noticed a pattern of no one exiting the arriving vehicles or entering them while the garage doors are open. That's not normal, especially since the garage is located in the back, and the estate is fenced off, so no casual passersby, either on foot or in a vehicle, have a direct line of sight to the entrance of the garage. That's taking precautions to the next level."

"They're protecting the identity of the so-called guests," one of the Guardians said.

Onegus nodded. "Also, that of the owners. The estate is owned by a corporation, which also pays the utility bills, so the names of the residents could be fake, which we are assuming. The corporation is owned by another entity, which is owned by a trust and so on, and it seems that the actual owner is a foreign entity."

"What about the staff?" another Guardian asked. "Aren't we supposed to catch one, thrall him or her, and get the information we need?"

"Good question. The problem is that we didn't see any of the staff leaving the estate. We know they are on the premises because we've seen uniformed maids throwing out the trash and a gardener mowing the lawn. You were supposed to be the team that collected the necessary info, and you might still end up doing just that, but I have a gut feeling that you will be going in. That's why the backup team is much larger than we initially intended."

He switched to another screen. "These are the blueprints of the house. It has two main levels, a basement, and a finished attic. The service staff occupies the attic, and the children are most likely being kept in the basement. Given the increase in the comings and goings in the last few days, things are happening over there, and this mission is likely to turn into an active extraction."

Drova's hands clenched in her lap. Even knowing what they were facing, the reality of children being not only held captive but terribly abused, made her blood boil. She forced herself to take slow, steady breaths, remembering her mother's warnings about controlling her emotions.

"Tonight still might be reconnaissance only," Peter said, taking over from Onegus. "We need to confirm numbers, security protocols, and most importantly, verify the presence of children captives. If there are children in danger in there, we will move in. It depends on what we find when we get there and if we can detect Doomers on the premises." He turned to Drova. "In either case, your job is to observe and learn. Do not even think to engage unless directly ordered."

"Understood, sir." If she wanted to one day become one of the attacking team, she had to play the role of the obedient cog in the machine, no matter how she hated doing that.

Lyall, who was in charge of the surveillance van, leaned toward her. "I'll walk you through the systems when we're in position. For now, pay attention to the layout and access points just in case your help is needed."

A surge of excitement rushed through her that the Guardian was even thinking in terms of her being needed. It was so much better than the almost dismissive attitude Peter was showing her. To him, she was a nuisance, a crazy idea of Kian's he had no choice but to humor.

The briefing continued with detailed assignments for each team member, and Drova absorbed every detail, noting how Peter had positioned his people to cover all possible contingencies. These weren't just random patrol patterns—this was carefully orchestrated choreography.

"Questions?" Peter asked when he'd finished.

Drova had several but kept silent. Her role was simple enough—watch and learn. Asking questions now would only reinforce the impression that she was a burden rather than an asset to the team.

"Five vehicles," Peter said. "Four SUVs and the surveillance van, with standard dispersal pattern. Communications check at every waypoint."

As the team began gathering their gear, Pavel touched Drova's elbow. "Ready?"

She nodded, following him toward the parking garage where the vehicles waited. The surveillance van was marked with the logo of some cable television network, which was a good call. It explained the dish mounted on its roof.

"Are you nervous?" Pavel asked when they stood in front of the van's opened door.

"Not really. I want to prove that I'm not a kid who needs babysitting, but I'm grateful for the opportunity to be an observer. In the future, though, I hope they will let me help. I want to make a difference."

"No one thinks you're a kid who needs babysitting." Pavel's expression softened. "But everyone has to start somewhere. Even Peter had to learn surveillance protocols before leading missions. He got promoted to Head Guardian when he took over the Avengers."

"Time to get settled in, rookie," Lyall called from inside the van. "We need to move out."

She gave Pavel a smile. "Good luck. And if we get to see some action, be careful."

"I will." He patted her back. "Keep sharp, rookie." He winked before sauntering away.

She watched him head to his vehicle, taking a deep breath before climbing into the van. The interior was a masterpiece of technology, housing state-of-the-art surveillance equipment.

"Sit over there," the Guardian instructed while powering up the systems. "I'll walk you through each component once we're in position. After all, you are here to learn, right?"

She nodded. "I don't expect to become a surveillance expert, but I'm happy to learn what I can."

"You never know, kid." Lyall winked at her. "You might discover that you have a knack for it."

52

PETER

As they neared their target location, everything about this neighborhood screamed money and privilege—manicured lawns, luxury cars, and security that was meant to be seen. But knowing that beneath that polished veneer lurked something far darker made Peter think of a thin layer of glitter covering festering rot.

"Team One in position," Alfie's voice came through his earpiece.

Peter tapped his own piece once. "Acknowledged. Team Two, status?"

"Two minutes out," Bowen reported. "No suspicious activity on approach."

The backup teams would hang back and engage if and when needed. Peter had chosen his people carefully for this mission, balancing experience with the stomach for what they might encounter.

"Van moving into position now," Lyall reported. "Preparing to deploy the parabolic microphone."

The van was going to park in the neighbors' driveway. They were out of town, and last night, one of William's crew members had taken care of their front-facing camera, so it was delivering a prerecorded long loop of no activity so no one would notice the van parking on their property.

They didn't have a front gate, which was unusual for the neighborhood, but even if they did, it wouldn't have caused much of a challenge.

"Can you get anything from there?" Peter asked.

"The parabolic mic can reach, but it's tricky," Lyall said. "If the perps are upstairs or near a window, I'll catch it. If they're in the basement, though, it's more difficult."

Peter suspected that much of the illicit activity was happening in the basement, so that was a problem. "What's your issue with the basement?"

"Sound doesn't travel well through concrete," Lyall said. "We're looking at layers of insulation, stone, and probably a lot of ambient noise masking anything useful. I'll need to focus on external openings—basement windows, vents, maybe even the front door if it's ajar."

Peter rubbed a hand over the back of his neck. "I'm looking at the plans, and there is a basement window on that side of the house. If it's closed, I'll send a Guardian to open it."

"If they are really loud down there, I can hear it

even with the window closed," Lyall said. "It will also come through pretty clearly if they talk near the window."

"How long until you are all set up?"

"Two minutes. The tripod is already prepped. Once I get the dish aligned, I'll tune it in. You'll have live audio in about ten minutes. Let's just cross our fingers that no one wonders what a news van is doing at their neighbors' house."

"You know what to say if anyone comes to ask."

They could thrall the person, or Drova could compel them into silence, but the easiest solution was a good cover story. They were filming a segment about luxury properties for sale in Beverly Hills, and they were waiting for their anchorwoman, who was running late.

"Let me know the second you hear anything."

"I will."

Peter tapped his earpiece once. "Prepare for the initial scan. Team One, move to set thermal imaging."

"Roger that." Jay's voice was barely a whisper.

Through the bulletproof window of their vehicle, Peter watched as Jay moved stealthily toward the estate's eastern wall. Despite his size, the Guardian could be remarkably subtle when needed. They'd chosen this approach based on the surveillance—supposedly, it was a blind spot in the estate's security cameras' coverage.

"There are more patrols than usual," Alfie

murmured through the comm. "I count six visible guards. The pattern suggests at least four more we can't see."

That was double the previous observations obtained through drone surveillance, and Peter's instincts flashed a warning.

"They have guests," Theo's voice came through. "Three vehicles parked behind the garage. High-end. Recently arrived based on engine heat signatures, and given that there is an eight-car garage on the property, they are hosting many people."

Peter's jaw clenched. He'd hoped they'd have more time for reconnaissance, but it seemed like they were going in.

"Thermal imaging in place," Jay reported. "Activating now."

Peter tapped his comm. "Lyall, what are you picking up?"

There was a long pause, and then Lyall's voice came through, tight with controlled rage. "Audio confirms the presence of children. Multiple voices. They need help."

"What's going on?" Peter demanded.

"They're begging someone to stop," Lyall said flatly. "Crying. Enhanced audio is picking up at least three distinct young voices. I don't know if they are boys or girls. Not that it matters."

"Thermal imaging coming through now," Theo reported. "I'm patching it to you."

Peter activated his tablet, studying the heat

signatures. The basement level showed multiple bodies—three small forms with their arms clearly raised above their heads, suggesting restraints. Adult signatures moved between rooms.

"More activity than expected," Alfie said. "They're getting bolder."

Peter weighed his options. Their original plan called for extended surveillance, building a complete picture of security rotations and access points before attempting a rescue, which was the safe way to go. But with confirmed victims in immediate danger, he couldn't wait.

"All teams, maintain position," he ordered. "Lyall, keep me updated on anything you can pick up. Numbers, locations, and any names used. Team One, get me a count on visible security and probable positions of the others."

They didn't have enough information, but they had the advantage of surprise and, as a last resort, a powerful compeller.

A child's scream cut through his thoughts, picked up by the enhanced audio and relayed through their comms. The sound hit him like a physical blow, and he heard several sharp intakes of breath from his team.

"Commander..." Alfie's voice held a dangerous edge.

"I know." Peter forced himself to think tactically despite the rage burning in his chest. "Status report. All positions."

The reports came in rapidly. Ten confirmed security personnel. Three *guests* in the main house. Two more were arriving in a new vehicle. Surveillance showed systematic rotation patterns—professional security, not thugs with guns.

Below it all, through the enhanced audio, were the sounds of children suffering.

Peter hadn't felt this kind of fury since his first mission of rescuing the victims of trafficking. He wanted to storm the estate and tear every adult apart with his bare fangs. But just as he couldn't have done it then, he couldn't do it now. The success of the operation depended on him keeping a cool head.

He had to emotionally detach.

"New vehicle approaching the gate," Theo reported. "High-end sedan. Two occupants."

More *guests* were arriving. More monsters were coming to hurt children.

Peter tapped his comm. "All teams, prepare for immediate action. We're shifting to extraction protocol."

A chorus of acknowledgments came through. They'd all heard enough, and even though this operation might cost them crucial information they needed to get to the head of the snake, they had no choice.

"Teams One and Two, prepare for a simultaneous breach. Backup teams, move into positions." Remembering Onegus's directive about collecting vermin to bring to the keep, Peter took a deep breath. "As much as I want to kill everyone in there, we need some alive for questioning."

The fate of their broader mission to destroy these networks would have to take second place to saving the children currently suffering inside that house, and Peter knew it would cost them, but some lines couldn't be crossed.

Some crimes couldn't be observed and documented for later action.

Sometimes, you had to be the shield that stood between innocents and monsters, whatever the cost.

"All teams," he said. "Prepare to move on my mark."

53

DROVA

Lyall set up the parabolic microphone, carefully aligning the dish toward the basement window of the target house.

Drova leaned forward in her seat as Lyall adjusted the sound, bringing the basement conversation into sharp focus. Two male voices came through clearly, speaking in a harsh, guttural language she didn't recognize. It reminded her a little of Kra-ell, and she caught a word here and there, but it still didn't make any sense to her.

She looked at Lyall, who was turning red as a beet. "What language are they speaking?"

Lyall's fingers tightened on the controls. "Filthy Doomers," he muttered. "That's their dialect—a bastardized form of the gods' old language. Not many still speak it, but I learned it a long time ago, and I know enough to understand the gist of what's being said."

"What are they saying?" Drova asked, noting the angry shade of his skin and the hard line of his jaw.

"Nothing I care to repeat." His jaw clenched. "They're discussing their 'entertainment' for the evening."

The cruel laughter that filtered through needed no translation, and neither did the whimper that followed it. Drova's fangs lengthened at the sound. Prey. These creatures were prey, and they were right there, so close that she could tear them apart with her fangs, suck out their blood until there was nothing left in their rotting carcasses and spit it on the ground because it was too vile to consume.

Lyall tapped his earpiece once. "Peter, we have confirmed Doomers in the basement. At least two of them."

"Location?" Peter's voice came through their comms, although his question was directed at Alfie's team.

"My bet is that they are the two near the eastern basement window," Alfie said. "There are more monsters in there, though. I guess those are the *guests*."

"We could take them out with an RPG," Drova suggested. "Clean shot through the basement window."

Lyall regarded her with a raised brow. "There are innocents in there. We can't just throw a grenade inside."

"That's right." Peter's voice came through the

comm. "We can't storm the place either because the Doomers will use the children as human shields."

Drova's fangs itched as more laughter came through the audio. She could almost taste their blood and could imagine the satisfying crunch of bone beneath her hands as she twisted their heads off, but she had better tools at her disposal.

"Use me," she said. "Get me a loudspeaker, and I'll compel everyone in that house to walk out with their hands up."

"No loudspeaker equipment in the van," Lyall said. "Why didn't I think of bringing a damn loudspeaker?"

"Don't you have something in the van you can use?" Peter asked. "But it has to be very loud."

"I don't. I can probably rig up something, but it will take too long."

"What about the guards' radio network?" Alfie's voice came through. "If we grab one of their transmitters, Drova could command them all at once."

"The Doomers might not be on the network," Peter said after a moment. "We need to get her inside somehow."

Drova's pulse quickened at those words.

Finally.

She could already imagine tearing into her prey. "I can compel them to stop breathing," she offered, running her tongue over her extended fangs.

Lyall shot her a sharp look. "Did you forget?

There are innocents in there who could hear you and also stop breathing. Leave the killing to the Guardians."

She managed a terse nod, though it cost her. He was right about the risk to the children, but there were other ways to kill that wouldn't rely on verbal commands. She could snap the Doomers' necks and tear their heads off with her fangs. They were just ordinary immortals, and she was stronger and faster.

The Doomers were still speaking in the background, their harsh language intercepted with bouts of cruel laughter. Drova's nails dug deeper into the arms of her seat, leaving deep gouges in the material.

"Control," Lyall said, noting her reaction. "Don't let rage cloud your mind. Angry people make mistakes."

"I am in control." Her voice came out as more of a growl than she'd intended. "I can follow orders. But when the time comes—"

"When the time comes, you'll do exactly as instructed." His tone left no room for argument. "This isn't about satisfying bloodlust. It's about saving souls."

Drova forced her fingers to loosen on the handles, but her fangs remained extended. The Guardian was right, but that didn't make it any easier to suppress her instincts. The Doomers triggered something primal in her, an urge to hunt and kill that grew stronger with each word they uttered in their ugly language.

Through the earpieces, Peter continued coordinating with the teams, and she tried to focus on the tactical details instead of her fantasies of violence, but the audio feed kept pulling her attention back to her prey.

"They're discussing prices now," Lyall translated grimly. "Setting up the bidding for—" He cut himself off, jaw tight.

Drova didn't need to hear the rest. Her fingernails pierced through the fabric of the seat arms, the pain of them digging into the wood underneath helping her maintain focus.

"We'll need a distraction," Peter's voice came through. "Something to draw their attention while we get Drova into position."

She could give them one hell of a distraction. Just let her loose for thirty seconds...

But no. She had to prove she could follow orders. Had to show them she wasn't just a predator acting on instinct, no matter how much those instincts screamed at her to hunt.

As more cruel laughter filtered through the audio, Drova closed her eyes, imagining in vivid detail exactly how she would silence those laughs.

But she would wait.

She would follow orders.

54

PETER

After forming a plan and asking for an immediate delivery of more vehicles, Peter climbed into the surveillance van while still mapping out the tactical sequence.

As Lyall shifted to make room, Drova watched him with barely contained intensity, her predatory nature evident in her extended fangs and the way her fingers flexed against the chair arms.

"I have a plan," he said, settling into the seat across from her. He tapped his earpiece. "Team One, I need two guards eliminated quietly. Strip them for uniforms and equipment. Bring one of the comms to the van." He paused for acknowledgments before switching channels. "Team Two, move into position to secure the control room. Wait for my signal."

Turning back to Drova, he pulled out his tablet.

"This is going to require precise timing and control. Can you handle that?"

Her fangs retracted slightly as she focused. "Of course. What do you need me to do?"

"Once we have the guards' equipment, you'll use their communication channel to order everyone on that frequency to report to the control room for a briefing." He zoomed in on the building layout. "That way, even if the Doomers aren't on the same channel, they won't immediately suspect anything when they see guards moving through the house."

Drova leaned forward, studying the floor plan.

"You'll enter through the kitchen door." He pointed at the spot on the plan. "Two of ours will accompany you dressed as the mansion's guards. As you head to the basement, you compel anyone you encounter—staff and guests who most likely will not be wearing comms—instructing them to get outside through the kitchen door and stay there. Quietly." He traced a path on the tablet. "This is your route to the basement. Speed is crucial. We need you to reach the Doomers before they realize what's happening."

"I can do that." She sounded eager, her eyes focused on the display. "What about the guards in the control room? Won't they start to wonder what they are doing there?"

"Team Two will handle them as soon as they're gathered." Peter studied her expression carefully.

"The guards are most likely human and easy for our Guardians to control."

She looked disappointed. "What are we going to do with them after we get the kids out and eliminate the abusers?"

He knew exactly what she wanted him to say, and if he could, he would have promised her that every monster in the place would be killed with extreme prejudice, but that wasn't conducive to their larger mission.

"This isn't about killing, Drova. It's about control and precision. You need to control your bloodlust."

"Even the Doomers? Can I at least kill them?"

"We need them alive to interrogate. We will take many prisoners tonight, and after we are done questioning them, we will eliminate some and use others as moles. Your services might be further required."

Her eyes brightened at that. "Good thinking. They can feed us more information." She squared her shoulders. "Got it. Quick, quiet compulsion. No excessive force unless absolutely necessary."

"Exactly." He switched channels again. "Status report."

"Two guards down," Jay reported. "Collecting equipment now."

Peter expanded the building schematic. "Memorize the layout. If anything goes wrong, you need to know every exit point."

Lyall spoke up from his station. "The Doomers are still in the basement. Their conversation suggests they're not planning to move anytime soon."

"Good." Peter turned back to Drova. "When you reach them, your priority is preventing any harm to the children. Compel them to stand down and remain still. Nothing else until we secure the area."

She nodded. "Understood. I thought to order them to get on the floor and lie face down."

"That's good," Peter approved.

Thankfully, every Guardian and even the Kraell participating in this mission wore earpieces that filtered out compulsion so none would be affected by Drova's commands.

She lowered her eyes, suddenly looking unsure. "What do I do about the children?" she whispered.

"Nothing. The Guardians will secure them and thrall them to sleep. We will take them to someone who will take care of them."

Drova let out a breath. "You've thought of everything."

"Of course. That's my job." He patted her shoulder. "If the uniforms fit, I'll get Pavel in one of them. Your mother wanted one of hers to make sure you are safe."

"Thank you." She gave him a smile that betrayed how young and unsure she was despite her bravado.

"Who do you want in the uniforms?" Alfie's voice came through.

"Pavel, if he can fit in one of them, and whoever fits into the other."

"Roger that. Approaching the van now, with the comm for Drova."

A moment later, the van's side door opened, and Alfie passed in the comm to Peter.

"Thank you."

His friend saluted and closed the door.

Peter handed the comm over to Drova. "Get ready. Once you're in position, everything moves fast."

Peter watched as Drova efficiently donned the tactical vest and comm gear.

"Remember," he said as she checked the comm, "Quick, quiet, precise. No deviations from the plan unless I give the order. Clear?"

"Crystal." Drova's voice was steady, and her fangs had receded to almost their dormant size.

She seemed focused on the mission now rather than her predatory instincts.

He tapped his comm again. "All teams, prepare for simultaneous execution on my mark."

55

DROVA

Drova's first task had been to send all security personnel to the control room for an "urgent briefing" and stay there with their backs to the balcony doors until told that they could leave. That had gone without a glitch. The room was located on the second floor, and the Guardians had used the trellis to climb to the adjacent balcony. Thralling the human guards was an easy task for the immortals.

Then, it was walking into the house through the kitchen door with Pavel and Theo, who were wearing the stolen uniforms. Pavel had put on a pair of sunglasses, so his Kra-ell eyes were hidden, but hers weren't. The two cooks who were working in the kitchen gasped as they registered her features.

"Walk out through the side door," she said

quietly but firmly. "Stand against the side wall and wait until someone comes to collect you."

Their eyes glazed over, and they moved as one toward the door without pausing to turn off the stoves and ovens.

Thankfully, Theo had the presence of mind to take care of that.

Neither she nor Pavel cooked, so it hadn't even occurred to them that, left unattended, it could cause a fire.

Not that she cared if the house burned to the ground after they extracted the children, but Theo quietly explained that the fire could spread to neighboring houses and cause damage and endanger innocent lives.

Through her earpiece, she heard Peter directing the team outside to guide the kitchen staff to the waiting van.

Where had that van come from? She pushed the question aside, focusing on the mission.

From there, the three of them continued through the mansion's lavish hallways.

A *guest* emerged from a side room, his expensive suit reeking of entitled privilege and other things she didn't want to think about.

Her fangs ached to extend, but she kept her voice steady. "Walk outside through the kitchen door. Keep walking until you are collected."

He obeyed without question, following the same path as the kitchen staff. Two more expensively dressed men appeared, likely drawn by her voice. Drova repeated her quiet command, satisfaction coursing through her as they too obeyed.

"Continuing to basement," she murmured into her comm.

The acknowledgment came as she reached the stairs, Pavel and Theo moving smoothly to cover her descent.

The basement's lighting cast harsh shadows, and the first thing that hit her was the smell—fear, pain, and something else that made her want to kill. But when she rounded the corner and saw the children, all predatory thoughts fled.

They were so small. So young. Tied to metal frames that looked like medical equipment, their tiny bodies showed marks of...

She swallowed bile, forcing herself to focus on the two Doomers who were turning toward her. Before they could speak, she snapped, "Face down on the floor. Don't move."

They dropped instantly, and Pavel rushed to secure them. The sound of footsteps on the stairs announced more team members arriving, and they immediately rushed to free the children.

Drova started forward to help, but the sight of the restraints, the—

Strong hands gripped her shoulders, turning her away. "You've done your part," Pavel said quietly. "Let's go."

She started to protest, but the words choked in

her throat. Tears spilled down her cheeks as Pavel guided her toward the stairs. Behind them, she could hear the Guardians speaking softly to the children, their gentle tones a stark contrast to what those young ones had endured.

"I want to kill," she whispered, her voice raw. "I need to—"

"I know." Pavel's arms went around her as they reached the top of the stairs. "And you will, but not today. You did exactly what was needed. You got us in clean, controlled the situation, and saved those kids. That's a win. Embrace it. You have proven yourself tonight."

She pressed her face into his chest, shoulders shaking. "How could anyone—" She couldn't finish.

"I know." He stroked her hair. "I know. But you helped stop it. You did good."

The predator in her screamed for blood, while another part wanted to go back and comfort those children. Instead, she stood there crying like a useless little girl.

"You did good," Pavel repeated firmly as if reading her thoughts. "Perfect control, perfect execution. Peter will be proud. Let's get out of here."

She lifted her head. "The children—"

"Are being taken care of by people trained to handle what they have gone through. They are taking them to the sanctuary. To Vanessa. You know Vanessa, right? My father's mate. That's what she does."

Of course she did. Pavel was talking to her as if she was the one suffering a trauma.

He led her outside through the front door instead of the one they had come in through. "The best thing you can do now is take care of yourself. Take deep breaths and repeat in your head that you did something good. You not only saved these children but probably also prevented Guardian casualties. Thanks to you, everything went smoothly."

She nodded, letting him lead her back to the van.

"That's our girl," Lyall greeted her with a grin and a high five. "You are this mission's hero."

Funny. Drova didn't feel like a hero right now. All she wanted to do was to go home, get in bed, cover her head with the blanket, and never come out.

56

PETER

The mansion's grand foyer served as Peter's command center while he coordinated the cleanup operation. The children were already gone, whisked away while thralled to sleep so they could be transported to the sanctuary where they would receive professional help.

The Guardians were not equipped to deal with traumatized children, so that seemed like the best solution. The last thing Peter wanted was to add to the damage that had been done to them.

Now came the methodical work of erasing the immortals' presence while securing evidence and prisoners.

"Teams Three and Four, status on prisoner transfer?" he asked, tapping his earpiece.

"Loading the last of the *guests* now," Alfie reported. "All secured and sedated."

"The Doomers are double dosed as per Julian's instructions," Jay added.

They had ended up with many more prisoners than Peter had ever expected to bring to the keep, but he wasn't an interrogator, and he preferred to leave the selection of who to leave alive and who to eliminate to the pros.

None of these sick fucks deserved to live another day and harm another child.

Peter climbed to the second floor, checking the Guardians' progress. In what had clearly been a security office, Theo and Bowen were disconnecting and packing computer equipment. There were countless hours of surveillance recorded on those, evidence of perversion that was no doubt meant to be used for blackmail and extortion.

He wondered how many politicians, Hollywood elites, and other public personalities had visited this house of horrors.

Peter wanted to develop a new side hobby and personally go after each one and tear their throats out with his bare fangs.

He could just imagine the news headlines.

"A reign of terror has the elites scrambling for cover!"

Other headlines came to mind, but he pushed them away. He had a job that needed to be done.

"Everything gets tagged," he reminded the Guardians. "The intel team will need to know which machine came from where."

"Already on it." Theo held up a labeled hard drive. "Looks like they were recording everything."

"Of course. That's why they do it. The big rewards come later with the extortion. They are paid with money and influence."

It was always about money and power, and the ones who paid the price were the most powerless, the innocent, the defenseless. Peter's jaw tightened. "Pack it all. Every backup drive and every cable. Make it easy for the hacker team. Their job will be hard enough just watching these recordings."

Theo nodded. "I'm glad I won't have to do that."

"Yeah, me too." Peter barely suppressed a shudder and continued to the mansion's office, where similar activity was taking place.

The office spoke of big money and no taste, with its leather furniture and pseudo-pornographic obscene artwork. Peter's attention was immediately drawn to the gaudy painting hanging on the wall behind the desk. "Did anyone check that thing for a safe?"

"Not yet," Gordon said. "I'm still busy tagging and packing the computer equipment and the various items from the drawers."

Peter walked over to the painting, and as he'd suspected, there was a safe hidden behind it.

"Need a safe-cracker in the second-floor office," he called through the comm.

Jay appeared moments later, tools already in hand. "Finally, something fun to do."

While Jay worked, Peter helped Gordon go through the desk drawers and check the undersides for hidden items and hidden compartments. Everything went into evidence bags—files, notebooks, loose papers, even random receipts. The intel team would sort through it all later.

"Got it," Jay announced as the safe swung open. "Oh, hello. Look at all this money and drugs."

Peter glanced inside. Multiple stacks of hundred-dollar bills were bound with paper ribbons, and the large bag of white powder was enough to drug an army. There were also several external hard drives, paper files, and ledgers.

"Bag it all," he told Jay.

The Guardian arched a brow. "Even the drugs?"

Peter nodded. "We will dispose of them safely. I don't want to leave them lying around."

He wondered if it was okay to just flush the stuff down the toilet. It was worth hundreds of thousands of dollars, but it was poison that had to be destroyed.

After the office, Peter continued to the third floor, where the staff quarters were located.

He found Randel in the staff common room, finishing the thrall work on the household servants. The Guardian's face was grim as he gave them their last marching orders and sent them to their rooms.

"It's done per your instructions," he reported. "Tomorrow morning, they'll walk into the nearest police station and confess to knowing about the operation and not reporting it sooner."

"Were they threatened?" Peter asked.

That was the only explanation he could think of that would prompt normal people to stay silent about the atrocities committed under their noses.

"Of course. But they were also well paid. So that was a double whammy. I made sure that they will have no memory of us or how their employers disappeared."

Peter nodded. Since there were no signs of forced entry or any struggle inside the house, the authorities would assume that the perpetrators fled with the children and all the incriminating equipment.

The monsters were already on their way to the clan's warehouse, where they would be checked for trackers before being taken to the keep's dungeon. They were going to get what was coming to them. As for the staff, Peter was fine with letting the human authorities deal with their complicity.

He tapped his comm. "All teams, final sweep of your assigned areas. I want every piece of evidence, every surveillance device, anything that wasn't part of the original house tagged and bagged. Search under and behind furniture, hidden cameras inside bedposts, statues, and artwork."

Confirmations kept coming in as he continued his own sweep. The house had to look untouched as if its occupants had simply left, so everything had to be done carefully.

"Perimeter team, status?"

"Area's clear. No curious neighbors, no patrol cars."

Of course not. In this neighborhood, people minded their own business, and most lived behind tall fences and electric gates. It's what had allowed this operation to flourish.

"Van is loaded with all equipment and evidence," Theo reported. "We're ready to move out."

Peter did one final walk-through, checking each room. Satisfied, he headed for the front door. "All teams, move out. Standard dispersal pattern."

When everyone other than his personal team was gone, he climbed into the seat beside Alfie and tapped his comm to Onegus's private channel. "Mission complete. Evidence and prisoners secured. No casualties."

"Excellent work," Onegus responded. "Kian's here with me. I've already given him a report, but he wants to hear it from you to get your impression."

As Alfie eased the SUV onto the road, Peter summarized the operation, emphasizing the smooth execution and Drova's crucial role. "Her performance was exemplary. She did exactly what she was asked to do and didn't crack under pressure."

She cracked after it had been done, but that was to be expected of a young woman who hadn't been hardened by life yet. Igor's compound might have been a harsh place, and some of the things that had gone on there were deplorable, but even that sociopath hadn't sunk this low.

"Jade will be proud," Onegus said. "Julian is en route to the warehouse with a fresh team of Guardians. They'll handle prisoner transfer and processing so your people can go home. Debriefing can wait for tomorrow."

"Appreciated," Peter said as he clicked his comm off.

His team had done good work tonight. Saved lives. Gathered evidence that would help them take down more operations like this.

But they also needed to talk about what they had seen, and they needed him to help them process it. Once they transferred the prisoners to the intake team, he was going to gather them for a quick pep talk before sending them home.

57

MORELLE

Morelle stared at her laptop screen, her cheeks warming as she read the next section of questions. The earlier parts about favorite foods, vacation spots, hobbies, favorite movies, favorite books, and moving scenes from movies and books had been mostly impossible to answer because she hadn't seen any Earth movies or read any Earth books. The videos she'd watched back on her home planet and the stories she'd read were so entirely foreign to human culture that the Perfect Match computer wouldn't know what to do with them even if she could somehow feed them into it.

Still, all of that was nothing compared to these intimate inquiries, which made her previous struggles seem trivial.

"Do you prefer to be dominant or submissive in

intimate encounters?" she read aloud, then quickly glanced around even though she was alone in the bedroom. The multiple-choice options included strictly dominant, mostly dominant, switch, mostly submissive, and strictly submissive.

She had no idea. Her limited experience with Brandon had been fairly balanced, with both of them taking turns initiating and leading their encounters. Did she have a preference?

Should she have one?

The next question asked about preferred locations for intimate encounters. The options ranged from traditional bedroom settings to exotic outdoor locations to public places with risk of discovery.

Her blush deepened. She'd only experienced intimacy in the bedroom and bathroom, but the idea of making love in nature held a certain appeal. She could imagine a magical meadow steeped in shadows with only the moon and stars providing illumination. A blanket on the grass, next to a body of water...

She shook her head. Focus. There would probably be a section on that later. The questions needed to be answered in order because they affected those that followed them.

Mother above, this was much more complicated than she'd thought it would be.

"Role-playing scenarios that interest you—select all that apply," she read. The list that followed made her eyes widen. Some were fairly tame, like professor/student, healer/patient, or encounters with strangers. Others were more elaborate, involving complex power dynamics and fantasy scenarios she couldn't even visualize.

"What is a pizza delivery person?" she muttered, puzzling over one of the options. She knew what pizza was, but why would anyone pretend to be delivering pizza to initiate an intimate encounter? It had to be quite popular if it was included in the questionnaire.

The bedroom door opening made her jump.

Brandon poked his head in. "How's the questionnaire going?"

Her heart was still racing from the surprise intrusion, even though it shouldn't have. Brandon had given her privacy to work on the questionnaire and had gone to work on his ideas in the living room, but he'd promised to check in on her from time to time to see if she needed help.

"It's...informative." She shifted the laptop slightly, not quite hiding the screen but not openly displaying it either. "I'm learning about many Earth customs I wasn't aware existed."

"You know that it's almost midnight." He crossed to the couch and sat beside her, leaning to glance at the screen. "Ah, you're using the Kra-ell translation. If you need help understanding the options, you'll have to read them to me or switch back to the original English."

She narrowed her eyes at him. "Have you gone through the questionnaire before?"

"No, but I heard it was quite racy. I'm curious to see how it earned its reputation."

That was a relief. For some reason, it made it a little less embarrassing to work on it together when it was the first time for both of them.

She scrolled back up to a section she'd intended to return to later. "What exactly is meant by light bondage versus moderate bondage? And why would anyone want to be tied up during intimate moments?"

Brandon smiled reassuringly, but there was a mischievous gleam in his eyes. "It's about trust and surrender. Some people find it arousing to give control over to someone they trust completely or to be trusted with that kind of control over someone else."

"Oh." Morelle considered this. "Like when you told me to put my hands above my head and hold them there?"

"That was a hint of that. What we did was very mild compared to what some of these options are suggesting."

She scrolled down. "'Sensation play incorporating temperature variations.' What does that even mean?"

He seemed unsure. "I'm not an expert on fetishes, but I assume that it could involve ice cubes or warming oils..." He trailed off as

Morelle's eyes widened with interest. "Is it something you think you would enjoy?"

She shrugged. "I don't know. The adventure would let us experience different sensations safely and find out if we like them or not."

He nodded, even though he hadn't yet agreed to join her on a virtual adventure. Still, talking about it as if it was a given was a great negotiation tactic. It would acclimate him to the idea without him even realizing what was happening.

Was that underhanded of her?

Maybe a little, but it was for a good cause. Brandon was a creative person, and he should not limit his experiences because of irrational fears. She was convinced that a virtual trip would recharge him and give him a lot of new ideas.

Morelle scrolled to another section. "Exhibition and voyeurism scenarios. What does that mean? Watching others or being watched?"

Brandon nodded. "In the virtual world, you can explore those fantasies without involving other people. It's actually an intriguing possibility."

She frowned. "Which one interests you? The watching or being watched?"

"Being watched. I like a little fake danger."

"If it's fake, it's not dangerous."

He chuckled. "I guess that's the beauty of the virtual experience. In the simulation, the danger will feel real. You will feel anxious, but in reality, it will be safe."

Morelle wanted to do a victory dance, but she stifled the urge and limited herself to a small smile. "You sound like you actually approve of it."

"I'm warming up to the idea." He wrapped his arm around her shoulders. "We can schedule a meeting with William tomorrow, if he has time, and get an extensive explanation of how it all works, or as extensive as I can understand without my eyes glazing over."

She lifted her hand and cupped his cheek. "I love you."

He dipped his head and kissed her lips eagerly, passionately, as if he couldn't wait to get her naked in bed.

She felt the same. He wouldn't even have to warm her up. She was already burning from reading those questions and letting her imagination run wild.

When they came up for air, his eyes were glowing, and his fangs were slightly elongated. "So, am I forgiven?"

She frowned. "Forgiven for what?"

"Keeping my suspicions from you and sharing them with Kian first."

The questionnaire had been so absorbing that she'd forgotten all about being angry at Brandon. The truth was that she'd already forgiven him last night, but she'd needed some time and distance to put her feelings of disappointment in proper perspective. After all, she'd kept things from him as well. She hadn't told him about Ell-rom's talent. Kian was the one who had revealed the secret.

"I've mostly forgiven you already, and now that you are willing to conquer your phobia for me, I can no longer be angry at you."

58

BRANDON

"It's not a phobia," Brandon protested. "It's a perfectly logical objection to having a foreign entity take over my mind. But if William convinces me that it's safe..." He smiled. "I will be thrilled to create a sexy fantasy with you. The possibilities are virtually limitless."

Just thinking of some of those possibilities was making him uncomfortably hard, and he had to shift to make room for his growing erection.

Morelle regarded him from under lowered lashes. "What if what I want is a little...unconventional?"

Dear merciful Fates, what did his lustful vixen have in mind?

"Like what?"

She scrolled back up to an earlier question. "Well, there's this option about role-playing supernatural creatures. Vampires, dragons, and other mythical creatures. Given what I can do, I thought it might be interesting to explore that dynamic in a controlled environment. It would help me accept it and maybe be a little less apprehensive about using it."

That was a little disappointing. He didn't want to go on an adventure to explore Morelle's paranormal abilities. He wanted to explore her sexual fantasies. But this wasn't about him. He'd resolved to talk to William even before coming into the room and helping her with the questionnaire.

She was his mate, and she deserved his maximum effort, not just what neatly fit inside his comfort zone.

"Go on."

"Maybe I could be a vampire queen, and you could be..." She faltered. "This is really silly."

"Your willing thrall?" he suggested. "Surrendering my energy to you willingly and letting you feed off my essence?"

"Yes." She sounded breathy. "Exactly that."

"We could craft a custom adventure together." He rubbed his hand over her arm. "Design exactly how we want it to play out. The setting, the scenario, every detail."

That was what he had done for decades. It would be a walk in the park for him to design the perfect experience for his mate, the love of his life.

Morelle's fingers closed over his knee. "I'd want it to be somewhere exciting and foreboding. A dark temple or a palace...but not like the ones back home. More luxurious, with beautifully crafted furniture and gorgeous outfits."

"Naturally." Brandon's thumb traced patterns on her arm. "As a vampire queen, you'd need something suitably regal."

She closed her eyes. "A deep red velvet gown. Floor-length but with a high slit, so my leg was showing. And you..."

"Let me guess—shirtless and at your mercy?"

It was amazing that she was imagining things she'd never seen. Was it possible the themes were universal and part of some galaxy-spanning genetic memory?

"Maybe a cape if it's cold," she said.

"It's our fantasy." He kissed her temple. "We can make it exactly what we want, including the temperature in the palace."

She returned to the questionnaire. "There's a whole section about preferred atmosphere and setting details. We can specify everything from the lighting to the background music, but I will leave those details to you. I wouldn't know where to start." She leaned against him, bringing the laptop with her. "We could also switch roles partway through. You could become the vampire king who captures me..."

That was more up his alley. "We could design two different scenarios and link them together. Experience both sides of the dynamic."

"You seem excited about this idea." She studied his face.

"I find the mutual trust enticing, the shared exploration."

Morelle leaned and kissed his cheek. "Thank you for being willing to try it with me."

Her innocence, combined with her curiosity and fearlessness, was incredibly arousing, but more than that, her eagerness to take this journey with him made his heart swell.

He'd been so stubborn about this, letting his fears override what could be an incredible opportunity to deepen their connection. Watching her work through the questionnaire and seeing her excitement about crafting shared experiences made him question his stance.

"We could incorporate actual blood drinking, but in the virtual world, it would be safe, symbolic rather than literal."

She was half Kra-ell, but she didn't have fangs and had no desire to drink blood, and yet the thought of experiencing her bite sent zings of desire through him.

Morelle's eyes widened. "You want me to bite you?"

"Yes." He traced his fingers along her neck where he usually bit her. "It would be interesting to experience it from the other side. We talked about it. Switching roles? I don't think I could go all the way to experience lovemaking as a female, but I can definitely see myself being bitten by you. In fact, it's incredibly arousing."

"I think so, too," she whispered, her hand sneaking under his shirt to caress his bare chest.

He snorted. "If just talking about it arouses us, imagine what will happen inside the adventure. We might set the machines on fire."

Her eyes widened. "Is that one of the risks?"

Brandon laughed. "I was speaking figuratively, but when we talk to William tomorrow, I'll ask him about the safety features. I want to understand exactly how the program protects users' minds. Now that I can see the appeal, I'm motivated to explore the virtual world with you."

They had a chance to experience things that might never be possible in reality, to explore aspects of their relationship in a controlled environment where they could push boundaries safely.

Morelle turned to face him fully. "I'm proud of you. It's not easy to get over irrational fears."

"My fears are perfectly rational, but let's leave it at that." He brought her hand to his lips. "Still, you are correct about fears holding me back from something that could be amazing. Relationships are about growing together and trying new things for each other." He lifted her and pulled her onto his lap. "Here is an idea. We could practice some elements in reality first. Get a feel for what we might want to explore virtually."

She looked at him with hooded eyes. "What do you have in mind?"

Instead of answering, he leaned in to kiss her.

Brandon marveled at how quickly his perspective had shifted. From being adamantly opposed to checking out the virtual world, he was now eagerly helping design their first adventure.

That was one of the many things he loved about Morelle. She challenged him to grow, to push past his comfort zone, and to discover new aspects of himself.

Their relationship wasn't just about compromise. It was about mutual evolution and becoming better versions of themselves together.

The whole was greater than the sum of its parts.

59

KIAN

Kian's home office was mostly dark, with only his desk lamp and his laptop screen providing illumination. He could have turned the lights on, there had been no reason not to, but it somehow felt fitting to watch this filth in the dark.

In fact, he regretted getting out of bed and going to his office to check on the progress of the intelligence team instead of waiting until tomorrow. Even just letting the recordings of these horrors play tarnished the sanctity of his home.

Once the human prisoners had awakened and had provided the passwords to the file with a little motivation from the Guardians, the team had cracked the encrypted files with ease.

Now, he sat surrounded by evidence of depravity that made his blood boil.

The surveillance feeds from the keep's cells

showed their newest occupants. The Doomers lay unconscious, heavily sedated on Julian's orders. The other prisoners—the *guests* or rather clients—were in separate cells, and most of them were awake and terrified.

Good. They should be.

Kian had memorized each of their faces. Wealthy men. Respected men. Monsters hiding behind expensive suits and carefully crafted public personas.

He clicked through another folder of files. A senator he'd seen on a televised event. A studio executive who'd given inspired speeches on social issues. A federal judge whose reputation for harsh sentences against child traffickers now seemed like the darkest form of irony.

The videos were worse than the photos. He wished he could believe they were computer-generated fakes, but the timestamp data and background verification proved their authenticity. His fangs had extended involuntarily, and his nails were scoring grooves in his desk as he forced himself to watch everything.

How many more were out there? How many children still suffered while these creatures walked free? The network appeared vast, with tendrils reaching into every level of society, but mostly the elite, the powerful, and the influential, who had gotten bored with every other form of depravity before selling the last piece of their souls to the devil.

Kian didn't even believe in the devil.

Perhaps he should.

It seemed like the devil not only existed but also rewarded his minions with extraordinary wealth and health. Some of these creatures were so well past their prime that they should have been residents of retirement homes and dementia centers.

Kian switched back to the live feed from the cells. The Doomers were the key. He had no doubt of that. The sickening operations would have existed without their involvement, but they facilitated the spread into an international operation because they didn't limit themselves to the ruin of just one country. They wanted to bring all of humanity to its knees so they could take over and enslave it.

He clicked through more files. Financial records showed massive payments flowing through shell companies, but the money trail disappeared into cryptocurrency transactions the team couldn't trace.

As with everything else, crypto was a tool that could be used for good or for evil, so blaming it for these crimes was like blaming safe deposit boxes in banks. The people who hid their blood money were the perpetrators of evil, not the vehicles they used.

As the door burst open, startling him from his

dark thoughts, he lifted his head and looked at his wife who was standing in the doorway wild-eyed and pale, clutching her robe around her.

"Syssi?" He rose immediately, concern replacing rage, and rushed to her. "What's wrong?"

"I had a dream or a vision. I'm not sure what it was, but I saw Kyra again. Or rather, for the first time. She didn't have a scarf on, and I heard her name spoken, so I knew it was her without a doubt."

He wrapped his arm around her and led her to the couch. "What did you see?"

Syssi opened her mouth to speak, then suddenly went rigid, her eyes glazing over, which indicated another vision was taking hold.

"Syssi?"

Her hand clutched his arm with bruising force. "Oh, dear Fates," she whispered. "The poor woman. We have to help her."

COMING UP NEXT
The Children of the Gods Book 92
DARK REBEL'S MYSTERY

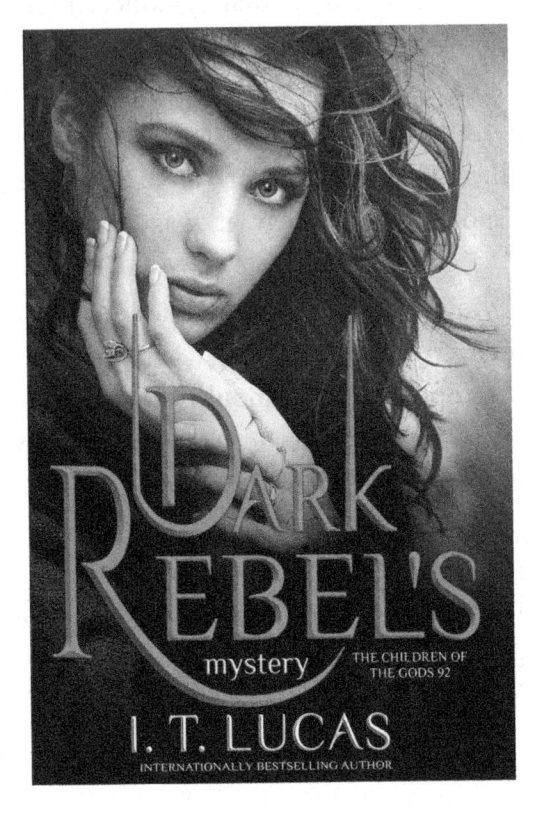

Some warriors are born. Others are chosen by fate and forged by circumstances. In the mountains of Kurdistan, a mysterious woman fights for freedom while her own past remains locked away.

Stay tuned as the truth about Kyra's disappearance begins to unravel.

JOIN THE VIP CLUB
To find out what's included in your free membership, flip to the last page.

NOTE

Dear reader,

I hope my stories have added a little joy to your day. If you have a moment to add some to mine, you can help spread the word about the Children Of The Gods series by telling your friends and penning a review. Your recommendations are the most powerful way to inspire new readers to explore the series.

Thank you,

Isabell

Also by I. T. Lucas

THE CHILDREN OF THE GODS ORIGINS
1: GODDESS'S CHOICE
2: GODDESS'S HOPE

THE CHILDREN OF THE GODS
DARK STRANGER
1: DARK STRANGER THE DREAM
2: DARK STRANGER REVEALED
3: DARK STRANGER IMMORTAL

DARK ENEMY
4: DARK ENEMY TAKEN
5: DARK ENEMY CAPTIVE
6: DARK ENEMY REDEEMED

KRI & MICHAEL'S STORY
6.5: MY DARK AMAZON

DARK WARRIOR
7: DARK WARRIOR MINE
8: DARK WARRIOR'S PROMISE
9: DARK WARRIOR'S DESTINY
10: DARK WARRIOR'S LEGACY

DARK GUARDIAN
11: DARK GUARDIAN FOUND
12: DARK GUARDIAN CRAVED

13: Dark Guardian's Mate

Dark Angel
14: Dark Angel's Obsession
15: Dark Angel's Seduction
16: Dark Angel's Surrender

Dark Operative
17: Dark Operative: A Shadow of Death
18: Dark Operative: A Glimmer of Hope
19: Dark Operative: The Dawn of Love

Dark Survivor
20: Dark Survivor Awakened
21: Dark Survivor Echoes of Love
22: Dark Survivor Reunited

Dark Widow
23: Dark Widow's Secret
24: Dark Widow's Curse
25: Dark Widow's Blessing

Dark Dream
26: Dark Dream's Temptation
27: Dark Dream's Unraveling
28: Dark Dream's Trap

Dark Prince
29: Dark Prince's Enigma
30: Dark Prince's Dilemma

31: Dark Prince's Agenda

Dark Queen
32: Dark Queen's Quest
33: Dark Queen's Knight
34: Dark Queen's Army

Dark Spy
35: Dark Spy Conscripted
36: Dark Spy's Mission
37: Dark Spy's Resolution

Dark Overlord
38: Dark Overlord New Horizon
39: Dark Overlord's Wife
40: Dark Overlord's Clan

Dark Choices
41: Dark Choices The Quandary
42: Dark Choices Paradigm Shift
43: Dark Choices The Accord

Dark Secrets
44: Dark Secrets Resurgence
45: Dark Secrets Unveiled
46: Dark Secrets Absolved

Dark Haven
47: Dark Haven Illusion
48: Dark Haven Unmasked

49: Dark Haven Found

Dark Power
50: Dark Power Untamed
51: Dark Power Unleashed
52: Dark Power Convergence

Dark Memories
53: Dark Memories Submerged
54: Dark Memories Emerge
55: Dark Memories Restored

Dark Hunter
56: Dark Hunter's Query
57: Dark Hunter's Prey
58: Dark Hunter's Boon

Dark God
59: Dark God's Avatar
60: Dark God's Reviviscence
61: Dark God Destinies Converge

Dark Whispers
62: Dark Whispers From The Past
63: Dark Whispers From Afar
64: Dark Whispers From Beyond

Dark Gambit
65: Dark Gambit The Pawn
66: Dark Gambit The Play

67: Dark Gambit Reliance

Dark Alliance
68: Dark Alliance Kindred Souls
69: Dark Alliance Turbulent Waters
70: Dark Alliance Perfect Storm

Dark Healing
71: Dark Healing Blind Justice
72: Dark Healing Blind Trust
73: Dark healing Blind Curve

Dark Encounters
74: Dark Encounters of the Close Kind
75: Dark Encounters of the Unexpected Kind
76: Dark Encounters of the Fated Kind

Dark Voyage
77: Dark Voyage Matters of the Heart
78: <u>Dark Voyage Matters of the Mind</u>
<u>79: Dark Voyage Matters of the Soul</u>

Dark Horizon
80: Dark Horizon New Dawn
81: Dark Horizon Eclipse of the Heart
82: Dark Horizon The Witching Hour

Dark Witch
83: Dark Witch: Entangled Fates
84: Dark Witch: Twin Destinies

85: Dark Witch: Resurrection

Dark Awakening
86: Dark Awakening: New World
87: Dark Awakening Hidden Currents
88: Dark Awakening Echoes of Destiny

Dark Princess
89: Dark Princess: Shadows
90: Dark Princess Emerging
91: Dark Princess Ascending

Dark Rebel
92: Dark Rebel's Mystery

PERFECT MATCH

Vampire's Consort
King's Chosen
Captain's Conquest
The Thief Who Loved Me
My Merman Prince
The Dragon King
My Werewolf Romeo
The Channeler's Companion
The Valkyrie & The Witch
Adina and the Magic Lamp

TRANSLATIONS

DIE ERBEN DER GÖTTER
DARK STRANGER
1- DARK STRANGER DER TRAUM
2- DARK STRANGER DIE OFFENBARUNG
3- DARK STRANGER UNSTERBLICH

DARK ENEMY
4- DARK ENEMY ENTFÜHRT
5- DARK ENEMY GEFANGEN
6- DARK ENEMY ERLÖST

DARK WARRIOR
7- DARK WARRIOR MEINE SEHNSUCHT
8- DARK WARRIOR – DEIN VERSPRECHEN
9- Dark Warrior - Unser Schicksal
10- Dark Warrior-Unser Vermächtnis

LOS HIJOS DE LOS DIOSES

EL OSCURO DESCONOCIDO
1: EL OSCURO DESCONOCIDO EL SUEÑO
2: EL OSCURO DESCONOCIDO REVELADO

3: EL OSCURO DESCONOCIDO INMORTAL
EL OSCURO ENEMIGO
4- EL OSCURO ENEMIGO CAPTURADO
5 - EL OSCURO ENEMIGO CAUTIVO
6- EL OSCURO ENEMIGO REDIMIDO

LES ENFANTS DES DIEUX
DARK STRANGER
1- Dark Stranger Le rêve
2- Dark Stranger La révélation
3- Dark Stranger L'immortelle

The Children of the Gods Series Sets

Books 1-3: Dark Stranger trilogy—Includes a bonus short story: **The Fates Take a Vacation**

Books 4-6: Dark Enemy Trilogy —Includes a bonus short story—**The Fates' Post-Wedding Celebration**

Books 7-10: Dark Warrior Tetralogy
Books 11-13: Dark Guardian Trilogy
Books 14-16: Dark Angel Trilogy
Books 17-19: Dark Operative Trilogy
Books 20-22: Dark Survivor Trilogy
Books 23-25: Dark Widow Trilogy

Books 26-28: Dark Dream Trilogy
Books 29-31: Dark Prince Trilogy
Books 32-34: Dark Queen Trilogy
Books 35-37: Dark Spy Trilogy
Books 38-40: Dark Overlord Trilogy
Books 41-43: Dark Choices Trilogy
Books 44-46: Dark Secrets Trilogy
Books 47-49: Dark Haven Trilogy
Books 50-52: Dark Power Trilogy
Books 53-55: Dark Memories Trilogy
Books 56-58: Dark Hunter Trilogy
Books 59-61: Dark God Trilogy
Books 62-64: Dark Whispers Trilogy
Books 65-67: Dark Gambit Trilogy
Books 68-70: Dark Alliance Trilogy
Books 71-73: Dark Healing Trilogy
Books 74-76: Dark Encounters Trilogy
Books 77-79: Dark Voyage Trilogy
Books 80-81: Dark Horizon Trilogy

MEGA SETS

The Children of the Gods: Books 1-6
includes character lists
The Children of the Gods: Books 6.5-10

Perfect Match Bundle 1

CHECK OUT THE SPECIALS ON

ITLUCAS.COM
(https://itlucas.com/specials)

FOR EXCLUSIVE PEEKS AT UPCOMING RELEASES &
A FREE I. T. LUCAS COMPANION BOOK

Join my *VIP Club* and gain access to the VIP portal at itlucas.com

To Join, go to:
http://eepurl.com/blMTpD

Find out more details about what's included with your free membership on the book's last page.

TRY THE CHILDREN OF THE GODS SERIES ON
AUDIBLE

2 FREE audiobooks with your new Audible subscription!

FOR EXCLUSIVE PEEKS AT UPCOMING RELEASES &
A FREE I. T. LUCAS COMPANION BOOK

Join my *VIP Club* and gain access to the VIP portal at itlucas.com
To Join, go to:
http://eepurl.com/blMTpD

INCLUDED IN YOUR FREE MEMBERSHIP:

YOUR VIP PORTAL

- Read preview chapters of upcoming releases.
- Listen to Goddess's Choice narration by Charles Lawrence
- Exclusive content offered only to my VIPs.

FREE I.T. LUCAS COMPANION INCLUDES:

- Goddess's Choice Part 1
- Perfect Match: Vampire's Consort (a standalone Novella)
- Interview Q & A
- Character Charts

If you're already a subscriber and you are not getting my emails, your provider is sending them to your junk folder, and you are missing out on important updates. To fix that, add isabell@itlucas.com to your email contacts or your email VIP list.

**Check out the specials at
https://www.itlucas.com/specials**

Made in the USA
Middletown, DE
18 January 2025